CW00432753

CUTTING
EDGE

Owen Carey Jones

First Published in 2017

Copyright © Owen Carey Jones 2017

ISBN: 978-1-54951-633-7

All rights reserved.

No part of this book may be reproduced or transmitted in any form
or by any means, electronic or mechanical, including photocopying,
recording, or by information storage and retrieval systems, without
written permission of the publisher, except where permitted by law.

All characters and events in this publication, other than those clearly
in the public domain, are fictitious and any resemblance to real
persons, living or dead, is purely coincidental.

Published by: Rotorua Publications

Chapter 1

It wasn't the first time Carter Jefferson had delivered a lecture about diamonds to a lecture theatre full of students, and it wouldn't be the last. As he looked around the room and waited for them to stop talking, he wondered whether they would be interested in what he had to say. Without doubt, it was the single most important issue facing the diamond industry and yet they were probably barely aware of it.

When silence eventually prevailed, the students looked at him expectantly. He smiled as he began to speak.

"So, how can you tell whether the diamond you have in your hand is a natural gemstone made in the bowels of the earth millions of years ago, or a man made object created in a lab in Silicon Valley yesterday?"

The room remained silent but, to Carter's surprise, one student, a blonde haired young man sitting at the back of the room, raised his hand.

"Yes," responded Carter, "Please do enlighten us with your knowledge of this subject."

The student lowered his hand and began to look a little nervous. "Well, if it was man made it would have a different spectrographic curve because of the evenness of the impurities in the crystal." He lowered his hand and looked at the students around him nervously before smiling.

Carter was impressed. "That's right!" he said. "Well done. And your name is?"

"James, Sir, James Oppenheimer."

Carter smiled. "Well that would explain your impressive knowledge. Are you planning to join the family business?"

"No Sir, definitely not! But they don't know that yet."

A titter ran around the room as the students smiled and looked at each other before Carter responded, "When are you going to tell them?"

"I'm not sure. Maybe when I'm a successful writer, like you, Sir."

The whole room exploded into laughter and Carter joined in. He liked people with minds of their own and James seemed like he was just such a person. Carter had written several books, most of them academic tomes about geology but also a couple of novels based on his personal experiences.

"OK, moving on, no one has yet come up with a reliable, easily affordable way to tell the difference between natural and synthetic diamonds. Today, it still requires the kind of equipment you will only find in a lab." Carter looked round the room as he paused and smiled before continuing, "So, if any of you ever comes up with a cheap sure-fire way to differentiate between them, not only will you save the natural diamond market, you will become a millionaire."

An hour and a half later, with his lecture over, Carter came out of the building in New York which houses the Education Centre of the Gemological Institute of America and headed along Madison Avenue to a lunch meeting with Isaac Sternberg. Isaac was the head of the New York Federation of International

Diamond Traders, for whom Carter occasionally did some investigative work. An established expert in diamonds, Carter also had a keen and logical brain and these two qualities made him a natural choice when the FIDT needed someone to look into something discreetly for them. The cases where he was brought in to help usually involved misconduct of some kind by people involved in the diamond business and Carter's detailed specialist knowledge of certain aspects of the industry, particularly the development and use of synthetic diamonds, made him unique. Most of these cases also involved liaising with the local police across national boundaries and Carter's life history, which included living in Belize, the UK and the USA meant that he had no difficulty in getting alongside people from different cultures. Added to that, his imposing appearance made it easy for him to command respect from those he had dealings with. Carter Jefferson was a tall black man in excellent physical shape for his fifty one years.

By the time Carter arrived at the restaurant, Isaac was already there. He stood to greet him, shaking him by the hand warmly. When they had ordered their food and were waiting for it to arrive, Isaac opened the conversation.

"Did you hear that John had left us and moved to Oxford in England?"

Carter was more than a little surprised to hear Isaac's news and his eyebrows lifted. John Sprague had been a key employee of the FIDT and he was someone with whom Carter had worked on numerous occasions and for whom he had the greatest respect. John's knowledge of the diamond industry and of the processes involved in synthetic diamond production, in particular, was second to none and he had worked for the FIDT for nearly ten years. Carter was shocked to hear that he had left and crossed the Atlantic.

"No, I didn't know that," he responded. "Why did he make the move?"

"Well, you know what he had been working on, don't you?"

"Last time I spoke to him, which was about a year ago, he said he was looking into synthetic detection systems."

"Yeah, we asked him to do that. But then, kind of out of the blue he called me to say he wanted to do some research, to see if he could find a new way, one that the average jeweller could afford."

"And…?"

"Well, you know how important this whole area is to the market in natural diamonds," Carter nodded and Isaac continued, "so we decided to sponsor him to do some investigative work."

"So why did he end up in Oxford? Not that I have anything against Oxford. Far from it, I have a lot of good memories of my own time there."

Carter's mind drifted back in time as memories came back into his head. He and his wife, Nicole, had been boyfriend and girlfriend while they had been at university in Oxford but they had split up after about a year and not been reunited until fate had brought them together again more than twenty five years later. It had been a highly emotional re-union with a lot of sadness and misery being mixed in with the joy of seeing each other again. Ultimately, they had been able to overcome the bad parts and had then got married, almost at the same time as Nicole's daughter, Eloise had married a Frenchman called Jacques, whose yacht she had hired for a works conference in the South of France. Carter returned to the present as Isaac explained why John had made the move.

"He said there were some good opportunities there for him to do some lecturing, as well as the research, and that would help with the costs of running his lab."

"Sounds good. Maybe I'll drop in and see him on my way back from Paris in June."

"Paris!" A broad smile covered Isaac's face. "Is it your wedding anniversary?"

Carter chuckled. "No, that's already been and gone. We're going to visit Nicole's daughter and son-in-law for a few days."

"Well, John's visiting family in Santa Monica next month but I think he's heading straight back to England after that, so he should be back by June."

The waiter arrived at their table with their food and the two men settled down to enjoy their meal.

———————————————

A month later, John Sprague and his twelve-year-old son, Mikey, walked through the trees between Ocean Avenue and Pacific Coast Highway, the road which bordered the beach in Santa Monica, as they made their way towards the pier. As they did, they encountered several homeless men camped out under the trees with their meagre possessions.

"Why doesn't someone get these people out of here and find them somewhere to live?" Mikey asked.

"Probably because everyone thinks it's someone else's responsibility to do that," answered his father.

"That's stupid! Someone should do something."

"Yeah, I agree." John smiled, pleased that his son had feelings for those less fortunate than himself.

When they reached the pier, they turned down onto it and headed towards the café which was half way along. The sun was shining brightly and crowds of people were thronging the pier.

As they approached the café, John and Mikey saw a fashionably dressed couple vacate a table and Mikey made a dash for it, getting there just before a more casually dressed group of men could beat him to it.

John watched and smiled as Mikey sat down at the table. He recalled the time he had been able to spend with his son on this visit, it was precious. He missed Mikey terribly. When John's wife Izzy, Mikey's mother, had died, Mikey had still been a baby and looking after him would have been impossible for John unless he had given up his job, which wasn't a feasible option. Instead, he had asked his wife's mother, Alice McGill, who also lived in New York, to take over, something she had been only too willing to do. Having lost her only daughter as a result of SUDEP, sudden unexplained death from epilepsy, she needed someone on whom she could lavish all the love she had felt for Izzy. Later, when Alice had decided that she could no longer cope with living in the city where her daughter had died, she had moved to Santa Monica in California. There, she had family who would be able to help her but, as a result of the move, John had lost touch with Mikey for several years, only seeing him very occasionally on family get-togethers like Thanksgiving and Christmas. Although in recent years he had tried hard to visit whenever he could, it was still a source of sadness for him that he saw so little of his son.

As father and son enjoyed a beer and a soda, they caught up with each other's news.

"I wish you hadn't moved to England," said Mikey, a serious look on his face.

John smiled. "It's not that much further away than New York," he said, trying to lighten the tone of the conversation. "And I get to bring you special presents, ones I wouldn't be able to get in New York." He gave Mikey an enigmatic look.

"You got me a present?" guessed Mikey.

"Sure did," responded John.

Mikey looked at his father expectantly, waiting for him to produce the present but John just sat there looking at him and smiling. Eventually Mikey could wait no longer.

"So where is it?" he asked.

"I haven't got it with me," taunted John. "It's back at the hotel."

"What is it?"

John smiled. "If I tell you that, it will spoil the surprise," he said.

Without a moment's hesitation, Mikey got up from his seat and waited for his father to do the same.

"Going somewhere?" asked John. Mikey sighed as John picked up his glass. "We haven't finished our drinks yet."

Mikey sat down again and picked up his half finished soda before quickly pouring it down his throat and banging the glass down on the table. John laughed and followed suit with his beer.

"Right! Where shall we go now?" asked John.

Mikey gave his father an 'I don't believe you' look before he spoke. "Your hotel?"

"Oh, yeah, right! You wanted to see if they've given me a good enough room, didn't you?"

At this, Mikey slapped his father hard on the back and they both broke out into a laugh as they walked back along the pier towards Ocean Avenue and the Ocean View Hotel, where John was staying.

Following the short flight to Los Angeles LAX airport, which had landed at 3:00pm, Pierre LeBlanc, a Frenchman in his mid thirties who was wearing dark blue jeans and a brown jacket, picked up a hire car, a

Ford Focus, and drove along the San Diego Freeway before turning left onto the Santa Monica Freeway. He had booked a room at the Hotel California and was soon checking in at the hotel reception desk and asking for a room with a sea view.

Once he had settled into his room at the hotel and checked the quality of the view from the window, which was everything he could have hoped for, Pierre removed his phone from his jacket pocket, selected a number, and pressed the call button.

Lucy Adams was in her office at a company located on the outskirts of Los Angeles, where a team of scientists, employed by the company, were continuing their research into the use of synthetic diamonds in the construction of computer processors. When the phone on her desk rang and she picked it up.

"Hello," she said.

"Lucy, ma chérie! I have arrived in town," said Pierre, using his most seductive French accent.

"Pierre?" said Lucy, not quite sure it was him. "Is that you?"

"Oui, c'est moi!" answered Pierre. "How are you, ma chérie?"

"I'm good," answered Lucy, a broad smile covering her face. "How about you?"

"I am good too. Is it still OK for us to meet tomorrow?"

"Yes, of course. Do you have the stuff?"

"It is with me now, as we speak."

"OK, well I'll see you in the morning then," said Lucy.

"As I am in town, would you like for me to buy you dinner tomorrow night?" asked Pierre; he did not want to spend any more evenings alone than he had to, especially not if the gorgeous Lucy was available.

"Yeah, OK, why not," responded Lucy. She liked Pierre and they had often dined together in the past. In fact, they had often done more than dine together but the relationship was a casual one, they both knew that.

As she put the phone down, Lucy's thoughts drifted back a couple of months to when she had been manning the company stand at a science fair in Silicon Valley in March. That was when she had first met John Sprague. Sure, he was a good bit older than her but as far as she was concerned he was gorgeous. Not only did he keep himself in good trim physically but he shared her interest in diamonds. Inevitably, given the mutual attraction, a drink turned into two drinks, and then three drinks and then four, before they eventually agreed to have dinner together. For both of them, the food had been irrelevant; what they had both wanted was to spend time with each other, as much time as possible, and when Lucy had woken up in bed alongside John in his motel room the next morning, she had been unable to prevent a big smile covering her face. It had been the most perfect evening and night and she had not wanted it to end. So it hadn't. Lucy had managed to convince her assistant to mind the stand on her own the next day while she and John spent a second day in each other's company, and then a second night in each others arms.

The next morning, as the time approached 9:00am, Lucy was waiting in her office for Pierre to arrive. Memories of the two days she had spent with John, when they had met at the science fair, were constantly in her mind and it was difficult for her to concentrate on work. Since then, they had been able to spend time together on a number of occasions and their relationship had grown deeper and stronger.

As Lucy's thoughts flitted from work to John and back to work again, Pierre appeared at the door to her office. Lucy was leaning back in her chair with her eyes closed when he knocked on the open door and waited for her to invite him in. The knock on the door brought Lucy quickly back into the present. She stood up behind her desk and smiled at the tall but quite slightly built man.

"Pierre, come in," she said, "You're early!"

Pierre looked at his watch. "By two minutes maybe," he said with a broad smile on his face.

Lucy came round from her desk and she and Pierre embraced. He kissed her on the lips before pulling back a little and looking into her eyes. "I have missed you," he said, almost in a whisper.

"I'm sorry, but you know how it is. A girl's gotta do what a girl's gotta do."

"Before we get down to work, are we still OK for dinner tonight?" asked Pierre.

"Of course! I'm looking forward to it. I've missed you too."

Pierre and Lucy settled into their chairs. She sat behind her desk and he sat in the visitor's chair, which he pulled round the desk so that he could be a little bit closer to her. He reached down to his bag and removed a large box, wrapped in brown paper, which he handed to Lucy.

"Here are the diamond wafers you ordered."

"Oh yes, thank you," said Lucy as she took the box from him and placed it on her desk. "Is the invoice inside?"

Pierre nodded before speaking, "I could send the stuff to you by courier but then I would not get to come and see you."

Lucy smiled at this but her smile was a little less inviting than Pierre was used to. He decided to change the subject.

"So, how did it go? At the fair in March?" he asked as he stroked Lucy's hand hopefully. "I was sorry not to be there."

"It was good. I really enjoyed it." She paused before continuing. "And I met this really interesting guy."

"Interesting? In what way interesting?" queried Pierre, a touch of frostiness apparent in his voice, which wasn't lost on Lucy.

"Well, like us, he works in the diamond industry, he's sort of a research scientist."

"Research? What kind of research?"

"He wasn't too specific about that but I worked out that it has something to do with the detection of synthetic diamonds."

"Well, that is interesting. What else did he tell you?"

"Nothing much really. But he did say that he thought it was only a matter of time before someone developed a cheap piece of equipment for distinguishing between synthetic and natural diamonds. In fact he was very interested in the work we have been doing here. You know, into miniaturisation of scientific equipment. And he's now using some of our latest processors in his work."

Pierre shifted in his seat and stopped stroking Lucy's hand. "What is his name?" he asked, fairly abruptly. "Maybe I know him."

Lucy smiled as she spoke, recalling once again her time at the fair. "John," she said, "John Sprague. He lives in England. That's where his lab is. At Oxford University."

Pierre rose from his chair, a distant look now on his face.

"Lucy, je suis désolé, but I have just remembered that I have to meet a work colleague in San Francisco this afternoon. Can we postpone dinner?"

Lucy was surprised at this, and more than a little taken aback, but she hid it well. "Yes, of course we can. How about tomorrow instead?"

"Tomorrow would be good. I will be back from San Francisco by then."

"And you can take me to the movies to make up for letting me down tonight."

Pierre took Lucy's hand in his and drew it to his mouth. He kissed her hand and then looked her in the eye. "It will be my pleasure," he said

Pierre blew Lucy a kiss as he left her office.

Lucy watched as he walked out of the door. She understood that the existence of another man in her life might have thrown him a little. She and Pierre had enjoyed a close relationship but both had accepted that it wasn't exclusive. After all, she lived in California and he lived in France.

Pierre's brain was melting as he left the building. He was employed by a man who had owned a business in the south of France which had specialised in the cutting of rough diamonds, ready for use in jewellery. These high quality gem diamonds had then been sold on to jewellery manufacturers around the world.

In addition, unable to resist the temptation, the business had become involved in selling gem quality synthetic diamonds mixed in with natural diamonds, using it's established business as a supplier of natural diamonds as a cover. These gem quality synthetic diamonds had been sourced illegally, through a complicated chain of supply, from a factory in Russia. As it was rare for gem quality diamonds to be tested to verify that they were natural diamonds, because the process required a laboratory full of very expensive equipment, it was relatively easy to mix synthetic and natural diamonds without being found out. But they had been unlucky. As a result of a mixed batch of diamonds which they had sold to a dealer in New York being sent for testing, the scheme had gone horribly wrong and resulted in a number of deaths.

Having been convicted of involvement in the deaths that had occurred, though not of actually killing anyone, Pierre's boss had been sentenced to a five year term in prison and was sent to the Prison la Farlède, located near Toulon, to serve his term. In his absence, Alphonse, who was his right hand man, had been given the job of running the business for him with Pierre's help. Following their boss's imprisonment, the company had lost its source of uncut natural diamonds and had moved into the distribution of synthetic diamond materials, such as the synthetic diamond wafers which Lucy's company was using. These were sourced from Russian manufacturers who also produced synthetic gem quality diamonds and Alphonse had decided to distribute these as well, mainly to manufacturers in other countries such as the USA who were unable to meet the fast growing demand for them from jewellery companies.

Later that day, American Airlines flight 1928 from Los Angeles approached runway one at San Francisco International Airport from the east, crossing San Francisco Bay as it descended towards the runway. On board, sitting in a window seat on the left hand side of the plane, was Pierre. He looked out of the window as the airport building came into sight, with a mass of cars parked on its roof, and a spaghetti like collection of roads leading to and from the airport from Bayshore Freeway.

Once the plane had landed, Pierre collected his bag from the conveyor belt. He then went through security into the main building and, before long, he was heading along the freeway, towards the city centre, in the red Chevrolet Cruze he had hired. Half an hour later he parked in the visitors' car park at The Shiny New Diamond Company, one of the companies which his company was supplying, quite legitimately, with the synthetic diamonds it was buying from the manufacturers in Siberia. He locked the car, leaving his bag in the boot and approached the modern, mainly glass, building with just his leather briefcase, as he had done on many previous occasions.

Having asked for Daniel Blundell at the reception counter inside the main door of the building, Pierre wandered over to the visitors' seating area but he did not sit down. A few minutes later, he saw Daniel, dressed in a dark suit, as usual, come out of the lift and walk towards him.

"You're two days early! I wasn't expecting you until Friday," said Daniel.

"I know, but my plans changed at the last minute. I'm sorry."

"No problem, come on up."

Daniel's office was on the top floor of the four storey building. As one of the founders of the company, he had a spacious corner office and the views out across San Francisco were eye-catching. The large office was furnished with everything you would expect to find in a top executive's office, including a large flat screen television and a sumptuous seating area near the window with two sofas and two armchairs, all in soft light brown leather.

As Daniel and Pierre sat in the two armchairs, there was a knock at the door and Angelica, Daniel's very attractive young blonde PA came into the room.

"Good morning Monsieur LeBlanc," she said, a beautiful smile on her face, before turning her attention to Daniel. "Can I get you both some coffee?" she asked.

"Yes, thanks, Angelica, that would be great," replied Daniel before looking at Pierre. "Coffee OK for you, Pierre?" he asked and Pierre nodded.

After Angelica had left to go and make the coffee, Daniel looked at Pierre.

"So, what have you got for me?" he asked, smiling.

Pierre opened the top of his briefcase and removed a polished wooden box measuring about nine inches by six inches and three inches deep. He put the box on the wooden table between them before taking a key from the pocket of his jeans. He used the key to open the box and then turned it towards Daniel. Inside, the box was lined with soft black velvet cloth and it was full to the brim with bright shiny colourless gem quality synthetic diamonds.

"It is as we agreed," began Pierre. "One thousand stones varying between a quarter of a carat and one carat, making six hundred carats in total."

Daniel smiled and nodded. "They look good, don't they," he said.

"They are from the same source, so they should be of the same quality, but if you find any problem with them, just let me know."

"Russian?" queried Daniel and Pierre nodded as Angelica returned with a tray, bearing their coffee and some biscuits, which she put on the table before leaving the room.

Daniel removed an envelope from the inside pocket of his suit jacket and handed it to Pierre. "One million dollars, as agreed," he said.

Pierre opened the envelope, looked at the cheque, and nodded before returning it to the envelope, which he then put deep into the pocket of his jeans. He handed the key to Daniel.

"Good to do business with you again, Daniel," said Pierre, smiling.

Daniel smiled back. "Let's get some of this coffee," he said as he started to pour it out into the cups. "And then you can tell me what's new in the diamond business in Europe." Daniel passed a cup to Pierre and then picked up the other cup and sipped his coffee as he looked expectantly at Pierre.

"Nothing much to tell you about," he said. " I haven't heard of anything new since I last saw you."

"No new cheap synthetic diamond detection devices appearing then?" asked Daniel, cocking his head.

Pierre looked away for a moment and then turned back to Daniel. "Well, the last one I heard of, officially, was the one from Japan. But that has pretty much been discounted as unreliable now." They both sipped their coffee.

"You said the last one you had heard of, officially. Do you have some unofficial information?"

Pierre looked away again, not sure if he should tell Daniel what he knew, and Daniel became a little impatient.

"Is there something you're not telling me, Pierre?" he asked, looking at Pierre sternly.

"Well, the thing is, there's this girl I know in Santa Monica, her name is Lucy. She works for a company which makes computer processors from synthetic diamond material."

"Yeah, and…?"

"Well, she has a boyfriend …" began Pierre.

"And it's not you?" interrupted Daniel, a smile on his face. Pierre looked Daniel in the eye, a serious look, and Daniel's smile disappeared.

"It used to be me, but not any more. She met a guy called John Sprague a little while ago at CompTech and fell for him."

"Well, I guess that was bad news for you but what's it got to do with me, or with our business?"

"After what Lucy had told me, I checked him out," opened Pierre, " I made some phone calls and found out that John Sprague used to work for the FIDT in New York. But for the last year, he has been working in Oxford, doing research, possibly aimed at developing an inexpensive synthetic diamond detector."

Daniel sat up in his chair. This was not good news, at least not if John had been successful in his work. But, then again, he wasn't the only person in the world trying to achieve that.

"Him and half the world!" he said, the smile returning to his face as he relaxed and leaned back into his chair again.

Having spent the night in San Francisco, Pierre drove the Chevy back along the freeway, heading back to the airport. There he took a flight to Los Angeles and made his way back to Santa Monica, where he was expecting to be having dinner with Lucy. When he got back to his hotel, he decided to give Lucy a call just to confirm that she was still happy to meet him for dinner.

"Lucy, Hi, "he began when she answered his call. "I'm back. Are we still OK for dinner tonight?"

"Yes, of course, I'll meet you at your hotel at seven. Are you staying at the California again?"

"Yes, I am. And seven is good for me. I will wait in reception for you." Pierre threw the phone onto the bed and frowned. He knew that he needed to find a way to get Lucy to tell him more about John's work and, more specifically, where he had got to with it.

By six o'clock that evening, Pierre had unpacked, been for a stroll along Venice Beach, where he had stopped at a bar for a beer, and returned to his room. He took a leisurely shower before putting on black jeans and a dark blue shirt and heading for reception. He knew he was going to be early but he wanted to make sure he was there when Lucy arrived.

When, at five past seven, Lucy walked into the Hotel California, Pierre's head was not the only one that turned. It wasn't that she was particularly dressed up, although she was wearing a quite tight fitting knee length blue dress, it was just that she was a stunningly attractive woman. She saw Pierre at the same time as he spotted her and he got to his feet to greet her. They both smiled and hugged each other, kissing each other on the cheek in typical French fashion. When they separated, Lucy spoke.

"So! Where do you want to go for dinner?" she asked.

Pierre was a bit surprised by Lucy's question. "I thought we could eat here. In the hotel restaurant," he said, indicating the entrance to the restaurant with a sweep of his hand.

Lucy nodded. "OK, sounds good. Shall we?" she said expectantly and Pierre responded by leading the way to the restaurant.

Chapter 2

At his house on the beach in Ambergris Caye, an island in the Caribbean, just off the coast of Belize, Carter sat on the veranda and surveyed the beautiful scene before him. Steps from the veranda led directly down onto the beach, his beach, and beyond that to the sea and one of the largest coral reefs in the world. He never tired of the view and would never regret making the move from New York.

As he sat gazing out across the gentle surf, Nicole came out of the house onto the veranda beside him.

"Well, I'm all packed and ready!" she said as she too looked at the picturesque scene.

Carter turned to look at her, a degree of shock apparent on his face. "We're not due to leave for another three weeks!"

"I know, but I can't wait to see Eloise," she said and smiled inwardly as she thought about her daughter. "And Jacques of course. It seems like ages since we last saw them."

"Nikki, it was only two months ago! They were here with us for two weeks in March, remember?"

"Like I said, ages ago."

They smiled at each other and Nicole put her arm round Carter's neck as she stood beside him. He took her hand and kissed it.

"We'll be there with them in Paris before you know it."

"I know. I just wish we didn't have to go to Oxford on the way."

Carter and Nicole had met in Oxford when they had both been students there, Carter doing a Master of Science degree in geology and Nicole a Batchelor of Arts degree. Their relationship had lasted for about a year until Nicole's father, not happy with his daughter being in a relationship with a non-Frenchman, had brought it to an end by threatening to pull her out of university and take her back to France.

Carter sighed, but it was a good natured sigh. "Well, I want to pay John a visit," he said. "And Jacques and Eloise will still be at Claudine's when we get to Paris anyway. And you like Oxford, you know you do. It's got lots of memories for both of us."

"Not all of them good ones."

"No, but it's where I first met you. And that's enough for me."

Nicole smiled. It had been a wonderful time when she and Carter had been an item while they were in Oxford. They had spent a lot of time together and experienced many things. As her mind drifted back and she listened to the waves breaking on the beach, she remembered one particular occasion when they had hired a punt. Carter had had the idea when they had been sitting beside the Thames in Christ Church Meadow, one of their favourite meeting places. They had walked back to Magdalen Bridge and hired the punt with the intention of punting down the River Cherwell which, after a few hundred yards, leads into the River Thames.

The fact that Carter had never hired a punt before or, for that matter, ever been on a small boat on a river, did not seem to him to be a problem. As they set off from the boat hire quay, Nicole was surprised at how good he was at moving the boat forward in a straight line, sticking the pole into the water until it reached the river bed and then pushing the boat forward. Carter continued to repeat his punting action while Nicole sat at the front of the little boat, enjoying the view. Before long, they reached the Thames. Although the Thames is a wider and busier river than the Cherwell, Carter did not see any reason why they shouldn't venture out onto it with the punt; he was confident that he knew what he was doing.

As they turned into the Thames, Carter continued to punt along, keeping fairly close to the bank, but then he began to drift towards the centre of the river, just as a large pleasure boat, carrying about a hundred passengers, appeared, heading towards them. The pleasure boat was making quite large waves as its bow ploughed through the water, so Carter tried, quite desperately, to move the punt closer to the river bank; he wanted, quite rightly, to keep a good distance between the punt and the pleasure boat, but it was then that his inexperience showed.

As Carter tried to turn the punt towards the bank of the river, he suddenly lost his balance and fell into the water. Nicole screamed before covering her mouth with her hands, fearing the worst. A few moments later, the pleasure boat sounded its emergency siren as it slowed down and came to a halt next to Nicole in the punt. By this time Carter had surfaced and was swimming towards the punt as fast as he could. All the passengers on the pleasure boat had gathered on the side of the boat, where they could see Carter; they were laughing their heads off as he struggled to climb back into the punt. When he had, and was safely back on board, the Captain of the pleasure boat sounded his siren again, in a sort of celebratory way, before re-engaging the engines and moving on along the river again.

Nicole recalled the embarrassment Carter had felt as he had wiped some of the water from his face and clothes. He had looked at the pleasure boat and shaken his head in disbelief at what had happened before turning back to look at Nicole. By then, her face had been covered with a huge smile, partly because of the hilarity of the event and partly because Carter was back in the punt, safe and sound.

Now, standing next to Carter on the beach in Belize almost thirty years later, Nicole sighed. It was true that if it had not been for Oxford, she would never have met Carter. She leant down and kissed him on the forehead.

As Pierre waited in the departure lounge for his flight home from Los Angeles LAX airport, he decided to give Daniel a call and update him on what he had found out from Lucy. During dinner, he had been able to extract some more information about John's work from her.

"I had dinner with Lucy last night," he began when Daniel answered the call.

"Yes, and …?" queried Daniel.

"I have some more information about John Sprague's work." Pierre paused and looked round the departure lounge before continuing "She told me that John had made good progress and was close to achieving his objective."

"What? You mean close to making a cheap detector that works?"

"Yes."

Daniel shook his head. "If that's true, if he does succeed in doing that, it would be catastrophic for us. The market for gem quality synthetics would dry up completely."

"I will be seeing Lucy again before too long. If I find out any more, I will be sure to let you know."

"Thanks, but I hope you don't have to bother. Otherwise, we will have to act to protect our business."

"I understand. And if it becomes a problem, we will work out what to do about it." said Pierre, as he ended the call.

When he got back to the south of France, Pierre noticed in his diary that his boss was due for release from prison in a few days time, having served two years of his five year sentence. Pierre had repeatedly promised him, during visits, that he would pick him up from the prison when he was released.

The Prison la Farlède, near Toulon, was surrounded by a twelve foot high concrete wall, topped with barbed wire, and it looked as bleak on the outside as it undoubtedly was, for its inhabitants, on the inside. It was only a short distance from Toulon but more than forty miles from Pierre's boss's home in Sainte Maxime so he had received few visitors, apart from Pierre, during his time there. Inside the concrete wall, prisoners were housed either in one of three L-shaped buildings, each having three floors of cells, or in the main building which was three hundred yards long and also had three floors of cells. Outside there was a recreation area which prisoners could use during the short time they were allowed out of their cells each day.

When his boss was due to come out of the main prison door, Pierre was waiting for him. He looked at his watch and, as he did, the door opened and his boss emerged. As he came out of the prison, he looked up at the sky and smiled and then noticed Pierre. The two men greeted each other with a hug before walking towards the car park, which was only a short distance away. Before long they were walking between the parked cars, heading for where Pierre had parked his black BMW.

"How are you, Pierre?" asked his boss.

"I'm good, thank you," responded Pierre but his boss could tell, from the look on his face, that all was not well.

He stopped walking and turned towards Pierre. "Something I should know about?" he asked.

Pierre also stopped walking and sighed deeply. "Not really. It is a personal matter."

Pierre's boss looked at him enquiringly. They knew each other well enough to share personal matters and, after a few moments, Pierre relented and reached into his pocket. He pulled out a gold locket and handed it to his boss. "Here, you can have this. I have no more use for it."

Pierre's boss took the locket from him. He could tell from the weight and feel of it that it was made of plastic not gold but he didn't think that was what was concerning Pierre. He opened the locket. Inside was a small picture of Lucy. He ran his finger over the picture affectionately, mentally stroking her face, before looking up at Pierre, enquiringly.

"Her name is Lucy. I thought she was my girlfriend," said Pierre, "She lives in Santa Monica."

"She's nice, very nice!" said his boss as he closed the locket and offered it back to Pierre.

Pierre gave him a disbelieving look. "I don't want it back. I just found out on this trip that she has a new boyfriend now. You keep it," he said. "Maybe you can change the picture and give it to *your* girlfriend."

Pierre's boss took over the disbelieving look. "Pierre, I have been in jail for two years!" he responded, "I don't have a girlfriend anymore." His look turned to one of disgust as he continued walking through the car park. After a few moments, feeling a little calmer, he spoke again, changing the subject in the hope of a more upbeat conversation.

"So, how is business?" he asked

"Business is good," responded Pierre, "But I think there may be a problem."

Pierre's boss stopped walking again, a look of consternation on his face as he turned to look at Pierre. "A problem? What kind of a problem?" he asked.

"Don't worry," replied Pierre, "I have talked to Blundell about it and we know what has to be done to fix it, if it comes to that." Pierre put his hand behind his boss's back, gently encouraging him to continue walking to the car. "Let's get in the car and I will tell you all about it on the way to Sainte Maxime."

"OK," nodded Pierre's boss as the two men got into the car and drove out of the car park, round the roundabout and off through the tunnel under the railway line. He looked back at the prison as they drove away towards the junction with the main road, which would take them in the direction of Sainte Maxime. He was pleased to be a free man again and on his way home.

Three weeks later, June having finally arrived, Carter and Nicole boarded the six-seater propeller powered aircraft which would carry them from San Pedro on Ambergris Caye to Belize City airport. Nicole particularly loved this part of any journey they went on. The plane seemed to fly close to the water and she could see the boats making their way to San Pedro from the mainland; it was as if she had wings and was flying herself there.

From Belize, a Boeing jet aircraft took them to Miami before they boarded a huge Jumbo Jet for the longest part of the journey to London. By the time they had arrived at Heathrow airport and collected their luggage, it was almost 9:00pm so they went straight to the Holiday Inn, which was close to the airport and where they had booked a room for the night.

The next morning, Carter took a taxi to the Hertz car hire depot at the airport and picked up a dark blue Peugeot before returning to the hotel to collect Nicole and their bags. Before long they were driving along the M4 motorway on their way to Oxford to meet John.

When they reached Oxford, Carter parked the car on Woodstock Road, near the city centre. He and Nicole parted company almost immediately. He needed to get to South Parks Road, the location of Oxford University's Department of Earth Sciences, where John had set up his research laboratory, whereas Nicole had decided to carry on into the centre of Oxford and revisit some old haunts. Carter kissed Nicole on the cheek as he turned to head towards the Department of Earth Science's buildings. Nicole continued along the main road south towards the river, keen to see some of the places where she and Carter had spent time as students nearly thirty years earlier.

When Carter reached the Earth Sciences building, a modern building constructed of glass and concrete in an interesting if not particularly beautiful design, he went in and approached the reception desk.

"Good morning, Sir. Can I help you?" the male receptionist asked.

"Yes, my name is Carter Jefferson. I'm here to see John Sprague," responded Carter, smiling.

The receptionist smiled back and picked up the phone on the desk in front of him before pressing a few buttons and waiting.

"Hello Sir, Carter Jefferson is here at reception to see you." The receptionist replaced the phone and looked at Carter. "He's on his way down."

Carter nodded and wandered away from the desk, looking around the very spacious hall in which he now found himself and wondering how John was liking working in this environment.

A few minutes later, Carter heard footsteps coming down the long staircase. He looked round to see John come down the last few steps and walk across the hall towards him.

"Carter! You found it OK then?" said John as they shook hands warmly.

"Sure, no problem," answered Carter, "I was here for four years as a student, remember."

"Of course. But I don't think this building was here then."

Carter took another look around as he spoke. "Absolutely not! The geology department didn't have anything like this back then. It's very impressive!"

"Wait till you see my lab; it's small but perfectly formed. And, exactly what I wanted. Come on, I'll show you."

John's lab in Oxford was not located within the Department of Earth Sciences building; that was reserved for research being undertaken by the department itself. Although John delivered lectures about the diamond industry for them from time to time, this only qualified him to have a small room in the building, which he hardly ever used. When it came to conducting research into the subject which he had become so passionate about, finding an inexpensive portable device capable of distinguishing between synthetic and natural diamonds, he used a couple of rooms in a building a little way further along South Parks Road. Using money provided by the FIDT, who were sponsoring his research, he had transformed the larger room into his lab, filling it with a couple of work benches and all the specialist equipment that he thought he would need. The smaller room functioned as his office and it was from there that he prepared his lectures and dealt with the administrative necessities of running a research laboratory.

The two men settled into the chairs at John's desk and started to reminisce about the things they had worked on together, the most recent of which, two years earlier, had been the sudden appearance of some synthetic diamonds in a parcel which was supposed to have contained only natural diamonds. Carter had been called in to find the source of the synthetic diamonds and the case had become a deadly game of cat and mouse as Carter had tracked down the source of the illicit gems. Along the way, Nicole had lost her father, who had been involved in the scheme, and also her son, before the mastermind of the scam had been caught and sent to prison. It had been a traumatic time for both her and Carter but ultimately it had brought them together again, after more than twenty-five years apart.

As they moved on to the present, Carter quizzed John about his move to Oxford. "It must make contact with Mikey even more difficult," he said.

"Not really," responded John. "OK, so it's a few extra hours travelling compared with getting to Santa Monica from New York but I see just as much of him now as I did before the move."

"And how's the research going? Are you making any headway?"

John nodded and smiled. "Yeah, I am," he said before pausing for a moment, "As it happens, I'm going to be doing a presentation at the Royal Society in London in a couple of weeks time. I've given it the title: Diamonds – Natural or Man-Made? What's the Difference?"

Carter cocked his head and stared John in the eyes. "Does that mean you've made some significant progress?"

John stared back at Carter before looking away and smiling. "Maybe you should come to the presentation and find out," he teased.

"You're not going to tell me, are you?"

"I'll tell you after I've done the Royal Society presentation."

"So you have got somewhere with it, then?"

"It's a work in progress," said John enigmatically.

Carter gave up and the conversation moved on to other subjects. Maybe John was embarrassed to tell Carter how little headway he had made with his research, despite working fairly continuously on the problem for nearly a year. Or maybe he just didn't want to talk about work.

"Anything else happening in your life?" asked Carter. "Mikey OK?"

"Yeah, he's fine. In fact I visited him a few weeks ago. He was just as bright and single-minded as ever!"

"Takes after his Dad, I guess."

"Yeah, well, maybe," responded John, a look of sadness on his face. "But there is something else I should probably tell you about," he continued, changing the subject.

There was a pause and a smile appeared on John's face. Carter had seen the look once or twice before.

"Let me guess," he said. "There's a new woman in your life?"

"Yup," replied John.

"She got a name?"

"Lucy. She lives in Santa Monica."

Carter was surprised to find that John's new girlfriend lived so far away and wondered how serious the relationship could be.

"How important is she to you?" he asked

"Important enough for me to have given her a solid gold locket with my picture inside it. She's into things like that and I knew she would appreciate it"

They both laughed and, after they had spent another hour sitting in the office adjoining John's lab, catching up on the rest of each other's news, Carter and John made their way down to the hall of the building. They promised to make sure that they stayed in touch more regularly in the future before they hugged and Carter left. Once outside the building, Carter took his phone out of his pocket and called Nicole.

Before long, Carter and Nicole were back on the motorway, heading for St Pancras International Station in London where they planned to drop off the hire car and catch the six o'clock Eurostar train to Paris. In a few hours, they would be meeting Nicole's daughter, Eloise, and her husband, Jacques, at the Gare du Nord railway station in the centre of Paris. Jacques and Eloise were on holiday, staying with Jacques' mother Claudine in her house on the south bank of the Seine, which she had bought following her move from Port Grimaud on the French Riviera. Once aboard the train, as Carter and Nicole relaxed into their seats, the journey from Belize finally caught up with them and they slept soundly throughout the journey.

Chapter 3

Carter and Nicole woke from their slumbers shortly before their Eurostar train arrived at the Gare du Nord railway station in Paris. When it stopped at the platform, they were already at the door waiting to get off and when the doors finally opened, they were amongst the first passengers to leave the train.

Almost as soon as they were on the platform, they saw Nicole's daughter, Eloise, running towards them, a broad smile lighting up her face. Eloise was an attractive slim twenty-two year old girl with blonde hair and, now that she lived in the South of France, her skin was lightly tanned. Jacques, her husband of one year was following her but he was running more slowly. Jacques was handsome and well toned and Eloise had fallen for him almost as quickly as he had fallen for her.

Eloise had already embraced both her mother and Carter by the time Jacques had caught up with her. He shook hands with Carter and kissed Nicole on both cheeks before they all started making their way to the exit.

"It's so good to see you, Mum," said Eloise, still grinning from ear to ear. "I know it's only been a couple of months but it feels like ages since I saw you."

"I know, it does, doesn't it. But we're here now, and with enough time to do some serious catching up." Nicole looked at Jacques as she finished speaking. "How is your mother, Jacques? Well, I trust?"

"Yes, she is well, thank you. She loves to live in Paris," answered Jacques, "She misses Port Grimaud and the sea, of course, but there are many compensations for her to enjoy here. And she visits us regularly."

The little group made their way to the taxi rank and got into the next taxi. Once they were all in the car, Jacques spoke to the taxi driver.

"Timhotel Louvre, s'il vous plait, et suivant, le Quai Voltaire," he said and the driver sped off along the Rue La Fayette in the direction of the hotel, near the Louvre art gallery, where Carter had booked a room for the week.

The morning after they had arrived in Paris, when Carter and Nicole were up and running, they set out to walk to Claudine's apartment, which was across the Seine on the upmarket, south bank of the river. As Carter and Nicole strolled through the gardens of the Palais Royale towards the Louvre, they both drank in the atmosphere. It was a sunny day, which matched their mood perfectly as they looked forward to a few days in Paris with Eloise and Jacques. After the Louvre, they took a slight diversion into the Tuilleries, where Carter insisted on having a ham baguette and a coffee at his favourite café in the gardens; Carter had visited the city many times and he never went to Paris anymore without indulging this obsession.

Half an hour later, they left the café and continued through the gardens until they reached the footbridge across the Seine. They strolled across the bridge, taking in the views up and down the Seine towards the Eiffel Tower in one direction and Notre Dame in the other. When they reached the end of the bridge, they turned left onto the Quai Anatole France and passed the entrance to the Musée D'Orsay, one of the most popular art galleries in Paris. As they walked past, Carter looked at the queues of people waiting to go in and then, suddenly, he stopped and turned to his right to stare at a statue of a rhino perched on a rock. Carter had seen a lot of the world but he had always been particularly taken by this statue; it was huge and towered above him. Nicole smiled as he stared at it and ran his hand over it.

"Hello, my old friend! How are you doing?" he said as he walked round to face the rhino and look it in the eye. Needless to say, it did not respond, except in Carter's mind. In his mind, it was as pleased to see him as he was to see it.

Nicole smiled and took his arm as she led him away from the statue. They continued their walk along the road, which would soon turn into the Quai Voltaire, where Claudine lived.

When they arrived at the door to Claudine's apartment, it was opened within seconds of Carter knocking on it, as Eloise yanked it open to let them in. She guided them into the living room, a spacious room with a huge window and balcony overlooking the Seine. Jacques was in the room when they arrived and, taking his turn after Eloise had hugged both her mother and Carter, he also hugged Nicole and then shook hands with Carter. A few moments later, Claudine came into the room from the kitchen and she too hugged them both, a big smile on her face.

"Welcome to my new home," she said. "Please sit down. I am making some coffee for us and Jacques has been out for some nice pastries."

Carter wished he hadn't had the ham baguette but smiled warmly as he sat in an armchair. "Coffee and a pastry would be lovely," he said.

Nicole and Eloise chatted away to each other in a corner of the room, catching up on each other's news, while Claudine disappeared into the kitchen to finish making the coffee, leaving Jacques and Carter to talk to each other.

"How's the charter business doing?" asked Carter, trying to make conversation.

"Good, it is good. We have as many charters as we want."

"And are you still enjoying it?"

"Oh yes, I like being on the sea. But the best times are when Eloise and I go off together, on our own. Those are the most special times."

Carter nodded. "I'm sure they are. Are you still living in Philippe's house?"

"Of course! It is the best house in Port Grimaud! Only if we were to leave Port Grimaud would we not live there."

A shocked expression crossed Carter's face as he spoke, "Are you thinking of leaving Port Grimaud?" he asked.

Jacques considered for a moment before answering. "Not at the moment. But when our family position changes, then maybe."

"Your family position?" queried Carter, not quite sure what Jacques meant by that, but before Jacques could respond, Nicole let out a loud 'Whoop' and started jumping up and down. She turned to look at Carter, who was now staring at her, and came over to him.

"I've just had some wonderful news!" she said, unable to prevent a huge smile from spreading across her face. "Eloise is pregnant! Jacques and Eloise are having a baby. Isn't that great!"

Carter rose from his chair and hugged Eloise. "Congratulations," he said and shook Jacques hand, "I'm delighted for both of you.

Just then Claudine came back into the room with a tray bearing the coffee and pastries.

"Ah, so you have heard the news!" she said, smiling broadly at Nicole, "It seems we are to be grandmothers!"

"Indeed we are! What wonderful news!" Nicole looked at everyone in turn, finishing with Claudine, before continuing. "Much as I would like a cup of coffee, I think this calls for champagne! Do you have any champagne, Claudine?"

Claudine smiled. "But of course! This is Paris! I will get it. And we can have the coffee afterwards."

Moments later, Claudine returned from the kitchen with a bottle of champagne, which she gave to Carter to open as she set out the champagne flutes on the coffee table. As Carter pushed the cork up with his thumbs, it flew out of the bottle with a loud bang and the champagne began to gush out of the bottle; there was no way he was going to open the bottle in a more controlled way on this occasion! Carter quickly aimed the bottle at the glasses, hoping to waste as little of the champagne as possible

---

Back in Oxford, John Sprague was continuing his work. He was a hardworking man, not only because he enjoyed his work but because he also felt that it was important; work that needed to be done by someone. As a result, he would do all the necessary office work in the evenings, leaving the days free for him to focus on his research. His typical practice, unless he had something better to do, was to work on his research project until the end of the normal working day and then take a break for something to eat. After that, he would return to the office to deal with the less interesting tasks, including admin and preparing for any lectures he was due to deliver. It was also the time of day when he might hear from Lucy and spend some time Skyping with her. But he would keep working until everything was up to date, often resulting in him working until quite late, and that was the case on the evening of the day after Carter had visited him.

As John beavered away at his desk, trying to make his finances add up, the intercom from the front door of the building beeped. It was 10:00pm and the rest of the building had emptied several hours earlier. Annoyed and frustrated, John pressed the button on the intercom on his desk.

"Yes, can I help you?"

"Am I speaking to John Sprague?"

"Yes, what do you want?"

"Hi, my name is Tom. I have something for you."

"Do you know what time it is?" John was not enthusiastic about letting someone he didn't know into the building at that hour, when he was there alone.

"Yes, I am sorry it is so late, I have only just arrived in Oxford from London and I have to leave early in the morning tomorrow," said the voice at the other end of the intercom. There was a few moments' silence before the voice continued. "Lucy asked me to call in on you while I was here; she had something she wanted me to give to you. She said you always worked late and that it would be OK."

"You know Lucy?" John queried, shocked and unsure who his late night visitor was, or whether he should let him in.

"Yes. My company supplies her company and I had a meeting with her in Santa Monica last week. That was when she asked me to do this favour for her. It was to be a surprise."

"Well, it's certainly that!" The reference to Santa Monica satisfied John that this late night visitor was telling the truth. "OK, come on in. I'm on the first floor. I'll meet you at the top of the stairs." He pressed another button on the intercom, which resulted in a continuous buzzing sound until he removed his finger a few seconds later.

John was waiting at the top of the stairs as his visitor ascended them. He was wearing gloves and in his left hand, was a large heavy sports bag, in his other hand was a small gift-wrapped package. As he reached the top step, a smile appeared on his face.

"So, what's the surprise?" asked John.

"Lucy asked me to give you this," the man said holding out the small package.

John smiled as he took the package from the man and began to open it. He wondered what Lucy could possibly have wanted to send him, without warning, via this anonymous courier. When he realised what it was, his smile broadened even further and turned into a laugh. Contained in the wrapping paper was a small gold coloured plastic locket. John opened it to find a small picture of Lucy inside. He closed the locket and looked at the man.

"Thank you, that's great. Would you like to come in for a coffee?" he said, holding out his hand, expecting the man to shake it before joining him in the office. The man smiled but then, instead of accepting John's offer, his face hardened. He dropped the sports bag on the floor and placed his left hand on John's shoulder, behind his neck. Then he pulled John towards him as, with his other hand, he pulled a large knife out from its sheath at the back of his trousers. Looking directly into John's shocked eyes, he thrust the knife deep into John's chest. John gasped and stared at the man in astonishment but all he saw was a self-satisfied grin. The man pulled the knife out and then thrust it in again, this time driving the knife into John's side. As John crumpled to the floor, gasping for air, the man walked past him and went through the door into John's office. Once inside the office, a brief glance through the door from the office to John's lab assured him that there was no one else there. He returned to the top of the stairs, where John was panting for breath as blood poured out of the two knife wounds. The man put his hands under John's arms and pulled him across the floor into the office. Then he collected his bag from the top of the stairs and went back into the office, closing the door behind him. He looked at John and reached down to grasp the chain attached to the locket, which John was still holding. He pulled hard, expecting to retrieve the locket but the chain snapped, leaving the locket still clasped tightly in John's hand. Frustratedly, the man threw the chain on the floor and went into the lab.

As John held onto the locket, with the blood draining out of his body, he tried to understand what was happening and his thoughts went back to when he had first met Lucy, three months earlier. He had been on one of his many visits to see Mikey and had then gone on to the CompTech fair in San Francisco. He had driven the three hundred miles from Santa Monica to Silicon Valley in San Francisco where he was due to attend the science fair, partly thrilled at having been able to see Mikey, of whom he was justly proud, and partly sad because he would not be seeing him again for two months. His convertible hire car sped along the freeway in the sunshine and, as evening drew in, the coolness of the air made him shiver slightly. A few minutes later, he pulled in to the car park at the motel where he would be staying for the next two days.

John wasn't prone to attend science fairs but when he had heard about this one, close enough to justify a visit to Santa Monica, and his beloved Mikey, he had decided he would go.

Having checked into his motel and made his way to the conference centre where the fair was being held, John walked into the building and collected his badge. Reluctantly, because he hated wearing badges, he put the tape, from which the badge was hanging, round his neck and made his way to the exhibition hall. Not surprisingly, given the location, this particular science fair was an event sponsored and run by suppliers to computer manufacturers and was focussed on the latest research into computer science.

Almost as soon as John had entered the hall, his eye was drawn to one of the stands. According to the sign above it, this was the stand belonging to NewChip Corp which, if it's prominent sales pitch was to be believed, was the front runner in the use of synthetic diamond wafers in the manufacture of computer processors.

Although John was attracted by the mention of synthetic diamonds, it was the person manning the stand that had particularly caught his eye. As he stood and watched her talking to the people who came up to the stand, he was struck by her appearance, not so much because she was particularly beautiful but because, to him, she was the image of perfection. Her long light brown hair ran down her bare shoulders and lay gently on her small breasts. The yellow dress she was wearing was quite close fitting and clearly demonstrated her slim figure. But more than any of that, it was her smile which John found so captivating.

After John had been standing watching this angel of a woman for several minutes, a quiet period came when she had no one approaching her stand and talking to her. Before John could make a move, she spotted him staring at her and smiled at him. That was enough of an invitation. John started walking towards the stand. When he arrived in front of the woman, he looked into her beautiful large brown eyes and smiled back at her before daring to speak.

"I see your company's work involves synthetic diamonds," he said.

"Yes, it does," she replied, "We are using them in the manufacture of computer processors."

"So I see. I was aware of diamond based material being evaluated for that purpose but I wasn't aware that anyone had actually gone into production."

"We haven't been in production long but we've reached the point now where we know that, as long as it can be acquired at the right price, diamond is the best raw material to use." The woman smiled at John and he smiled back.

"I'd like to hear more about your work," said John, "When do you get finished here?"

The woman chuckled. "Are you asking me for a date?" she asked.

"No, no, I couldn't do that. I don't even know your name."

"It's Lucy," she said, "What's yours?"

"John, John Sprague. I work with diamonds too." John held out his hand and Lucy shook hands with him.

"Really? Well, at least now you know my name." There was an invitation in the smile that Lucy gave John as she spoke.

John smiled back at her. "Is there any chance you would have time for a drink and a chat when you're finished here?" he asked

"Sure, why not? How about I meet you at ... " she looked at her watch, " ... at seven, in the bar? It's just round the corner from here."

"That would be great! Thank you." John held out his hand again, he wanted to feel the cool softness of hers again, and she obliged.

"See you at seven then, John."

"Seven it is."

Reluctantly, John turned away from Lucy and pretended to be interested in the other stands in the hall but his mind was racing. He had propositioned a woman he had only just met! He knew nothing about her, apart, of course, from how gorgeous she was. John looked at his watch, it was three-fifteen. He had nearly another four hours to wait!

John's thoughts were brought back to the present as the man who had stabbed him lit a match and threw it into the lab. The lab was quickly engulfed in flames as the petrol the man had liberally poured all over the floor and benches caught fire. As he turned back to face John, he reached down to John's hands, each of which was held tightly in a fist. He forced each hand open, expecting to find the locket in one of them, but when he found nothing in either of them, he started to examine the floor of the office, pushing John's body out of the way as he did. Finally, sighing and shaking his head, he lit another match, this time throwing it towards John. It landed on the floor next to John, who watched, impotently, as the petrol on the floor of the office caught light and the flames began to engulf him. He reached out his hand towards the man, but the man just smiled, shook his head and turned away, closing the door behind him as he left the office. John's eyes closed for the last time as the flames engulfed his body.

As the man who had stabbed John and set the lab on fire left the building, flames could be seen in the windows of the first floor and, within a few moments, there was the sound of breaking glass, followed by a loud whoosh as the fire in the lab sucked in air from outside to keep the flames burning brightly. The few people who were in the street turned to look at the building, now engulfed in flames. A couple of them extracted their phones to ring the emergency services.

The man who had set fire to the building, with John in it, walked away unnoticed.

By the time the fire brigade and the police had arrived at the scene there was little left of the building. Flames were still licking the walls but mostly it was just a charred ruin. Inspector Andy Ellis of the Oxford police looked at it. He shook his head as the firemen hosed water onto what remained of the flames.

Chapter 4

On their third day in Paris, having largely spent the second day revisiting old haunts, Carter and Nicole rose and breakfasted on coffee and croissants. This they did at one of their favourite cafés near the Pont Neuf, with Notre Dame Cathedral, on the Ile de la Cité in the middle of the River Seine, visible in the background. They had arranged to meet Jacques and Eloise, along with Claudine if she decided to join them, on the bridge, near the steps leading down to the jetty. From the jetty, they could hop onto a boat for a trip up the Seine as far as the Eiffel Tower and back again. It was something Carter had decided he wanted to do before they had left Belize.

As they sat at the café, at a table on the pavement outside, shielded from the sun by a canopy, they looked at each other and smiled. They had been together for two years now and the excitement had still not worn off. Having been apart for most of their adult lives, following their break up in Oxford, two years seemed hardly any time at all and they had both enjoyed every second of it.

Carter looked at his watch. "It's almost eleven," he said as he signalled the waiter over to collect the money he had placed on top of the bill. "We should be going."

They rose from their chairs and set out to walk the short distance to the Pont Neuf. When they got there, Jacques and Eloise were waiting for them, standing close to the steps which led down from the bridge, through a sort of tunnel, to the riverbank below. The four hugged each other before proceeding down the steps into the semi-darkness and emerging near the building which housed the boat operator's offices and ticket booths. As Carter queued to get their tickets, Jacques, Eloise and Nicole wandered towards the door leading to the jetty, where they had agreed to wait for Carter.

"Did you enjoy your breakfast?" asked Eloise of her mother, already knowing what the answer would be.

"Of course! What's not to like about a cappuccino and a croissant at a café in Paris overlooking the Seine?" came the response, followed by a smile.

"Are you still liking living in Belize?" asked Jacques, aware that it had been a big decision for Nicole to make the move from Yorkshire, where she and Eloise, and her now dead son, Rob, had lived for many years. Even after the death of her Yorkshire born husband, soon after they were married, she had decided to stay there but following her marriage to Carter, that had all changed.

Nicole nodded. "Very much," she said, "The people are kind and Carter's house, being right on the beach, is idyllic."

"But you must miss the cultural side of things a bit," said Eloise, "You know, parties, theatre, that sort of thing."

"Not really. Yes, the culture is different but that doesn't mean it doesn't exist," responded Nicole, "And, actually, I quite like the way things are in Belize. You know, very laid back and take it as it comes. I like the easy-going way of life they have there."

Carter interrupted their conversation as he arrived with the tickets in his hand. "The next boat will be leaving in ten minutes," he said as they went through the door onto the jetty. There was already a queue of people waiting to board the boat which was moored there.

Before long, they were all sitting in the sunshine on the top deck of the boat. The four of them were squashed into one row on the starboard side of the boat as it made its way west along the Seine. A tour guide stood at the front, providing a running commentary on what could be seen from the boat. Carter was struck by her sunglasses. They were huge, almost the size of saucers, and he could not stop looking at her.

"I think someone is quite taken with our guide," said Nicole, indicating who she meant to Jacques and Eloise with a jerk of her head. They smiled and looked at Carter and he became aware of the fact that he was being watched. He turned his head to look at them.

"What?" he asked, genuinely unaware that he had been staring at the attractive blonde girl in the huge red sunglasses.

Eloise chuckled. "Mum thinks you've got the hots for the guide," she said.

"Ridiculous!" responded Carter, "But I do like her sunglasses." He broke into a smile and they all joined him as Eloise spoke.

"They are a bit out there, aren't they?"

After ploughing along the Seine for about half an hour, the boat reached the Eiffel Tower where it made a big sweeping turn, keeping the tower in sight until the turn was completed and they were on their way back to the Pont Neuf.

As they all enjoyed the picturesque scene on both sides and drank in the sunshine, Carter's phone rang. Nicole gave him a disparaging look, clearly not amused at the interruption to the peace and calm surrounding them. He looked at his phone to see who was calling and then turned to Nicole.

"It's Isaac!" he said, "What the hell does he want? And at this time? It must be the crack of dawn in New York!"

Nicole shrugged as Carter pressed the receive call button and put the phone to his ear. "Isaac! Hi. What can I do for you?" Carter listened as Isaac spoke to him, a look of consternation rapidly crossing his face. When Isaac had finished, Carter responded. "Yeah, of course. I'm in Paris right now but I'll get on to it right away." Carter nodded as Isaac thanked him before ringing off.

"By the look on your face that wasn't a social call?" suggested Nicole.

Carter shook his head and tried to collect his thoughts. The news from Isaac had come as a big shock. "John's dead," he said, when eventually he found his voice.

Nicole screwed up her face, not quite comprehending what she had just been told.

"John as in John Sprague? Who you were with a few days ago in Oxford?" she asked. Carter nodded and Nicole continued, "Bloody hell! What happened?"

Carter looked away into the distance and Nicole realised just how much the news was affecting him. She put her hand on his shoulder and squeezed it gently.

"I am so sorry," she said. "I know you two were close." Carter nodded but continued to look away towards the bank of the river. He lifted his hand and wiped away a tear.

"How did he die? Did Isaac say?"

"He's not sure," said Carter, "He's only just heard about it, he says. All they know, at this stage, is that last night there was a fire at his lab and he was killed. Isaac says there wasn't much left of the lab, or of John, by the time the fire had been put out."

"So was it an accident? An electrical fault or something?"

48

"According to the police, it was deliberate."

"But why would John set fire to his own lab?"

"He didn't. Someone else did," said Carter before pausing and looking Nicole in the eye, "After they had stabbed him in the chest."

Nicole's hand went to her mouth in shock. Beside her, Eloise and Jacques were watching and listening, not sure who or what Nicole and Carter were talking about. She looked at them and then at Carter.

"Why would anyone want to kill him?"

Carter just shook his head and stared into the distance before closing his eyes and letting his head drop. Nicole took his hand and held it in both of hers as Jacques and Eloise looked on questioningly.

A couple of hours after Carter had received the news about John Sprague's death, he and Nicole were sitting in their hotel room, she on a chair and he on the edge of the bed. On the small table between them was a bottle of wine from which two glasses had been filled.

"Isaac wants me to go and talk to the police in Oxford. See what I can find out about what happened. Maybe help them to get to the bottom of it."

Nicole nodded. "OK. Do you want me to come with you?"

"No, that's not necessary," said Carter, shaking his head slowly, "And it wouldn't be much fun for you either."

"So, shall I head back to Belize and wait for you there?"

"No," Carter shook his head again, "Why don't you stay here with Jacques and Eloise?" He looked at her as she replied to his suggestion.

"They're going back home to Port Grimaud tomorrow," she said, "Do you think you'll be done in Oxford by then?"

"I don't know. Until I get there, I don't know what I'm dealing with. Or how involved I might get."

"Maybe I could go back to Port Grimaud and stay with them until you know what's what?

Carter nodded, "Good idea, if you think they'll be OK with that."

"I'm sure they will be. And it will give me a chance to catch up with some people again."

"OK. Give them a call and see what they say."

Nicole got up from her chair and went over to Carter. "I'll do that later," she said. "But first, I want you to promise me that you'll be careful. After all, you have me to consider now and I don't want anything bad to happen to you."

Carter smiled as Nicole sat on the bed beside him, an amorous smile playing on her lips. "I'll be careful," he said. "I promise."

Nicole put her arm around his waist as she stroked his cheek with her free hand. "Good," she said in as sexy a voice as she could.

Carter sighed and took a deep breath as, bit by bit, Nicole became more intimate in her ministrations. He wasn't sure this was the time for sex but any reservations he might have had were being eroded very quickly, especially when Nicole unbuttoned his shirt and began kissing his chest. Before long, they both fell back onto the bed and gave way to their passions.

The following morning, as Nicole was packing up her things in the hotel room in Paris, ready to leave and set off to meet Jacques and Eloise, Carter was on a Eurostar train hurtling along the track back to London.

As he reviewed the events of the last twenty-four hours, he started to apply his logical mind to them to see if he could come up with any answers.

The first possible scenario that he considered was that the Oxford police had got it wrong, that the fire had been an accident, but he quickly dismissed that thought as fanciful as it would not explain the stab wound in his chest. The second option was that John had set the fire himself and accidentally got caught in it, but that too failed to explain the stabbing. No, the only possible explanation was that he had been attacked and killed by an intruder who had then proceeded to torch the lab with John in it. But why? What motive could a killer have? Maybe he, or they, were after the diamonds which John kept in a small safe in the office, when he wasn't using them in an experiment. But they wouldn't be worth that much, not enough to justify murder, at least he didn't think so, and that ruled out theft as a motive.

As Carter turned these thoughts over in his mind, he recalled the time he had spent with John only a few days earlier. They had talked about old times, reliving some of their past escapades and adventures and they had talked about what they were both currently doing. Carter already knew about John's search for an affordable synthetic diamond detector so none of that had surprised him. Unlike Lucy! Now that had been a big surprise. As far as Carter knew, John had not had a serious relationship with another woman since his wife had died. Her untimely departure from his life had left him feeling deserted and he hadn't wanted to ever be in that desolate place again. True, he had had some girlfriends along the way but he had never let himself get seriously involved with them, not like he seemed to have done with Lucy.

From what John had told Carter, it had been very unexpected, a chance encounter at a science fair in California. They had hit it off from the start and the fact that they had shared interests in synthetic diamonds and miniaturisation just made it all seem right to John. He had explained to Carter how, after they had enjoyed a romantic dinner, they had gone to a bar and talked. Lucy had explained how the use of synthetic diamond wafers had made possible the miniaturisation of some quite bulky equipment and John had told her about his search for a small, relatively cheap synthetic diamond detector.

John had quickly recognised that what Lucy was working on could be helpful to him in his work. They had discussed the possibility of working together but it had gone no further than that, although John had started using her company's micro-processors as he had tried to develop an affordable solution. In the few months that had passed since they had met, most of their time together had been spent enjoying their relationship, not discussing their work. In fact they had only had the opportunity to be together on three occasions since the science fair, and these occasions had usually been combined with a visit by John to see Mikey. Of course their phone bills had climbed dramatically as they had spoken to each other on most days, exchanging idle chit-chat about what they were doing. And they would Skype each other regularly as well, just to enjoy seeing each other and being in each other's virtual company.

There was no doubt in Carter's mind that John and Lucy had been deeply in love with each other, if for no other reason than John had told him that he had given her a solid gold heart shaped locket with a photograph of himself inside it. If that didn't prove it, nothing would.

Only one other subject had come up in Carter's conversation with John that day, and then only for the short time that was left after John had stopped lyricising about Lucy. That subject was the matter of John's progress with finding a solution to the natural diamond industry's problem of not being able to distinguish between synthetic and natural diamonds without resorting to a lab filled with very expensive equipment. To Carter's surprise, John had refused to elaborate, despite Carter's insistent questioning, but the enigmatic smile on his face gave Carter the clear impression that he had made progress, maybe even that he had cracked the problem. Why else would he have been booked to present a paper at the Royal Society, one of the most prestigious scientific establishments in the world?

After disembarking from the Eurostar train at St Pancras station in London, Carter went back to the Hertz car hire office. Once he was seated in the car, he texted Nicole to say that he had arrived and then he set off to drive to Oxford.

Chapter 5

Mikey stared out of the window of his bedroom in Santa Monica. Downstairs, his grandmother, Alice, was in the kitchen doing the washing up following their breakfast of cereal and pancakes. Mikey loved pancakes and could become quite difficult if he didn't get his daily quota.

As Mikey watched the people walking along the street below, most of them heading towards the beach, he saw a man and a woman dressed in smart business-like clothes approach the house. As they knocked on the door, he turned from the window and went to the top of the stairs, getting there just as Alice reached the front door.

Alice pulled the door open and saw the man and the woman, both looking very serious. "Can I help you," she asked.

The man pulled a card wallet from his pocket and flipped it open to reveal that he was from the Santa Monica Police Department.

"I'm Detective Harrison and this is my colleague, Detective Chaney. We're with the SMPD."

Alice's expression changed to one of mystification. Why would the SMPD be calling on her?

"Are you Alice McGill?" asked the man as Alice just stood there looking at them.

"Yes, I am. Why are you here?"

"Can we come in?"

Alice looked behind her and saw Mikey standing at the top of the stairs. "Go back to your room, please, Mikey." Mikey reluctantly did as he was told and closed the door before Alice continued. "OK, come in," she said, stepping to one side.

Detective Harrison followed Detective Chaney into the hall and closed the front door behind him. Once they were all in the living room, Alice closed the door to the hall.

"Please sit down," she said as she sat on the sofa and indicated the two armchairs to them. "And then you can tell me what this is about."

The two detectives sat down and there was a pause before Detective Harrison spoke. "You are Mrs Alice McGill?" he asked.

"I already told you that," replied Alice as she sighed, a little offended by being asked the same question twice.

"And you know a man called John Sprague?"

Alice nodded. "He's my son-in-law. Why are you asking me this? What's happened?"

Detective Harrison sighed and dropped his head before lifting it again and looking Alice in the eyes. "I'm sorry, Mrs McGill, but we have some bad news for you."

Alice froze and her eyes stared at the man, her expression fixed, as he continued.

"We have been informed by the police in England that a man named John Sprague died in a fire in Oxford, the night before last."

Alice's whole body sagged on hearing the news and her eyes dropped to her hands as she twisted and turned them, her distress clear to see. After several moments, she looked up at Detective Harrison, and then at his female colleague, before returning her gaze to Harrison.

"Are you sure it was my John Sprague? Not someone else with the same name?" she asked, more in hope than expectation.

"You were named as next of kin on his passport."

Alice nodded and then began to cry. Detective Chaney moved to sit beside her. She put her arm on Alice's shoulder and stroked it gently.

"We are so sorry to be bringing you such sad news," she said, as comfortingly as she could. Alice looked at her, tears running down her cheeks, and then dropped her eyes again.

Suddenly they all heard a noise outside the room. Alice turned her head to look at the door. The detectives followed the direction of her gaze as Alice got up and slowly opened the door. Immediately, Mikey, who had been standing outside listening to the conversation, turned and ran back up the stairs, screaming and shouting.

"It's not true Grandma! I don't believe it! Tell them to go away!"

The door of Mikey's bedroom slammed shut and there was silence. Alice looked at Detective Chaney who screwed up her face and mouthed 'I'm sorry!' to her. As Alice turned back into the living room, a loud crash came from Mikey's bedroom. Alice looked back up the stairs and shook her head sadly. Detective Chaney put her arm around Alice.

"Would you like us to stay until he calms down a bit?" she asked but Alice shook her head.

"No, you should go. I'll take care of him. That's what I've been doing for the last twelve years since his mother died. When he was just a baby."

"I'm so sorry," said Detective Chaney as she and Detective Harrison prepared to leave the house.

As they reached the front door, Detective Chaney reached into her pocket. She removed a card and held it out towards Alice. "Here are my contact details. Please give me a call when you're ready and I'll provide you with more information and do whatever I can to help."

Alice looked Detective Chaney in the eyes as she took the card, appreciative of her concern and her offer of help. "Thank you," she said, "I suppose I'll need to arrange for his body to be brought home."

Detective Chaney nodded as Mikey appeared at the top of the stairs. She looked up at him and Alice, noticing this, looked behind her and saw him standing there, his hands gripping the banister and tears flowing from his eyes. As he went back into his room, she turned back to Detective Chaney.

"I don't know how he's going to cope, losing his Dad now as well. It's just not fair." Alice shook her head sadly as the two detectives went out of the front door and she closed it.

Upstairs in his room, the tears continued to flow from Mikey's eyes as he gathered up the pieces of the large brown clay owl his father had given him on his last visit with the advice to 'seek wisdom rather than fame'. They had been talking about Mikey's desire to be a famous actor. Living in Santa Monica, it was hard not to be attracted by the trappings of theatrical success. And now, the last present he would ever get from his father lay in pieces on his bedroom floor. When he had gathered all the pieces into a pile, he went to his wardrobe and extracted a shoe box. He dumped the shoes unceremoniously onto the floor and then knelt beside the shattered owl. Slowly he picked up the pieces and put them into the box; he could still treasure the present, even if it was broken into bits. As he picked up the last piece, he looked at it; it didn't look like a piece of the owl, it was just a bit of black plastic. He turned it over in his hands and then shrugged and dropped it into the box.

As Mikey put the box containing the pieces of the broken owl into his wardrobe, his grandmother knocked gently on the door. He went to open the door and when he did, she took him in her arms and they both let their grief pour out of themselves freely.

––––––––––––––––––––––––––––

As Carter drove from London to Oxford, Nicole, Eloise and Jacques boarded a train from Paris to Aix-en-Provence. Three hours later, they arrived in Aix from where they drove to Port Grimaud, parking in the residents' car park just outside the town.

Not long after, Nicole was reclining in a chair on the terrace outside what had once been her father's house, the largest house in Port Grimaud. Although the house had been inherited by Nicole after her father's death, she had given it to Eloise and Jacques when they had got married. As Nicole had, by then, moved to live with Carter in Belize, she had no use for the house and it seemed the most appropriate thing to do with it. On the table beside her was a bottle of Sancerre, her favourite white wine, and a half full glass. Nicole closed her eyes and drank in the sunshine. As she did, her mind drifted back into the past.

It had been a tumultuous few years for her, beginning with Carter contacting her after twenty-five years, something which had been quickly followed by the death of her son, Rob. A few weeks later, that had been followed by the death of her father, Philippe, as a result of his involvement in a diamond smuggling scam which Carter had exposed. She didn't blame Carter for her father's death in any way. Not simply because she was in love with Carter, and had been since they had met as students in Oxford, but because she now understood that her father had, perhaps unknowingly, got into bed with some very unsavoury people. One of them was Gilles Rénard, who, over the years, had been her father's right hand man in so many enterprises and who she had met on many occasions. She now knew that it had been Gilles who had encouraged her father to get involved in the scam. Although she had been aware that Gilles was not afraid of breaking the law when it suited him, Nicole had never seen him as particularly dangerous. But when Philippe had died in his attempt to save Jacques and Eloise from Gilles and his cronies, she had realised just how far into the criminal pit Gilles had descended. That Gilles had only been sentenced to five years imprisonment for his part in the deaths of four people had shocked and outraged her. Although it was true that the only crime the police had been able to pin on him was that of stealing a yacht, she knew he had been much more involved than that.

Nicole raised herself slightly and took a sip from the wine glass before looking out across the lake that formed the centre of the canal town of Port Grimaud in the Bay of St. Tropez. At the other side of the lake, was the Capitainerie and it was there that she could see Jacques' boat, the Esprit de Jacques, moored. The Esprit de Jacques was a sixty-four foot motor yacht which Jacques had bought, soon after his twenty-first birthday, with money from a trust fund. The trust fund had been set up for him by someone who believed he was his father but who, at the time, was unknown to Jacques.

In the distance, Nicole could just about make Jacques out as, with Eloise, he prepared the boat for a charter he had booked for the next day. She smiled as she recalled Eloise's excitement when she had phoned her to tell her that she had met this wonderful French man. And now they were married, and living and working together in Port Grimaud, where Nicole, herself, had grown up.

In one of the larger meeting rooms at the Oxford Police headquarters, two tables had been lined up, end to end, and several chairs placed behind them. In these chairs were several senior police officers in uniform along with a detective in plain clothes. Arranged in front of the tables, facing the police officers were three television camera crews and about fifteen other people, including both television interviewers and newspaper reporters.

The fire in the building on South Parks Road had already been widely reported, as had the death of the only occupant at the time of the fire, but this was the first official briefing from the police.

Following a brief introduction during which the Deputy Chief Constable had confirmed that the fire had been deliberately started and also that the man found dead in the building after the fire had been put out had been murdered, the press conference was opened to questions.

Immediately a young woman reporter jumped in. "Who was the man who was killed?" she asked.

"I can't give you his name yet. We're still in the process of contacting his relatives," answered the DCC.

"Was he local?"

"He was resident in Oxford although originally from the United States."

Another reporter, a middle aged man, tired of being upstaged by the young woman, stepped forward and spoke before she had a chance to ask another question.

"How was he killed?" he asked.

"He was stabbed prior to being burnt in the fire."

"Do you know what the motive for the fire was?" The young woman was in the driving seat again.

"At this stage, we have no information on that. Nor on the motive behind the murder. The investigation has only just begun."

The DCC looked along the line of police officers sitting at the tables to see if anyone wanted to speak. The detective in charge of the investigation nodded to him and he turned back to face the reporters again.

"Detective Chief Inspector Murray, who is leading the investigation, would like to say a few words," said the DCC, upon which DCI Murray began to speak.

"We would like to make an appeal," he began. "If anyone knows anything which might help with our enquiries, please contact us as soon as possible. At this stage, all information is valuable and will be kept entirely confidential. The number to call is 01865 230 230."

"Thank you Detective Chief Inspector," said the DCC. "Before we close this conference, I would like to extend the sympathies of all of us in the Thames Valley Police Force to the relatives of the victim of this appalling crime. Thank you."

The DCC, followed by the other police officers rose amid the flurry of camera flashes going off as the reporters got their last few photographs.

By the time Carter had arrived in Oxford, the police press conference was over. He parked the car on the road behind St Aldates police station before walking down Floyds Row and into the building. At the reception desk he asked for Detective Chief Inspector Murray and then sat on one of the seats provided for visitors. A few minutes later, DCI Murray appeared and went over to greet him.

"Carter Jefferson?" he asked.

"Yes," responded Carter. "And you must be DCI Murray."

"Indeed. Shall we go to my office?"

Carter nodded and they made their way to the staircase leading to the next floor of the three storey building. Once they were seated in DCI Murray's office, Carter took his FIDT identity card out of his pocket and passed it to Murray.

"Thanks for seeing me," he began, "As you can see, from time to time I work as an investigator for the New York Federation of International Diamond Traders, an industry body which seeks to protect the interests of its members, most of whom are dealers in diamonds."

Murray looked at Carter's identity card and then handed it back to him. "What can I do for you," he asked.

"Well," began Carter, "As I believe you know, my boss, Isaac Sternberg, the President of the Federation, asked me to contact you because one of the Federation's former employees, John Sprague, has been found dead in Oxford. He thinks I may be able to help with the enquiries into his death."

"And what do *you* think?" Murray leaned back in his chair and folded his arms.

"At this stage, I have no idea. All I know is that John is dead, that he was murdered and that his lab was torched."

"That's about the size of it. A murder inquiry is now under way but we've made little progress so far. Mr Sprague was working alone in the building when he was killed, at around 10:00pm. The fire was almost certainly a professional job, very thorough. There is very little left of the contents of the lab or of the victim for that matter."

"Do you have any leads at all?"

"Not really but the inquiry has only just begun. Having said that we are struggling to come up with a motive for either the murder or the arson."

"Do you know what he was working on?" asked Carter.

"According to the University's Department of Earth Sciences, it was something to do with synthetic diamonds. They say he was a bit of an expert on diamonds."

"He was more than that. He was one of the world's leading experts on the detection of synthetic diamonds. He was looking into ways of distinguishing between natural and synthetic diamonds."

"Interesting," responded Murray, "Was there anything about his work that could explain his murder?"

"Not that I know of for certain. He was always very secretive about his work but I can check with the FIDT who were part funding his research, if you like, and see if they know?"

"Yes, please do. And let me know what they say," said Murray, rising from his seat and offering his hand to Carter. "Thank you for your help Mr Jefferson. I'll await hearing further from you."

Carter rose from his seat and shook Murray's hand. "I'll be in touch as soon as I have any information," he said as Murray ushered him out of the office and towards the stairs.

An hour later, Carter had checked into the Old Parsonage Hotel. It was one of Oxford's better hotels and once he had settled into his room which overlooked a small wooded area between the Banbury and Woodstock roads, he called Isaac. He needed to find out how John's research had been progressing and Isaac was the only person he could think of who might know.

Although John had told Carter that he had made some progress, something which he had appeared to be very excited about, Carter had no idea how close to a solution John actually was. After a few rings, Isaac answered the phone.

"Isaac Sternberg," he said.

"Isaac. Hi, it's Carter here."

"Hi Carter. Tell me all," said Isaac, a sombre tone to his voice.

"Well, I just had a meeting with the detective in charge and, given that his lab was torched at the same time, it's looking like John might, possibly, have been killed because of what he was working on, although that's far from certain at this stage."

Carter waited for a response from Isaac. When it came it was subdued.

"I see," he said quietly.

"Isaac, apart from you and me, did anyone else know what John was working on?"

"Not that I know of," replied Isaac. "But he could have told other people about it, maybe people in the Earth Sciences Department."

"Yeah, maybe," responded Carter. "I'll check that out tomorrow." Carter paused for a few moments before continuing. "Do you know how he was getting on with his work? Any significant progress?"

"If he had made a breakthrough, he didn't tell me about it. I know that he felt he was moving forward with the research but that's all. But then he was always very hesitant to talk about where he was getting to with it. Did he tell you anything when you saw him?"

"No, not really. Pretty much the same as he told you, that he had made some good progress and that he was going to be making a presentation at the Royal Society in London about his work. But he didn't tell me specifically what progress he had made. It might have just been a step or two along the way."

"Well, see what you can find out, will you, Carter. John was a friend and I'd like to make sure the police find out who did this. Please give them any help you can and I'll send Conrad to join you in Oxford. You two make a good team."

Conrad was employed by the FIDT and had been Carter's partner in several of the investigations he had undertaken for them. He would be happy to have Conrad alongside him again.

Carter ended the call and threw his phone onto the bed before burying his face in his hands and taking a deep breath. It looked like he was back in investigation mode again, only this time he was investigating the death of a friend.

Chapter 6

Professor Ronald Thackeray had been a lecturer in the Geology Department of Oxford University at the time Carter was a student there and he now headed up the Department of Earth Sciences. In trying to find out what he could about John's death, Carter had decided that, as a first step, he should talk to the Professor. If he was to make any progress in finding out why John had been killed, he knew that he had to start at the beginning and fill in all the background he could about John's time in Oxford.

As Carter approached the entrance to the Earth Sciences building, he remembered, with some grief, that the last time he had done so had been to meet John, just a few days earlier. Once inside the building, he went to the reception desk, asked for the Professor and then wandered away towards the visitors seating area. He stood staring out of the large window overlooking the paved area outside the building and wondered if he would recognise the Professor after nearly thirty years. His thoughts were interrupted by a voice behind him.

"Carter! What a surprise!" Professor Thackeray was smiling and clearly delighted to see his former student.

Carter swung round on hearing the Professor's voice and he too broke into a smile as they shook hands. "Professor! It's good to see you," he said.

"Ronnie, please!" said the Professor with a slightly pained expression.

"OK. Ronnie," responded Carter. "Thanks for making time to see me."

"No problem. Shall we go up to my office and get some tea?"

Carter nodded and the two men set off towards the stairs. As they climbed the stairs, they reminisced and Carter noted that, despite the length of time that had passed since their last meeting, his former tutor had changed very little. That last meeting had been after Carter had graduated with a Masters degree in Geology. On that occasion, Carter had still been wearing his graduation gown and sub-fusc, the dark clothing worn beneath the gown, when the Professor had congratulated him warmly and sincerely. The Professor had considered Carter one of his best ever students and had told him so before they had parted company.

When they reached the Professor's office, Professor Thackeray picked up his phone and ordered some tea and cakes before they sat at a small round table. Both were still smiling and it was Carter who spoke first.

"So, Profess… sorry, Ronnie, you made it to the top of the heap?"

"If you can call being head of department the top of the heap. But I'm happy with that. I'm not sure I would want any more admin duties than I already have with the job I've got."

"Presumably you still do some lecturing?" asked Carter.

"Absolutely! That's what I enjoy and it's what ensures that I continue to learn. After all, I have to be one step ahead of the students, don't I?"

"You were always several steps ahead of me!"

There was a pause in their conversation as their tea and cakes arrived on a tray. Thackeray's P.A. put the tray on the table.

"Would you like me to pour the tea?" she asked.

Professor Thackeray smiled at her. "That's very kind of you but we can manage, thank you."

She smiled at them. "Enjoy your tea, gentlemen," she said as she turned and left the office.

The Professor began pouring the tea as he spoke. "So, tell me Carter, what have you been up to for the last … how many years has it been?"

"Thirty, give or take," responded Carter. "And I've spent most of that time working for the FIDT, on and off over the years."

Thackeray stopped pouring and looked up. "Really! We had a research fellow who was sponsored by the FIDT, John Sprague. He died recently. In addition to his research he also did some lecturing for us. Did you know him?"

"Yes, I did," answered Carter. "In fact I saw him only a few days ago right here in Oxford."

"Did you know he had …"

"Yes," interrupted Carter. "That's why I'm here." Thackeray looked confused as Carter continued. "One of the things I do for the FIDT, on a part time basis, is look into things that they are concerned about, things that they want to get to the bottom of."

"Really," said Thackeray as he continued pouring the tea. "What's that got to do with John's death?"

"Well, did you know that the police think John's death involved foul play?"

Thackeray shook his head. "No. All I heard was that there had been a fire at his lab down the road and that he had been killed by it."

"That's not strictly accurate," said Carter. "He was stabbed to death, before the lab was set on fire."

Thackeray looked at Carter, the shock he felt on hearing what Carter had just told him was evident on his face. "That's terrible," he said, shaking his head slowly from side to side. "Do they have any idea who killed him? Or why?"

"No. And that's why they're happy for me to be involved in the investigation. Because of the thoroughness with which the lab was torched, it may have been something to do with his work. Everything in the lab was reduced to ashes."

"OK, so this is not a social visit then."

"I'm afraid not. But I am pleased to see you, and to have the opportunity to talk to you about other things. But first I need to ask you if you know anything about John's research?"

Thackeray thought for a few moments before answering. " Not much, I'm afraid. His interaction with the Department was mostly to do with his lecturing role. I knew, of course, that he was doing research but, as it wasn't funded by the Department, it wasn't any of my business what he was looking into."

"And he never told you?"

"No, well, not much. Just that it involved diamonds. But that wasn't a surprise given who was financing the research. He said he would reveal everything when he had finished the work."

"So you didn't know that he was trying to find a cheap, portable means of distinguishing between natural and synthetic diamonds?"

"No, although most of his lectures dealt with the subject of synthetic diamonds; the ways in which they could be made and how the processes were developing and improving. I doubt that anyone in Oxford knew more about the subject than he did."

"Probably not even anyone in the whole world. He was at the forefront of knowledge about synthetic diamonds. I know this because, over the years, I've had dealings with him when I've been working on cases involving such stones."

Carter finished his cup of tea and started to get to his feet. "Well," he said to the Professor, "I've taken up enough of your time." He held out his hand as Thackeray rose from his seat.

"Let's try and get together for a drink while you're in town," suggested Thackeray. "I'd like to hear more about what you've been up to since you left Oxford."

"That would be great," agreed Carter as they shook hands. "I'll give you a call when I know what my movements are going to be and see how you're fixed." Thackeray nodded his approval of the idea as Carter continued. "I'll see myself out."

As he descended the steps to the reception area, Carter considered what he had learned from the Professor. It wasn't much really but that was no surprise. He knew from his meeting with John, three days earlier, that he was playing his cards very close to his chest. But if no one knew what he was working on, or what progress he had made with it, why would anyone want to kill him and destroy his lab?

The following day, Carter met Conrad, a man of medium height and build in his late thirties, at Heathrow airport and drove him to his hotel in Oxford, where he had booked a room for him. It had been quite a subdued reunion as Conrad and John had also been good friends. After Conrad had checked in and taken his suitcase to his room, he changed from the black jeans and grey jacket in which he had travelled to England and dressed more formally in a dark suit. He knew that Carter would be wearing a suit and that he would expect Conrad to be similarly clad.

Conrad and Carter had agreed to meet in Carter's room so that Carter could bring him up to date with the investigation. Once Conrad had unpacked the rest of the contents of his suitcase and thrown some cold water onto his face in the bathroom to wake himself up fully, he made his way to Carter's room on the floor below and knocked on the door. Carter opened the door. He indicated to Conrad that he should follow him into the room before turning away and walking back in himself. Conrad walked into the room and closed the door as Carter returned to the armchair he had been sitting in. Conrad sat opposite him, in the other of the two armchairs by the window.

"It's good to have you on board again," said Carter smiling warmly.

Conrad shook his head. "I'd like to say it's good to be here but, given the case we're working on, it isn't."

"I know what you mean," responded Carter. "But we owe it to John to find out what happened here, and why he's dead."

Conrad nodded. "Yeah, you're right, we do. So, what can you tell me?"

"Not much," said Carter. "Fact is, there's very little to go on. The police here in Oxford are struggling to find a motive. I mean, from where they're sitting, they can't think of any reason why anyone would want to kill John, let alone burn down his lab? From what they have found out so far, they believe he was an easy going sort of a guy, not the kind to make enemies. And they're right about that. I don't think I know anyone that didn't get on with him. So, unless it's got something to do with what he was working on, it just doesn't make any sense."

"What relationships did he have with people here in Oxford?" asked Conrad.

"According to the local police, their investigations have revealed nothing out of the ordinary, just what you would expect. He had dealings with people in the Earth Sciences Department, where he was doing some lecturing, but nothing personal. Nothing that could explain what's happened."

"He was always a bit of a loner after Izzy's death. He never really recovered from that."

"No, you're right, he didn't." Carter tapped his chin with his finger. "But there *was* something that had happened in that context," he said. "He had met someone recently, someone special. But it wasn't anyone local. He told me quite a lot about her when we met last week. And it was pretty obvious that he was in love with her."

"Could that have anything to do with his death?" asked Conrad.

"Don't know. But I wouldn't have thought so. He was here and she's in California."

"Where in California?"

"Santa Monica."

"That's where John's mother-in-law and son live."

"So … ?"

"Nothing really," Conrad shook his head. "But if he and this new girl were close, she might know something that could help us to get to the bottom of this. Maybe we should talk to her."

"Yeah, I guess. But I don't know much about her other than that her name is Lucy and that she works for a company called NewChip Corp that makes computer chips using synthetic diamond wafers. John did tell me that they had a common interest in computer miniaturisation."

"So might he have told her what he was working on?"

"It's possible. He was very secretive about it, even with me, but we all know how few barriers there are that can't be crossed during pillow-talk!" Conrad smiled and Carter got to his feet. "I could do with a beer. Let's go find ourselves a pub and maybe get some food as well."

Having spent an hour in the Crown pub near the hotel, and enjoyed a couple of beers and a sandwich whilst they caught up on each other's news, Carter and Conrad walked through the centre of Oxford. Conrad had never been to Oxford before and, as they made their way towards John's burnt out lab, Carter took some pleasure in pointing out some of the landmarks. Amongst these were Balliol College, which they passed as they walked down Broad Street, and the Bodleian Library on their right as they turned up Parks Road. The city centre was relatively quiet as it was the summer holidays and there were very few students to be found wandering the streets.

When they got to the building which had housed John's lab on South Parks Road, just past the Department of Earth Sciences building, Carter spoke to the uniformed policeman at the entrance and showed him his identity card. The policeman looked at it and then at Carter.

"DCI Murray said it would be OK for us to have a look round," said Carter, realising that the policeman had not been informed of his visit.

The policeman used his radio to contact the police station whilst Carter and Conrad looked at the damage to the building, which was quite extensive. When the policeman had finished on the radio, he walked towards them.

"That's OK. You're clear to go in."

Carter thanked the policeman and then he and Conrad went into the building and up to the first floor. As they entered John's office and looked into his lab, neither was prepared for the scene of utter destruction that confronted them. The fire had destroyed everything flammable and blackened everything that wasn't. Carter and Conrad walked slowly round the lab before returning to the office.

"I don't think we're going to find anything that's useful in here," said Conrad.

Carter nodded. "Whoever did this knew what he was doing, it's a pretty thorough job."

"What about his house, where he lived? Has anyone had a look there?" asked Conrad.

"Not that I know of."

"Looks to me like someone wanted to destroy all trace of what he was working on."

"Could be," responded Carter. "Seems likely that John's death is connected to his work rather than his personal life. When we met, he did mention that he had made some good progress recently. If that had taken him significantly closer to finding a solution, it could be the reason why someone would want him dead. But they would have to have known about it."

"Maybe there'll be some clues at his house," suggested Conrad. "Can we get access to have a poke around, see what we can find?"

"I'll ask," said Carter as he extracted his phone and pressed a few buttons before putting it to his ear.

"Chief Inspector," said Carter as DCI Murray answered his call. "I was wondering if you had searched John's house to see if there were any clues there."

"Yes, of course, it's routine in cases like this," answered Murray. "but we didn't find anything."

Carter thought for a moment before continuing. "Would you mind if I and my colleague, Conrad from the FIDT, had a look around?"

"Don't see why not. When did you have in mind?"

"This afternoon, if possible," suggested Carter.

"OK, I'll meet you there in an hour," responded Murray, agreeing to Carter's request.

Carter ended the call and put his phone back in his pocket before looking at Conrad.

"Next stop, John's house," he said and the two men left John's office and the building that had housed his lab, nodding to the PC at the front of the building as they passed him.

Chapter 7

Jacques saw the last two guests off the Esprit de Jacques before he closed and locked the door to the boat's saloon and left the boat. Eloise had crewed for Jacques on the charter as usual but she had left as soon as they had docked at the Capitainerie in order to join her mother, who had been on her own at their house during the charter.

Jacques strode across the quay at the Capitainerie in Port Grimaud and walked quickly towards Le Grande Rue, the road that led round to the Place du Marché. Feeling thirsty, when he reached the Place, he called in at the Café Poisson and bought a bottle of beer.

As he continued his walk home, Jacques took a swig from the bottle and then suddenly stopped in his tracks. He lowered the bottle and stared at the two men standing talking near the boules court in the centre of the Place. One of them was Gilles Rénard. Jacques had thought that Gilles was still in prison and was surprised to see him out and about, a free man again, so soon.

Jacques watched the two men talking for a few moments before continuing along the Rue des Deux Ports towards the Rue de L'Ile Longue, at the end of which was the house where he and Eloise lived, the house Nicole had given them after her father's death.

Once inside the house, Jacques walked across the large living room and onto the terrace which faced out across Le Lac Interieur, the small expanse of water which formed the centre of the canal town of Port Grimaud.

Sitting in a lounger on the terrace, enjoying the sunshine and the view, was Nicole. Jacques walked to the edge of the terrace and looked out across le Lac, his eyes focussed on the far distance, he was clearly deep in thought about something. Jacques and Nicole were soon joined on the terrace by Eloise, carrying two cups of coffee.

"All safe and secure on the Esprit?" she asked, smiling at Jacques as she put the cups on the table next to her mother. Jacques nodded but there was clearly something on his mind.

"What's the matter?" queried Eloise, concerned to see him frowning.

"Oh, it's nothing really. Just that on my way back from the Esprit, I saw Gilles Rénard in the Place."

Eloise and Nicole both turned to look at him, they looked shocked to hear what Jacques had just told them.

"I thought he was in prison," said Eloise as she sat in the seat next to Nicole.

"It seems not," replied Jacques.

"He must have got time off for good behaviour," suggested Nicole, clearly very upset about what she had heard. "But two years in jail for what he did doesn't even come close."

"The only thing they could prove against him was that he stole the Esprit," offered Jacques. "They couldn't prove he had been involved in anything else, not after Philippe's death."

Eloise and her mother slowly resumed their positions, laying their heads back as they soaked up the afternoon sunshine.

"The guillotine wouldn't have been enough for me!" said Nicole coldly. "He's a murdering bastard and I wish he was dead!"

"Well at least you won't have to see him around town once you go back to Belize," offered Eloise.

Her mother nodded. "That's true. But it doesn't really make me feel any better about it."

Carter and Conrad were walking across Oxford, on their way to the house where John had lived, when Carter's phone rang. He pulled it from his pocket and saw that the call was from Nicole. He pressed the receive button and put the phone to his ear.

"Nikki, hi hon. How's things in Port Grimaud?" he asked in an upbeat tone, fully expecting Nicole to be enjoying the time she was spending with her daughter and son-in-law.

"Oh sunny and beautiful, as you'd expect," replied Nicole, also in an upbeat tone before her voice turned more serious. "But there's something I wanted to ask you," she continued.

Carter picked up on her change of tone and became concerned. "What's up?" he asked.

"How long did Gilles Rénard get for what he did?"

"I think it was five years, wasn't it."

"Well, he's out! Jacques just saw him in the Place. And it's only been two years!"

"Yeah, well that's the justice system for you," said Carter trying to talk Nicole down from her agitated state.

"Carter! Two years is not justice! He was responsible for my father's death! And for Yvonne's rape and murder!"

Yvonne was Jacques' half sister. She had been killed during Carter's search for the source of the synthetic diamonds which Gilles had obtained from Philippe, Nicole's father, and which he had then fed into the natural diamond distribution system. But

Gilles' involvement in Yvonne's death could not be proved.

"Nikki, you know there was no evidence against him as far as Yvonne's death was concerned. And regarding your father's death, all they could prove was that he stole the boat that your father grabbed onto the back of, as it pulled away from the quay. Your father died of a heart attack."

"Yeah! A heart attack brought on by trying to save Jacques."

Carter sighed. "Look, sweetheart, you knew at the time of the trial that he didn't get what he deserved for what he did, or for what he arranged to be done by other people."

Nicole calmed herself a little before continuing. "Yeah, maybe. But I'm still not happy that he's a free man running around town again. I don't know what I'll do if I see him."

"You'll do nothing, OK? You will just ignore him. He'll get what's coming to him one day."

"Yeah, well, I hope he does. And I hope it hurts like hell!" said Nicole, her temper cooling. "Anyway, how are you getting on?"

"We're just on our way to have a look round John's house here in Oxford. But there's nothing significant to report yet. It looks to me like it was something to do with his work but I don't really have any evidence to support that theory."

"How long do you think you'll be in Oxford?"

"Not much longer, there's a limit to what I can find out here. But I'll let you know how things develop."

"OK. Should I stay here with Eloise for now then?"

"Unless you feel you would rather be back home, given what you've just told me."

Nicole considered this for a few moments before responding. "No, I'll stay here until you're ready to go home. I'm enjoying being with the kids and I'll probably get over … you-know-who being here. Either that or I'll just kill him."

They both laughed before Carter ended the call by sending Nicole a kiss over the phone.

Conrad looked at him enquiringly as he ended the call. "Everything OK?" he asked.

"Yeah, I think so. Apart from Jacques having spotted Gilles Rénard wandering about town, free as a bird."

Conrad nodded as he and Carter continued their walk to John's house. "Yeah, I think that would have an unsettling effect on any of us."

Carter and Conrad turned off the Woodstock Road onto Leckford Road where John had rented a two storey stone built semi-detached house. Carter checked the note he had made of the address and they found John's house about half way along the road. There was no sign of DCI Murray but it occurred to Carter that he might be inside the house so they approached it and Carter knocked on the front door. There was no answer, so they wandered the few yards back to the iron gate at the front and waited.

A few minutes later, a black saloon car drove down Leckford Road and parked near where Carter and Conrad were standing. DCI Murray got out of the car and walked towards them.

"Been waiting long?" he asked.

"No, only a couple of minutes," replied Carter. "Thanks for letting us have a look round."

"No problem. Actually, I'd appreciate any insight you can offer."

"We'll be pleased to help if we can, Inspector," said Carter

Murray headed for the front door of the house as he spoke. "At the moment we have no clue as to why Sprague was killed. We don't know whether he caught an intruder in the lab or if he, personally, was the target and the fire was just a cover, or a means of getting rid of evidence. There doesn't seem to be any motive for his murder. Certainly not theft. We found a stash of diamonds still there in the safe in the office."

Murray unlocked the door and held it open for Carter and Conrad. Once inside the house, Conrad began the search as Carter and Murray continued their conversation.

"We have some ideas about that," said Carter, "But nothing concrete."

"Care to share your thoughts?" asked Murray.

"The only thing that makes any kind of sense would be if John had actually achieved what he set out to achieve," said Carter as they walked through the hall into the living room at the front of the house. "There are people who would prefer that he hadn't and, if he had, they would prefer that no one found out about it. As you know he was working on synthetic diamond detection. He was trying to find a more effective way of distinguishing between synthetic and natural diamonds, one which would be both inexpensive and easily portable. And one which would be a hundred percent reliable without the need for special training in its use."

"Why would anyone have a problem with that? Surely it would be a good thing, wouldn't it?" asked Murray as Conrad left the living room to begin his search of the first floor of the house.

"Depends on who you are," said Carter, "And whether you're talking about industrial or gem quality diamonds. To the average jeweller, it would be a great piece of kit to have readily available. At the moment, the only known method of reliably distinguishing between natural and synthetic diamonds requires a lab with expensive equipment and trained operators."

"I see," responded Murray thoughtfully. "I think I'm beginning to get the picture. Basically, the people making the gem quality stuff would prefer that your average Tom, Dick or Harry jeweller isn't able to distinguish them from real ones."

"Oh, they're all real diamonds," corrected Carter, "But a natural diamond has been in the earth's crust since the beginning of time whereas a synthetic diamond could have been made in a factory last week. And the attraction of diamonds for jewellery is in that old saying that 'diamonds are forever' and that the supply of them is limited."

"So if you can't easily tell the difference between synthetic and natural diamonds, that's a big problem for the natural diamond market because there will be loads more gem quality diamonds coming into the market now and no one knows whether they're synthetic or natural?"

"Yes, and the converse is also true, in that if you *can* tell the difference, easily and cheaply, the bottom falls out of the market for gem quality synthetics."

"And in both cases, big money is involved," concluded Murray, nodding his head sagely. He considered this information for a few moments before fixing Carter with a stare. "So that could be a motive for Sprague's murder then, couldn't it?" he added, "If your friend *had* been successful with his work?"

Carter nodded. "It could. But it's still a bit of a long shot. The fact remains that lots of people have been trying to find a solution to this problem for a long time, so far without success."

"Yes, I get that. But this still puts a completely different spin on the case. Especially if someone knew his research had been successful. It might also explain why the lab was torched," observed Murray.

As Carter and Murray concluded their conversation, Conrad came down the stairs and into the room. The two men looked round as he approached them.

"There's nothing here," said Conrad. "Just the sort of stuff you'd expect to find in anyone's home. Nothing relating to his work." Conrad turned to Murray. "Did your people remove anything?"

The Inspector shook his head. "No," he answered. "We searched the place but nothing was removed. We didn't find anything that we thought might be significant."

"In that case, I would suggest that whoever killed John had already removed any items relating to his work before you got here."

"That's possible," said Murray. "We didn't find any keys on the body. We had to get the keys to the house from the landlord. So the killer could have taken the victim's keys."

DI Murray locked the front door as the three men left the house. Murray offered Carter and Conrad a lift back to the city centre but they declined, preferring to walk. As they made their way back along Leckford Road and onto Woodstock Road, not speaking, Carter finally broke the silence.

"It's looking more and more like the reason why John was killed was to do with his work."

"Yeah, but why?" queried Conrad. "As far as we know, he was no nearer to finding a solution than he was a year ago. And no nearer than anyone else working on the same problem. At least there's no proof that he was."

"Maybe that's the point. Maybe he had made a significant discovery." Carter reflected inwardly before continuing. "He told me he had made some good progress but maybe it was a bit more than that. Maybe he had actually cracked the problem."

"But how would anybody know about that. He never told us anything about it, and given how secretive he was, he probably didn't tell anyone else. I mean he didn't even tell you."

Carter stopped walking and touched his forehead with his hand. "I wonder," he said, almost to himself, as Conrad looked at him expectantly.

Carter didn't respond. Instead, he just began walking again and the two men continued the walk back to the hotel in silence, Carter deep in thought, Conrad not wishing to disturb his colleague's mental processes.

In the Place des Artisans in Port Grimaud, next to the main entrance to the town, was the yacht charter agency which had been Gilles Rénard's base and which he had nominally run for Philippe, Nicole's father, who was the owner, before Philippe had died. Subsequently, following Gilles' arrest and imprisonment, his assistant at the yacht charter agency had stepped up to the plate and kept the business running, something which, to be fair, he had been doing anyway, long before Gilles was arrested, even though Gilles was technically in charge. When Nicole had inherited the business, following her father's death, she had sold it to Gilles' assistant, with the hope of ensuring that Gilles would have no job to go back to when he was eventually released, something she would be more than happy about.

However, Gilles' main source of income had not been the salary he got for being in charge of the yacht charter agency, but his earnings from the diamond cutting business he had set up, with Philippe's help, some years earlier in Sainte Maxime. It was that business which had ultimately led to Philippe's death when Carter had been brought in to investigate the source of a batch of synthetic diamonds which had been fed into the natural diamond distribution chain.

Gilles had started the diamond cutting business because Philippe already owned a diamond mine in Guinea and was willing to supply him with the rough diamonds that came out of his mine. Quite by chance, Gilles had found out some years later that Philippe had a contact in England, a friend of Nicole's called Anna who, in turn, had a close friend who worked in a large synthetic diamond factory in Siberia. Somehow, Dimitri, this Siberian contact of Anna's, was able to secretly remove gem-quality synthetic diamonds from the production machines in the factory without anyone noticing. When he had discovered that Anna knew someone who not only owned a diamond mine in Guinea but was also connected to a diamond cutting business in France, he had persuaded Anna to act as a go-between. Dimitri knew that the diamond cutting business was the perfect route through which to distribute his ill-gotten gains as natural diamonds, and get the highest price for them, and he had wanted to make the most of the opportunity it presented.

In the first instance, Anna had done a deal with Philippe on Dimitri's behalf and then subsequently, whenever Dimitri had stolen enough stones from the machines to make it worthwhile, he would deliver them to Anna and then she would pass them on to Philippe. Although Philippe knew that what they were doing was technically illegal because of the source of the synthetic diamonds, he didn't feel that it was causing harm to anyone and was just a minor bending of the 'rules'.

Although he was in prison, Gilles had wanted to rebuild his business life so that he would have something to return to when he was released. He knew he would never be involved with the charter agency again so he had decided to focus his time on the diamond business. Before he had been sent to prison, Nicole had told him that she wanted nothing more to do with him or his business with the result that he had lost his source of natural uncut diamonds from Philippe's mine in Guinea. While he was in prison, the day to day operations of the business had continued to be managed by Alphonse, but he had struggled to find any new and reliable sources of uncut diamonds. Things had looked bad for the company but Alphonse was a man who had spent all his working life in the diamond business. With no uncut natural diamonds available, Alphonse had decided, with Gilles' approval, to buy synthetic diamonds, both industrial and gem quality, from a manufacturer in Russia and sell them on to companies in the USA and elsewhere which could not make enough to meet the demand for them. Whilst Alphonse had dealt with the sourcing of the synthetic diamonds from Russia and had handled all the paperwork associated with the import and export of gemstones, Pierre had dealt with the matter of finding buyers and of delivering the synthetic diamonds to them.

During the time that Gilles had been kept locked up, for the relatively minor crime of stealing a yacht, the only charge the local police had been able to make stick, Alphonse had managed to build up a significant business supplying gem quality synthetic diamonds, perfectly legally, to producers in the USA and elsewhere who could not meet the demand for them. The company also supplied industrial synthetic diamond material to, amongst others, Lucy's company in Santa Monica.

This synthetic industrial diamond material was specifically grown, using the carbon vapour deposition method, for the purpose it would be put to, the purpose being the making of computer processors. Because diamond is such a hard element it can withstand much higher temperatures than silicon, the usual material used to construct computer processors, and it can, therefore, cope with much faster processing speeds before collapsing into liquid.

When Gilles returned to the business, after his release from prison, he was very impressed with what Alphonse had achieved in his absence, both with the industrial side of the business and, especially, with the gem quality diamonds. Whilst there wasn't a vast amount of money to be made from the industrial side of the business, as they were only acting as a go-between, there was enough to justify doing it. But when it came to the gem stones, there was good money to be made as synthetic gem quality diamond values were not massively below those for their natural equivalents, largely because no cheap, hundred percent reliable means of distinguishing them from natural diamonds had yet been discovered. If it ever was, and most industry pundits did not believe it ever would be, then the value of synthetic gem quality diamonds would drop very sharply, as would the demand for them.

As Gilles waited outside his house, which was next door to the yacht charter agency he had once run, he looked at the people milling around in the Place. They were mostly tourists but many of them owned houses in the town and spent a considerable amount of their time there, especially in the summer. As he watched the people going to and fro, Pierre came through the stone archway into the Place and approached him. The two men greeted each other with a handshake but they both clearly had things on their minds.

"Come, let us take a walk," suggested Gilles. Pierre nodded and they made their way across the stone bridge leading to the road which would take them round the east side of the town to the Capitainerie. As they did so,

Gilles continued to speak. "Alphonse tells me that we have received another shipment from Siberia," he said. "It will need to be delivered soon."

Pierre nodded; he understood that his primary function, especially now that Gilles was back, was to act as a courier delivering synthetic diamonds, both industrial and gem quality, to the people Gilles' company sold them to. It wasn't a difficult task and he quite enjoyed it but, sometimes, Gilles expected more of him. Sometimes, Gilles wanted Pierre to do things that he would prefer not to do, despite his past as a member of a criminal gang. But it was exactly this past life of Pierre's that made him so valuable to Gilles. Because of it, he had contacts who could fix things. One of these, a man called Henri, was now in prison as a result of his involvement with Gilles, serving a life sentence for murder; it was Henri who had been convicted of the rape and murder of Jacques' sister, Yvonne.

A few minutes later, when the two men reached the Capitainerie and walked out along the breakwater, beneath the flags flying from the twenty or so flag poles which lined it, they were out of earshot of anyone.

"So now our customers can relax," said Pierre. "As there will not be a cheap detector on the market anytime soon."

"Which is good," added Gilles. "Not that they knew there was anything to be worried about anyway."

"No, maybe not, apart from Blundell, of course. But it is better for us that the matter has been dealt with," said Pierre. "The fire destroyed everything and the back up of all the research which was at Sprague's house has been disposed of as well."

"And you don't think he had any more backups of his work?" queried Gilles, wanting to be sure that his business was safe.

"Not that we know of. But it is possible, of course, likely even. I will be keeping an eye open for any indication that he did."

Gilles smiled and nodded as they both turned to return along the breakwater towards the Capitainerie.

"When will you make your next visit to California?" asked Gilles.

"I have already booked a ticket for tomorrow afternoon," replied Pierre, smiling; he had no objections to spending time in California, he liked it there and he was looking forward to seeing Lucy again.

Wanting to spend some time on his own, thinking through all the latest developments, Carter left Conrad at the hotel entrance and walked south along St Aldate's towards the river. After passing Pembroke College, he turned to his left to go into Christ Church Meadow where there was a pleasant walk through the park. It was a walk that he had enjoyed on many occasions in the past and he especially liked walking through the trees which lined the path leading to the river bank.

As he strolled along the path under the tall trees, Carter recalled the times he had spent there with Nicole all those years ago. At that time, they had been students at Oxford University, young and free, and very much in love. Until Nicole's father had ruined it all. Philippe had not been happy about their relationship and had threatened to take Nicole out of university and back to France if she didn't end it. So she had ended it. Nearly thirty years had passed since that moment on the river bank when she had told Carter the bad news. But then, two years ago, after all that time apart, they had met again and this time there was not going to be anything that would keep them apart. After Carter had concluded the case he was working on, which had led, not only to them getting reacquainted, but also to the deaths of Nicole's father and of her son, there had been a brief courtship, quickly followed by a wedding in Yorkshire. There had been no need for a honeymoon; as far as Nicole was concerned, going to live with Carter in his beach house on an idyllic island off the coast of Belize would be honeymoon enough. And it would never end!

When he reached the river bank, Carter sat on the grass and stared into the water, remembering. But it wasn't long before his thoughts returned to the present. Who, he wondered could possibly have wanted to kill John? But he knew well enough that the question was quite easy to answer, in general terms, if, as he now believed was the case, John had managed to find a guaranteed cheap way of distinguishing between synthetic and natural diamonds. If he had done that, there would be no shortage of people wanting him and his discovery buried forever. It would have to be something, a device, that would leave no doubt about the standing of the diamond being examined, something that would not require any further testing to be done to confirm the result. But had he created such a device? And, if he had, who knew about it? He hadn't told Carter and, as far as Carter was concerned, he considered them to be close friends; if he had told anyone, why wouldn't he have told him? And why wouldn't he have told Isaac, the man from the organisation which was financing his work, and with whom John probably had the closest working relationship. Who else would he have told?

And then it came back to him! What about Lucy? From what John had told him, Lucy had only been in his life for a few months but they had become very close. All sorts of private or secret information can pass between two people who have given their hearts to each other unreservedly and maybe, in one of their quieter moments, John had told her that he had been successful with his research. Carter was slightly offended at the notion that John might have told his girlfriend and not him. He wasn't sure how far John and Lucy's relationship had travelled, or whether John would have shared his biggest secret only with her and not with anyone else, but from the way John talked about her, he was clearly besotted with her.

Carter sighed and looked up along the river as a couple of students in a punt came downstream. Maybe he should speak to Lucy and try to find out what, if anything, she knew about John's work. Maybe a trip to Santa Monica was called for.

Chapter 8

After he had explained to Nicole before leaving Oxford that he had to go from there to Los Angeles, and having agreed with her that she would stay on with Jacques and Eloise for the time being, Carter's plane from London touched down at LAX airport at ten o'clock that Wednesday evening. More than an hour later, his cab from the airport dropped him outside the Ocean View hotel in Santa Monica. Once he had checked in, he went to his room and texted Nicole to tell her that he had arrived safely. Then, he undressed, splashed some water on his face and collapsed onto the bed; it had been a long journey.

When he awoke the next morning after eight hours of sleep, Carter felt refreshed, not quite firing on all cylinders but certainly a lot better than he had felt the night before. The Santa Monica Police Department had been advised by the Oxford police that Carter was someone who could be trusted and that it would be helpful to them and their case if they gave him every assistance. As a result, the Santa Monica police had left a message at hotel reception for Carter that morning and this was delivered to him in his room at nine o'clock. When Carter opened the envelope and read the message, he was pleased to see that, along with the contact details for the SMPD detective, Alex Birch, who had been assigned to liaise with him, it also gave details of Lucy's address and telephone number and confirmed that they had not yet been in contact with her. He rang room service and ordered some coffee and a Danish pastry before going into the en-suite bathroom for a refreshing shower.

Having enjoyed a leisurely shower, Carter dressed himself in black trousers and a white shirt, topped off with a lightweight tan jacket. He had decided that he would visit Lucy's apartment rather than telephone her; he didn't want to give her the news about John's death over the phone.

When Carter came out of the hotel entrance, the sun was shining brightly and his black leather bag hung from his shoulder. In his hand was the street map of Santa Monica which he had bought at the hotel reception desk. Carter opened the map and quickly found the address he had been given for Lucy's apartment. It was fairly close to the hotel, on California Avenue, in a block of apartments surrounded by trees, mainly palm trees. Carter estimated that it was about half a mile away and decided to walk there rather than take a cab.

As Carter walked along the narrow piece of parkland between Ocean Avenue and Pacific Coast Highway, which would take him to California Avenue, the sunshine lifted his spirits. But he was not looking forward to telling Lucy about what had happened to John. If he had understood John correctly, she was as enamoured of him as he was of her and Carter was not expecting her to take the news well.

Lucy's apartment block was only a short distance along California Avenue and it wasn't long before Carter was inside the white painted square block, looking at the swimming pool around which the apartments were arranged. He backtracked a few paces to the office in the archway leading into the central courtyard and asked where Apartment 16 was. The man in the office directed him across the central courtyard and up the steps to the top floor and said that, once there, he would find the apartment by walking along the balcony.

Carter made his way to the apartment and knocked on the door. When it was opened, a few moments later, he immediately understood why John had been so overwhelmed by Lucy. As she stood there, barefoot and wearing a simple short red dress, with her light brown, somewhat tousled hair falling round her shoulders, Carter's mouth dropped open.

"Can I help you?" she asked and, if Carter had not already been struck dumb by her appearance, the sound of her soft dulcet tones would have done the job. He quickly regained his composure and smiled.

"Are you Lucy Adams?" he asked, the purpose of his mission returning and quickly removing the smile from his face.

"Yes I am. And you are … ?"

"Oh, I'm sorry! I'm Carter Jefferson, a friend of John Sprague's. I was with him in Oxford last week."

Carter's composure dissolved again as Lucy smiled. "Oh, really?" she said, "That's so great. To meet a friend of John's. I just wish I could find the time to go over to England and visit him. I haven't seen him for weeks." Lucy paused, waiting for Carter to say something. When he didn't, and his eyes shifted away from her, she became concerned. "Is something wrong?" she asked. "Last time I spoke with him he was getting his presentation to the Royal Society in London ready."

Carter nodded, a serious and sad look on his face. "Yes, I'm afraid so. Can I come in?"

Lucy opened the door wide and let Carter into her apartment. Inside he turned to face her. She shut the door and looked into his eyes, as she spoke.

"It's something bad, isn't it?"

"I'm really sorry to be the one to bring you this news," began Carter. "But John is dead."

Lucy's knees gave way and Carter stepped towards her, putting his hands on her shoulders and guiding her to sit in one of the armchairs. He sat on the sofa next to her and took her hands in his. He was struck by their softness and mentally scolded himself for noticing such a thing at a time like that. She looked up at him, the tears running down her cheeks.

"What happened?" she asked, her voice faltering and almost inaudible.

Carter took a deep breath. "He died in a fire at his lab."

"But how? Why? I don't understand."

"Lucy," said Carter, gripping her hands tightly, "John was murdered. He was stabbed to death before the lab was set on fire. And everything in the lab was destroyed by the fire."

Lucy burst into tears and her head dropped, her chin hitting her chest as it did. She pulled her hands away from Carter and covered her face with them as she sobbed. Carter put his arm round her shoulders and held her.

"I am so sorry," he said. "He told me about meeting you, about how much you meant to him, and I can imagine how devastating this news is for you."

Slowly Lucy calmed herself and lifted her head to look at Carter. "Why?" was all she could say before her head dropped back into her hands and she dissolved into tears again.

"The police don't know for sure," said Carter. "But it looks as if it was probably something to do with his work."

Lucy nodded her head slowly as Carter got to his feet. "I'll make us some coffee," he said as he turned to look for the kitchen.

Lucy rose from her chair. She grabbed some tissues from the dresser and wiped her eyes. "It's alright," she said. "I'll do it."

"Are you sure?" asked Carter as he bent down a little to look into her eyes. She nodded and Carter followed her into the kitchen.

As Lucy set about making the coffee, having something to occupy her seemed to calm her emotions a little.

"Do you know what he was working on?" she asked.

"Yes," said Carter. "We were both in the same field of work, although I now spend most of my time writing."

"So you know that he was working on a synthetic diamond detector?"

"Yes. He told me last week that he had made good progress with it."

Lucy turned to look at Carter and fixed him with a stare. "Oh, he had done more than that!"

"What do you mean?"

"When I spoke to him last, when he was preparing his presentation to the Royal Society, he told me that the tests had been totally conclusive and that he was going to announce that at the presentation."

"What tests?" queried Carter. John hadn't mentioned any tests to him when they had spoken, just that his research was going well.

"You don't know, do you?" said Lucy and Carter shook his head; he had no knowledge of what Lucy was talking about. "He said he had to keep it quiet until after the presentation," she added.

"The presentation to the Royal Society?"

Lucy nodded. "He had done it," she said, waiting for Carter's reaction.

"What? You mean …" The penny had dropped and Carter realised that what Lucy was telling him was that John had achieved what he had set out to achieve, "You mean that he had made a totally reliable and affordable detector? One that met all the objectives he had set?"

Lucy nodded, a smile coming to her lips as she recalled the conversation she had had with John at the time. "When his final tests, a few weeks ago, proved beyond doubt that the new little black box he had created was one hundred percent reliable, he called me," she said. "He couldn't hide his excitement. It meant that he could now announce to the audience at the Royal Society that he had finally done it!" Lucy stopped talking as the reality of John's death hit her afresh and she began crying again. In between sobs, she tried to continue. "He was … so … happy! … And now … this! It's just … not… fair."

Carter took her in his arms and held her close. He didn't speak; there was nothing he could say that would make it any better for her.

Half an hour after Carter had broken the news of John's death to Lucy, they were sitting in the living room of her apartment, drinking their coffee and talking about John's work. Lucy was telling Carter how they had not only fallen in love with each other but had also become work colleagues. She described to him her work, which involved using synthetic diamond wafers to build faster micro processors, allowing equipment to be developed which was a fraction of the size needed previously, when cooling systems were necessary to prevent the micro processors from overheating. And she explained how this had enabled John to develop a

97

detection system for synthetic diamonds which was both portable and reliable, and which could be produced cheaply.

Carter listened intently as Lucy spoke. It was obvious that John had trusted her completely and unconditionally and that she was the one person with whom he had shared his discoveries. It was almost as if they had worked together on the project, but it was also clear that, while she understood the principles involved in the workings of this new black box which John had created, she had no knowledge of the fine detail. She simply knew that the detector used lasers in the application of mass spectrometry to the analysis of a diamond placed inside the box, that the detector gave an unequivocal result, natural or man-made, within a few seconds and that no special knowledge or training was required to operate the detector.

As Lucy continued to tell Carter all she knew about John's work, there was a knock at the door. She looked towards the door, where a man was standing outside.

"That's Pierre," she said as she got up to go and open the door. "Pierre's company supplies our company with the synthetic diamond wafers we use to make our micro processors," she added as she approached the door and opened it. "Hi Pierre, come on in. There's someone I want you to meet."

Pierre came into the apartment and saw Carter who was on his feet ready to greet him.

"Carter Jefferson," said Carter introducing himself and holding out his hand to Pierre.

"Pierre LeBlanc," replied Pierre with what Carter thought was a rather forced smile.

Carter wondered whether the time had come for him to leave but he had one more thing to tell Lucy before he did.

"Before I go, Lucy, I should tell you that John's body is being flown to L.A. today. The police in England don't need to keep it, so his mother-in-law has arranged the funeral for Friday, tomorrow. I'll be going so, if you like, I could pick you up and take you?"

Lucy's face turned sad again as she was reminded of the finality of John's death. "If you don't mind, that would be great. Thank you. I'd rather not have to go on my own."

Carter gave Lucy a final hug before shaking hands with Pierre again and leaving the apartment.

Back at his hotel, Carter went into the lounge and ordered a beer. Then he sat in a seat looking out across Ocean Avenue towards the Santa Monica pier. He had arranged to meet Detective Birch of the SMPD there but he was early and, as he sat waiting, his thoughts quickly turned back to the case.

If John hadn't given Lucy any detailed information about his little device, he wondered who else he might have told. Apart from Lucy and himself, the only person that came to mind was Isaac, so he decided to give Isaac another call. Although Isaac had been pretty clear with Carter that he was not aware that John had achieved his objective, that could have been for reasons of confidentiality.

"Hi, Isaac," he said when Isaac answered his call. "I'm in Santa Monica."

"What are you doing there?" asked Isaac.

"I had a meeting with Lucy this morning. You know, John's new girlfriend."

"Oh yeah, he did mention her to me. Was she able to throw any light on what happened?"

"She didn't even know he was dead. But she did tell me that John had actually completed his work and built a portable device which could reliably differentiate between natural and synthetic diamonds."

Carter heard Isaac's sharp intake of breath before he spoke. "Wow!" He said. "He certainly kept that quiet."

"Yeah, she also said that he was going to announce his success in a presentation to the Royal Society in London next week. I knew about the presentation, John told me about that, but not that he was going to be announcing that he had achieved his objective. I thought he was just going to tell them a little bit about his work."

"Man, that is so sad. Why didn't he tell me?"

"So you definitely didn't know about that then?"

"No, like I told you when you asked me before, I didn't know how far he had got. I knew he was moving forward, he told me that, same as he told you, but he didn't tell me that he had actually done it, that he had made the device and that it worked."

There was a few moments' pause as both Carter and Isaac considered the implications of John's lack of communication. Carter broke the silence.

"If he didn't give Lucy the fine details of how the device worked and he didn't confide in you, then the fire in his lab has destroyed all the evidence, everything we would need to build on his work and produce an affordable detector."

"No, way!" shouted Isaac. "If John had cracked the problem, he would have had a back up of everything. He was always Mr Backup Plan, you know that."

"Yeah, that's true. But where the hell could it be?"

"Maybe in his house somewhere?"

"No, we checked his house. If there was anything there, it had been taken by whoever killed him."

"Then I guess, they know and we don't."

"Maybe," said Carter. His mind was racing, trying to work out what John would have done to make sure he had a back up of all his work. "I'll let you know if I find out anything else."

Carter ended the call and stared out across the road. A constant stream of people passed the window, many of them turning onto the pier when they reached it.

"Carter Jefferson?"

Carter's attention was brought back from the tourists outside the window to the man standing over him in the hotel lounge. He looked up at him and nodded before getting to his feet.

"Yes, I'm Carter Jefferson. You must be Detective Birch," he responded, holding out his hand, which Birch shook warmly.

"Please, call me Alex."

"In that case, I'm Carter."

Both men smiled and sat down before Carter proceeded to fill Birch in on the details of what had happened in Oxford and his thoughts about why John had been killed. Then he told him about what Lucy had said regarding John having been successful with his work and outlined the implications of that.

The next day, the sun was shining as Carter drove from the hotel car park to Lucy's apartment. He parked outside and went into the building. When he got to Lucy's door, he knocked and waited for her to answer. Carter was wearing a dark grey suit and a dark blue tie, it was the nearest he had to black. When the door opened, he saw Lucy who, despite her sad face, looked gorgeous in a black knee length dress and black high heeled shoes. Around her neck was a black lightweight scarf.

"Are you ready?" he asked, even though he could see that she was. Lucy nodded and they headed towards the stairs.

The journey from Lucy's apartment to the church where John's funeral was to take place would not take long. Alice, John's mother-in-law, lived in a small but very pleasant house on Palisades Avenue, a road leading off Ocean Avenue about a quarter of a mile further along from Lucy's apartment. Being a devout Catholic, Alice attended the neighbouring St Monicas Church on California Avenue, only a short distance from her house.

As Carter and Lucy drove to the church, he decided to quiz Lucy about Pierre. The fact that Pierre worked for a company that supplied synthetic diamond wafers was enough to spark his interest.

"How long have you known Pierre?" he asked, as he drove slowly along Ocean Avenue.

"Oh, only about a year. He comes over from France four or five times a year to make deliveries, and I usually see him when he's in town."

"Whereabouts in France is he from?"

"The south. Near Cannes," answered Lucy, a broad smile on her face. "I was going to pay him a visit there this year but then I met John."

"And suddenly England became more attractive as a place to go to for a holiday than France?"

Lucy smiled. "Yeah, you could say that. I mean Pierre and I were never an item, as such. Just friends, and colleagues of course."

"I know the south of France a bit," said Carter. "I was in a small place called Port Grimaud a couple of years ago. That's in the bay of St Tropez."

Lucy's head whipped round. "No way!" she exclaimed. "That's where Pierre lives! Well, close by, in Sainte Maxime."

"It's a beautiful part of the world," responded Carter before changing the subject as St Monicas

Church came into view. "Have you ever been to this church before?" he asked.

"No. I'm not really a churchy sort of person," replied Lucy thoughtfully as Carter parked in the church car park. When he had, he and Lucy got out of the car and followed a group of people, who they took to be fellow mourners, into the church.

After the brief church service, the hearse carrying John's coffin, followed by the mourners, made its way to Woodlawn Cemetery between Michigan Avenue and Pico Boulevard. In this peaceful place, Carter and Lucy followed the coffin to the graveside where the priest said some last words before John was finally laid to rest.

Lucy had cried freely during the church service, especially when Alice had spoken about John, but her tears had now stopped and she just looked very sad. Carter checked that she would be alright on her own and then made his way over to where Alice was standing looking down into the grave. She dabbed her eyes with a tissue as Carter approached her.

"Mrs McGill," he said, "My name is Carter Jefferson. I worked with John, on and off, over many years. He was a fine man."

Alice nodded. Her hand had been on Mikey's shoulder throughout the burial ceremony and it remained there as she spoke. "Yes, I know who you are," she said. "John always spoke very warmly of you." She looked down at Mikey. "This man used to work with your Dad, Mikey."

Mikey looked up at Carter, screwing up his eyes a little as the sun shone into them. "You're the investigator, right?" he asked.

"I sometimes do investigation work, yes, but I do other things as well."

"So why is my Dad dead? Can you tell me that?" There was a degree of aggression in Mikey's voice but Carter dismissed it as a consequence of the traumas the boy had experienced in his young life; first his mother dying when he was a baby and now his father.

"Mikey!" admonished his grandmother, pulling the boy closer to her.

Carter held up his hand. "It's OK, Mrs McGill, I understand. And if I can find out who did this to him, I will."

Carter left Mikey and his grandmother to return to Lucy. As he did, he noticed a man he hadn't seen before standing under a tree a little way off, watching the proceedings but keeping his distance. He was quite tall, but not as tall as Carter, and he wore his black wavy hair long enough for it to reach his shoulders. As he was wearing a tan coloured jacket over a white shirt rather than being dressed in black, like most of the mourners, Carter concluded that he was probably a cemetery employee keeping an eye on things.

"She's taking it well," said Carter as he reached Lucy. "Mikey's not doing so good, though."

"I've never met them before," she said. "Even though they live just down the road from me. You would think I would have taken the trouble to meet my boyfriend's mother-in-law and son, wouldn't you?" She turned, angry with herself, and started walking towards the car. Carter followed her.

"Don't give yourself a hard time! You hadn't known him that long," he said as he caught up with her. "Maybe you can get to know them now. This is a time for all those who were close to him to support each other."

Lucy stopped and turned to Carter. "You're right. You are so right! And there's no time like the present." Lucy set off at a brisk pace back towards the grave, with Carter following on behind her. Alice and Mikey were still standing receiving the condolences of the mourners, which now included the man Carter had spotted under the tree.

Alice looked at Lucy as she approached, and ended her conversation with the man. "You must be Lucy," she said as Lucy reached her and stopped.

"Yes, I am," said Lucy.

"John showed me a picture of you. He talked a lot about you recently. In fact it was quite hard to get him to talk about anything else."

"Mrs McGill, I just wanted to say what an amazing man your son-in-law was," said Lucy before turning her attention to Mikey. "Your Dad was a very special person, Mikey. Clever, witty and very, very handsome. I hope you turn out like him."

Mikey gave Lucy an 'I'm not sure about you' look before speaking. "Did you work with him?" he asked.

"Yes, a bit," answered Lucy. "But more than that, he was my boyfriend. Your Dad and I had been going out together for a while. He was very special to me."

"OK," said Mikey and his grandmother smiled.

"I think he approves of you," she said to Lucy.

"Good! Because I would like to get to know the both of you," responded Lucy. "If that's OK with you, of course?"

Alice smiled again. "Of course it is. We'd like that, wouldn't we Mikey?"
Mikey nodded his approval and he also managed a smile as he spoke, "Just don't go dying on me, OK?"

"Mikey!" said Alice in a reproving tone "Please!" She began to cry and Mikey put his arms round her waist.

"I'm sorry Grandma," he said as he hugged her.

"It's OK, sweetie, I understand."

Carter and Lucy parted company with Mikey and his grandmother, with Lucy assuring them that she would be in touch.

Chapter 9

At 8:00am on the Monday after the funeral, Mikey came out of the front door of his home. He was dressed in his school clothes and had his rucksack on his back.

"Bye, Grandma. See you later," he called back through the door.

"Bye, Mikey," she called back. "Take care of yourself and have a good day at school."

Mikey closed the door and started walking to Lincoln Middle School, which he had attended for nearly two years. It was about half a mile from his home but it usually took him about twenty minutes to walk there as he always made a diversion to meet up with his classmate Joey who lived in an apartment on 4th Street. Mikey and Joey had been friends since attending St. Monica Catholic Elementary School and always watched out for each other.

Joey was looking out of the window of the apartment where he lived as he waited for Mikey to appear. He did this every school day, usually while he was finishing his breakfast glass of orange juice. Mikey was quite punctual, his grandmother saw to that, so Joey knew to within a few minutes what time he would see Mikey walking along the street with his rucksack on his back and his earphones in his ears.

As Mikey turned the corner onto 4th Street and came into view, Joey called goodbye to his mother and left the apartment. Joey was waiting for Mikey at the entrance to the apartment block when he got there, with his head turned away, looking at a car parked about fifty yards behind him.

"What's up?" asked Joey, noticing that Mikey's attention was being absorbed by something down the street.

"Nothing, I guess," replied Mikey, turning to look at Joey. "It's just that I think that maybe that car has been following me."

"No way!" exclaimed Joey, impressed by the drama of Mikey possibly being followed.

"Nah, it's probably nothing. Just some perv. that likes my arse." They both laughed at that and set off to complete the journey to school.

By the time Mikey and Joey reached the school, they had forgotten about the car, having busied themselves with discussing the physical merits of one of the female teachers who would be taking their first class, until morning break time.

Mikey and Joey were still talking about Miss Heaton when they, along with most of their classmates, came out of class and headed for the basketball courts which bordered Washington Avenue. Neither of them had any intention of playing basketball, that was for the sporty kids, all they wanted was somewhere to sit and enjoy a chocolate bar and some soda.

As the two boys sat with their backs against the wire fence which separated the basketball courts from the road, Mikey told Joey about the police arriving to tell his grandmother that his father was dead. As he was doing so, two men walked along the road behind them. When they were about six feet from the boys, they stopped under the trees which lined the road. One of them took a cigarette packet from his pocket, extracted a cigarette and lit it. As he smoked the cigarette, the two men drifted closer to the boys and were soon close enough to hear what they were saying.

"I was listening through the door, and when I heard them say my Dad was dead, I completely lost it," said Mikey. "I ran up the stairs to my room, took the big brown clay owl he gave me the last time he visited us, and threw it at the wall." Mikey fought back the tears as he told the story.

"You don't have to tell me if you don't want," said Joey, concerned for his friend.

Mikey sniffed. "It's OK. I just wish I didn't have done that. It's the last memory I have of him, when he gave me the owl and told me to look after it."

One of the men standing behind the boys coughed and Mikey looked round. Immediately, the two men started talking to each other and Mikey continued telling Joey his story.

"I collected up all the bits of the owl but there was no way I could fix it. So I got a shoe box out of my cupboard and put all the pieces in that."

When Mikey got home from school, he was shocked to find a police car parked outside the house. He opened the front door and went in. He could hear his grandmother talking to someone in the living room and he waited by the door, listening to what she was saying.

"I went out around one, like I do every day, to walk along the beach. I like the beach. And then, when I got back here, the door was open and everything was in a mess, as you can see."

That was enough for Mikey. He walked into the living room and stood looking at them, his grandmother first and then the two police officers and then his grandmother again.

"What's happened," he asked. "Is someone else dead?"

Alice got to her feet and went over to him, putting her arm around him as she spoke, "No, sweetie, it's nothing like that. Somebody broke into the house, that's all." She kissed him on the head and rubbed his shoulder. "It's nothing for you to worry about."

"OK," responded Mikey as he turned and walked towards the door, heading for his bedroom.

"Mikey!" called one of the officers as he went through the door. Mikey stopped and turned and went back into the room. "Have a look through your stuff and come and tell us if anything is missing, OK?"

"Sure."

Mikey went back through the door and up to his bedroom. As he entered the room, he was shocked by the mess he found. It looked like whoever had broken in had gone through every drawer and cupboard and emptied them onto the floor. He went immediately to the wall cupboard and pulled the door open; it was empty, like everything else. He searched quickly through the pile of his things on the floor, looking for the box containing the pieces of the clay owl, but it wasn't there. When he had finished, he sat down with his back to the wall and cried.

Downstairs in the living room, ten minutes later, the police officers were finishing interviewing Mikey's grandmother as Mikey entered the room. They all looked at him expectantly.

"They took the owl," he said.

Alice gasped and put her hand to her mouth. "No!"

Mikey nodded. "That's the only thing missing from my room."

"Can you describe it to us please," asked one of the officers, his pen poised to take notes.

"It was a big brown clay owl. It was a present from my Dad last time he was here." Mikey paused. He hadn't told his grandmother about throwing it against the wall. "It was in a green box, about so big." Mikey held out his hands to indicate the size. "I smashed it when I heard my Dad was dead. It was in bits." He looked at the officers. "Why would they take that? It's not worth anything anymore."

"I don't know, Mikey," said the officer. "But we'll keep an eye open for it."

Mikey nodded and the police officers took their leave as Alice approached Mikey and put her arm around him again.

As he had agreed with Alice, when he had telephoned her the day before, Carter arrived at Mikey's house soon after 6:00pm on the day of the burglary. He was completely unaware of what had taken place; he simply wanted to talk to Alice about the possibility of John having given her anything to look after for him.

Carter knocked on the door and Alice answered it. She led him into the living room where Mikey was still clearing up after the burglary, putting things in cupboards and on shelves.

"You having a bit of a tidy up?" he asked jokingly.

Mikey turned and gave him a scathing look. "We've been burglarized. They made a total mess of everything."

Carter was shocked at the news and it showed on his face. "What did they take? Have you had time to go through everything yet?"

"Yes," said Alice. "The cops wanted us to check while they waited. But as far as we can tell, the only thing missing is the clay owl that Mikey's Dad gave him on his last visit here."

111

Carter thought for a few moments before speaking. "Was there anything special about the owl?" he asked, whereupon Mikey rounded on him.

"Yeah! Course there was! It was *extra* special! It was the last thing he ever gave me!" He started to cry as he continued, "And he asked me to take special care of it. And now it's gone." Mikey started hitting Carter in the chest with his fists and his grandmother came over and calmed him.

"It's not Mr Jefferson's fault, Mikey," she said as he stopped crying and turned his back on them.

"Well, it's somebody's fault," he said.

"And I'm going to find out whose," responded Carter as he sat in one of the armchairs. Alice followed his lead and sat in the other.

Mikey turned back from looking out of the window and went out of the room into the hall. Alice looked at Carter sympathetically.

"Don't beat yourself up," she said. "He just needs someone to blame and you happened to be here."

"It's alright. I understand," said Carter as Mikey came back into the room with his school bag.

He put it on the coffee table and opened it. Then, after giving Carter a serious look, he reached into it and pulled out a computer memory stick. He held it in his hand as he looked at Carter.

"Maybe this was what they were looking for," he said. "It was inside the owl."

Carter gave Mikey an enquiring look, waiting for him to explain. Mikey took a deep breath before speaking again.

"When the cops came and told us Dad was dead I smashed the owl against the wall. And when I was clearing up the pieces, I found this. I didn't know why it was in there but I figured Dad must have put it in there for a reason, so I kept it with me."

Carter took the memory stick from Mikey. "Thank you," he said seriously. "This could help us to find out who killed your Dad."

Carter looked at Alice. "This could be very significant," he said. "I'd like to take it and have a look at what's on it, if that's OK with you?"

"Of course. Whatever you think is best. We just want to see that whoever killed John pays for it."

"I'll liaise with the SMPD and make sure they know everything that's going on," added Carter as he got up and began to leave. When they were in the hallway and Carter was half way through the front door, he turned to Mikey. "We will find them," he said. "They *will* pay for what they have done."

Later, in the hotel where Carter was staying, and where Conrad had joined him earlier that day, Conrad slammed the lid of his laptop shut and removed the memory chip from the USB slot. He held it up and looked at Carter.

"It's all encrypted," he said. "Unreadable without the key-code."

Carter sighed. He reached out and took the memory chip from Conrad. "Is that like a password?" he asked.

"No, not really. A password is usually something easily memorable but an encryption key-code is generated by the computer and could be any combination of letters, numbers or other characters."

"So we're no further forward then."

Conrad shook his head. "Not without the key-code."

Carter was disappointed. Following John's funeral, he had summoned Conrad to come to Santa Monica from Oxford because he felt that he would be of more use there with him, than back in Oxford. And, when

Mikey had given him the computer chip, he thought he had been proved right. He had expected that Conrad, with all his technical knowledge of computers, would be able to access the information on it and Carter was surprised to hear that he could not.

"If John went to all the trouble of creating a backup of his work and secretly hiding it with his son, he must have put the key-code somewhere."

"Unless he committed it to memory," said Conrad.

"But that would be a hell of a risk to take, wouldn't it?"

"Not if he had an unencrypted copy of everything somewhere else and just wanted to make sure he had a second, secure, backup copy."

"John was the master of the backup plan," said Carter. "He even had backup plans for his backup plans. If he did commit the key code to memory, he would have had a backup copy of it somewhere." Carter tried to think all this through but he wasn't really getting anywhere with it.

"Well if it was in his lab, it won't exist anymore, after the fire," observed Conrad.

"I don't think he would have kept it there. Or at his home. No, for maximum security, the backup of the key-code would need to be somewhere else, like the memory chip was. We just have to figure out where."

The next morning Mikey was walking along 4th Street again, on his way to meet Joey as usual, when a black car drove past him and pulled up twenty yards ahead of him. He glanced at it briefly before continuing to walk along the sidewalk. As he came alongside the back door of the car, it suddenly opened and an arm reached out and grabbed him. Mikey was shocked. He wriggled and fought and managed to free himself. He started running along the street as fast as he could. His attacker, a man of medium height and build, got out of the car quickly and ran after him. As they ran down the street, the car followed them, its rear door still open. Mikey ran as fast as he could towards Joey's apartment block, where he saw Joey, who was waiting for him as usual. Joey was using his iPhone to access the internet when he heard Mikey running towards him and looked up. Before Mikey could reach Joey, he was grabbed and pushed into the back seat of the car by the man who had been chasing him. The man then climbed into the car with him and slammed the door shut as the car sped off past a shocked Joey.

Not sure what to do, Joey decided to go back inside and tell his mother what he had seen. She immediately called the police who arrived at the apartment within minutes. Inside, the two police officers sat with Joey and his mother and tried to understand what had happened.

"And you don't have any idea who they were or why they would want to take Mikey?" asked one of the officers.

Joey shook his head. "No, but his dad was killed in England last week. I don't know if that could have anything to do with it." Joey was getting more and more worried about his friend and it showed in his face and tone of voice as he continued speaking to the police officers. "And his house was burglarised yesterday."

The officers sat up on hearing about the burglary and looked at each other before one of them spoke to Joey's mother. "OK, we need to report in with the information you've given us and see if there is any connection between these incidents. Thank you for your help."

"What about Mikey?" piped up Joey, as the police officers got up to leave. "You need to tell his Gran what's happened."

"You don't need to worry about that, Joey," said one of the officers, raising his hand as he spoke. "That's our next job, just as soon as we've radioed in."

Joey was relieved but still concerned as he watched the two police officers follow his mother to the door. Then, just as they were about to leave the house, he remembered something.

"Officers, wait!" he called after them. "There's something else." The officers came back into the hall and waited for Joey to continue.

"I think I got a picture of the guy who was chasing him," he said as he searched for the picture on his mobile phone. "They didn't see me take it."

Joey held up his phone and turned it towards the police officers so that they could see the picture. The officers smiled and one of them reached out and took Joey's phone.

"No kidding," he said as he looked at the picture. "Is it OK if we keep this for now?"

Joey nodded his head vigorously. "Sure, no problem. If it helps to find him. It will help, won't it?"

"Yeah, I think maybe it will."

The officers left the house and Joey's mother closed the door. She put her arm around Joey and guided him back to the living room.

Having received a telephone message asking him to call in to see Detective Birch, Carter left Conrad at their hotel, where he was still trying to find a way to access the computer chip, and walked the short distance from the hotel to the Santa Monica Police Department's main office on Olympic Drive. When he arrived at the building, he went in and approached the reception desk where there was a police officer in uniform.

"Hi," said Carter, "I'm Carter Jefferson. I'm here to see Detective Birch."

The officer looked at Carter for a few moments without speaking and then picked up the telephone handset and punched in a few numbers.

"Detective Birch?" he paused waiting for the response. "There's a Carter Jefferson here to see you." The officer looked at Carter as he replaced the handset. "He'll be down in a few minutes." Carter nodded and took a few steps back from the counter to wait.

When Detective Birch came out of the lift, he walked towards Carter and greeted him with a handshake.

"Thanks for coming over," he said. "There's been a new development."

Birch led Carter to the lift and they both got in, with Carter wondering what the new development could be.

By the time they had reached the interview room, which was in the corner of the large office shared by Birch and about a dozen of his fellow detectives, Carter had established that the new development was to do with Mikey. Birch had informed him that the twelve year old was missing and that there was evidence to suggest that he had been abducted. Carter and Birch sat down at the table in the interview room.

"Why would anyone want to kidnap Mikey?" queried Carter.

"I was hoping that you would be able to tell me that," responded Birch. "Your case revolves around his father's murder so I thought you might be able to throw some light on what the motive might be."

Carter thought for a moment and then decided to come clean. He hadn't yet had an opportunity to inform the local police about the memory chip Mikey had given him but he had also thought that there was probably no point in doing so until he had established exactly what information it contained. Now things had changed.

"As far as I know, the only connection that Mikey has with my case is that John Sprague was his father. John was doing research into the detection of synthetic diamonds with the aim of building a piece of kit to do the job reliably and affordably, so that any jeweller, or diamond owner for that matter, could make use of it."

Birch looked at Carter. "You know Mikey's house was broken into yesterday, don't you?" Carter nodded. "And that the only thing taken was a broken clay owl that his father had given him?" Carter nodded again as Birch waited for him to respond.

"I can maybe add something to that," said Carter, eventually, as Birch took a deep breath. "When I went to see Mikey and his grandma after the robbery, Mikey told me that he had found a black plastic memory stick inside the owl. He found it when he smashed the owl. Initially, he didn't give it a second thought and just put it in a box with all the other pieces. But then he realised it was a memory stick and decided to put it in his school bag."

Birch nodded. "OK, it's starting to make a bit of sense now. Looks like the kidnappers maybe want the memory chip. But how the hell did they know it was in the owl? Or that Mikey even had an owl, for that matter?"

"That I can't answer," said Carter. "Mikey gave me the chip and I and my computer geek friend, Conrad, have been trying to find out what's on it. But it's all encrypted. And without the key-code it's unintelligible"

"So you don't know what's on it?"

"No, not at this stage. But I can make an educated guess." Carter paused as he gathered his thoughts. "In my opinion, it almost certainly contains a back up of all John's research files. If and when we eventually manage to decrypt it, I believe it will show that John had succeeded in making a cheap, portable and reliable synthetic diamond detector."

"And that's a big deal?"

Carter laughed. "Massive!" he said. "If such a thing were to be readily available it would do two things simultaneously. It would secure the natural diamond market and it would knock the bottom out of the market for gem quality synthetic diamonds. And that means billions of dollars on both sides."

"So you reckon they abducted Mikey because they wanted to know if anything had been inside the broken owl they stole from his house?"

"Why else? That's the only possible explanation. Somehow, they must have guessed that it contained something important." Carter shook his head sadly. "This is bad, really bad. If he tells them about the chip, he's dead and if he doesn't … God knows what they'll do to him."

"Well, if he does tell them, you'll be next to get a visit from them," said Birch.

Carter nodded. "And we still have no clue as to who *they* are."

Birch sat back in his chair and took a deep breath. He opened the file in front of him and removed a photograph.

"That's not entirely accurate," he said. "We have this." He pushed the photograph across the table towards Carter. "This picture was taken by Joey, Mikey's best friend at school. Mikey and Joey meet up every day and walk to school together."

Carter looked at the photograph. It was not the sharpest image he had ever seen but it showed quite clearly the face of a man driving a car. He looked up at Birch, waiting for him to continue.

"Joey was waiting for Mikey in the front yard of his apartment block when he saw this car pull up alongside Mikey and a man try to drag him into the car. He's a quick thinking lad and he had his iPhone in his hand – he was probably on Facebook or Twitter." They both smiled at the idea before Birch continued. "So he took this picture. As you can see it shows the driver's face quite clearly."

Carter looked at the photograph again. The man was white with dark hair and looked to be middle aged, maybe about forty years old.

"Do you recognise the man?" asked Birch

Carter shook his head. "No, I can't say that I do. But then there's no reason why I would. Can I have a copy of this?"

"Sure, you can keep that one. The original's safely filed away."

Carter put the photograph in his pocket. "Anything else I can help you with?" he asked. Birch said that there wasn't and he escorted Carter back to the reception area and signed him out.

―――――――――――――――――――

In the basement of the building where he was being kept, Mikey sat in the corner of the room, with his knees pulled up to his chin. The room had no windows and the only light came from a small lamp on the floor in the opposite corner. Although there was a table and two chairs in the centre of the room, Mikey felt safer sitting in the corner.

This wasn't the first place they had taken him to after they had grabbed him off the street. For the first few hours, he had been held in another basement, a bigger one. And then, in the middle of the night, he had been blindfolded again and moved to this other place.

On the table was a plate bearing a couple of sandwiches which Mikey had not touched and had no intention of touching. He had been in the room for twelve hours and had not eaten anything. He would not have drunk anything either but his thirst had got the better of him and he had taken sips from the bottle of water he had been given. The bottle was beside him as he sat and wondered why he was there.

Mikey looked towards the door as he heard a key being inserted into the lock. In the silence of the basement, the noise it made was deafening, and it frightened him. The door creaked open slowly and two men came into the room. One stayed by the door while the other approached Mikey. The one by the door looked mean and strong, very strong, to Mikey. The other man, the one who had walked across the basement floor, now stood over Mikey, looking down at him, smiling.

"You like sitting in the corner, don't you, Mikey?" he said.

Mikey didn't look up, in fact he didn't move at all. After a few moments had passed, the smile disappeared from the man's face. He reached down, grabbed Mikey's arms and lifted him to his feet. Mikey stood there looking at the floor, not moving, so the man took him by the hand and dragged him over to the table.

"Sit down!" he said abruptly. Mikey did as he was told but continued to look at the floor as the man sat down opposite him. "It's time we had another talk," said the man. "And this time you're going to tell me what I want to know."

Mikey looked up, his eyes showing how frightened he was. "I don't know anything else," he pleaded. "I've already told you everything I know."

"So you don't know why your stupid fucking father gave you the owl?"

Mikey's eyes blazed at the insult. "He's not stupid!" he shouted. "If he was, you wouldn't want to know all this stuff!"

The man let his shoulders drop as he spoke. "OK, so let's both just calm down, shall we?" he said. "All I need to know is what you did with whatever was inside the owl."

"What makes you think there was anything inside it?"

"You told me that when you found out your dad was dead, you smashed it against the wall and there was nothing inside it."

"Yeah, that's right. There wasn't anything inside it."

"Why would you expect me to think there was something inside it?"

"Eh?" responded Mikey, not quite understanding what the man was getting at.

"Yesterday, you made a point of telling me that there was nothing inside the owl. That tells me that there *was* something there." The man leaned forward and reached out his hand. He grabbed Mikey roughly by the chin and looked into his eyes. "Now tell me, you little runt. What was inside the owl? Because if you don't, your Grandma is history. Understand?"

Mikey nodded his head. His grandmother was the only family member he had left. If anything happened to her, he would have nobody and he didn't want that. And what did he have to lose anyway? His father was dead and nothing he said would change that. He looked the man in the eye and knew instantly that he was quite capable of killing his grandmother. He sighed as he decided to tell the man what he wanted to know.

"There was a computer memory stick inside it," he said.

The man let go of Mikey's chin. He leaned back in his chair and smiled. "At last!" he said. "And where is it now?"

"Where is what?"

The man's face turned nasty again. "Don't try to be clever, Mikey. Where's the memory stick?"

"I gave it to someone," said Mikey, looking away from the man in front of him, at the man standing by the door.

"Who?" continued the man in front of him.

"I gave it to Mr Jefferson. OK?"

Without a word, the man who had been questioning Mikey got up and left the room, closely followed by the man who had been standing motionless by the door. Mikey heard the key turn in the lock and looked at the door. Then, he got up and went back to the corner of the room, resuming the position he had been in before the men had entered the basement.

Chapter 10

The next morning, as Carter got out of the shower, he decided it was time he called Nicole to see how she was getting on in Port Grimaud with Jacques and Eloise. He had been away from her for more than a week and he didn't like being separated from her. After they had broken up on the river bank in Oxford, they had not seen each other for more than twenty-five years and every day spent away from Nicole was a day lost as far as Carter was concerned.

As he was getting dressed, Carter looked at his watch. The time difference between Los Angeles and the south of France was such that there were only a few hours during which he and Nicole would both be awake. It was 7:30 in the morning, which would make it 4:30 in the afternoon in Port Grimaud.

Once Carter was fully dressed and ready for the day, he picked up his phone and selected Nikki from his list of contacts. A few moments later, she answered his call.

"Hi Nikki," he said warmly, "I'm missing you like crazy."

"Me too!" responded Nicole.

Wearing a pale blue bikini which displayed her still shapely figure, Nicole was walking along the beach, heading towards the Capitainerie. Ahead of her was the breakwater with all its flags blowing in the gentle refreshing breeze as she stopped to talk to Carter.

"Jacque and Eloise OK?" asked Carter.

"Yes, they're fine. I'm just about to join them on the beach. I can see them now."

"Doesn't sound like you're missing me *that* much," teased Carter.

"Well I am, you'll just have to take my word for it." Nicole smiled and somehow Carter knew that she was smiling and he smiled back.

"If Jacques is there, can I have a quick word with him, please?"

Nicole carried on walking towards where Jacques and Eloise were lying on their towels on the busy beach. Eloise was also wearing a bikini but hers was pink; it went well with her long blonde hair and tanned skin. Jacques, on the other hand, was wearing shorts and a T-shirt and was partially shaded from the sun by the parasol he had erected and planted in the sand.

"Jacques," said Nicole as she arrived beside the parasol. "I've got Carter on the phone. He wants to talk to you."

Jacques sat up and took the phone from, Nicole.

"Carter, Bonjour," he said.

"Hi Jacques, can I ask you something?"

"Of course."

"I've met a French guy here in Santa Monica. He says he's from Sainte Maxime and I wondered if you knew him. His name is Pierre LeBlanc."

Jacques thought for a few moments before replying to Carter's enquiry. "I know many people here called Pierre," he said. "But Pierre LeBlanc does not mean anything to me. Would you like me to make some enquiries?"

"Yeah, if you don't mind. But don't go to a lot of trouble."

"I will ask some people I know if they have heard of him."

"Thanks, Jacques. Can I speak to Nicole again, please?"

Jacques handed the phone back to Nicole before picking up a handful of dry sand and letting it run through his fingers onto Eloise's stomach. She reacted with a slight shiver and opened her eyes to look at him.

"You never get tired of doing that, do you?" she said as she smiled and sat up.

Jacques smiled back at her. "You like it, you know you do. So don't pretend that you don't."

Eloise hit Jacques on the arm before he put it around her shoulders and drew her to him, giving her a peck on the cheek. They both laughed as Nicole, who had been watching them, ended her call with Carter and sat down beside them.

"Please! Behave yourselves?" she said jokingly. "This is a public place!"

Carter put on his jacket and looked in the mirror. It was quite early. He hadn't slept well and, after speaking to Nicole, he decided that he would go for an early morning stroll along the beach and see if that made him feel any less tired. It occurred to him to invite Conrad to go with him but then he thought better of the idea as he knew that Conrad liked his bed. As Carter came out of his hotel bedroom, he shut the door behind him. He walked along the corridor, past a couple of maids busying themselves with tidying the room next to his, and down the stairs to the lobby, preferring not to wait for the lift to arrive. As he came out of the stairway into the lobby, he noticed that it was busy with people milling about close to the reception counter, most of them waiting to pay their bills. Carter approached the counter and dropped his key-card through the slot designed for that purpose before checking his watch. It was 8:00 am. He left the building, exiting onto Ocean Avenue which was busy with people bustling along, on their way to work. The sun was shining and he took a deep breath of the sea air before crossing the road and making his way onto the beach.

As Carter left the hotel, a man dressed in a dark suit, who had been sitting in a remote corner of the lobby, saw him leave and got to his feet. It was Pierre. Through the window, he watched Carter cross the road and then went to the reception desk.

"One-o-six, please," he said to the busy receptionist who reached behind her to get the key-card from the rack where all the key-cards were kept when they were not in the possession of a guest. Not finding it there , she looked under the counter in the box below the slot through which Carter had posted it. She retrieved the key-card from the box and handed it to Pierre.

Up on the first floor, the two maids were still working on the room next to Carter's when Pierre came out of the lift and walked along the corridor. He smiled at them as he let himself into Carter's room and closed the door. The two maids stopped what they were doing and looked at each other. They exchanged a few words in Spanish before one of them, the older of the two, put down her cleaning tools and set off along the corridor.

Inside Carter's room, Pierre started going through the drawers. One by one he emptied them before moving onto the next but he found nothing other than Carter's clothes, a few English pounds and some Euros, which he left in the drawer. Then he opened the wardrobe and saw Carter's laptop computer resting on the bottom under the clothes hanging there. He smiled to himself and was just about to pick up the laptop when he heard a key-card being inserted in the door. His head whipped round as the door opened and the hotel's security officer came into the room and stood blocking

127

the doorway. The two maids peered around the security officer, trying to see what was going on.

"Is this your room, Sir?" asked the security officer and Pierre looked at him for a moment before deciding what to do. Then he made a run at the security officer, hoping to knock him out of the way and make his escape. But the security officer was experienced and had anticipated that. He blocked the doorway and smiled.

"Not so fast," he said. "You haven't answered my question."

Pierre looked at him and, without hesitating, gave him a sharp kick between the legs. As the security officer bent forward in pain, Pierre shot another kick at him, this one catching him on the chin and sending his head sharply backwards. Before he could recover from the attack, Pierre pushed his way past him, and past the two maids, before running down the stairs and out of the building. The security officer pursued him, despite being in considerable pain but, by the time he reached the hotel entrance, Pierre had disappeared.

Having returned to the hotel to be informed, as he was being given his key-card, that his room security had been compromised, Carter ran up the stairs and opened the door. He went to the wardrobe and looked inside it. He relaxed slightly when he saw that his laptop was still there. Satisfied that the most valuable item in the room was safe, he looked round the rest of the room. Everything was as Pierre had left it, drawers open, clothes on the floor and, to his surprise, the foreign currency still sitting there in the open top drawer. He picked it up and stared at it. If the thief hadn't pocketed the money when he had found it, why had he bothered to break into his room? The security officer, who had followed Carter at a more leisurely pace, came into the room as Carter was pondering this question.

"Anything missing?" he asked.

Carter shook his head. "Not as far as I can tell," he said before holding up the currency, which was still in his hand. "Not even this. Doesn't make any sense."

"Maybe we got here before he could take anything," suggested the security man.

Carter paused, his mind racing. "Unless ... " He looked at the security guard and reached into his jacket pocket. "Unless this is what he was after." Carter held up the memory stick.

"A memory stick?" questioned the security man.

"Yeah, but not just any memory stick. This one could be the key to the case I'm working on."

"You're working on a case? Are you a cop?"

Carter shook his head. "Private investigator. But I'm working with the SMPD on this case. I'll call them and tell them what's happened."

The security man nodded, a sad look on his face. "OK, but we got onto it as soon as we knew something was wrong." He said defensively.

Carter smiled. "Don't worry, I'll tell them you did good."

The security man smiled back weakly. "Thanks," he said. "I guess you don't need me to report it then?" he asked.

"No, I'll take care of it," responded Carter and then, as a thought crossed his mind, he continued, "Can you describe the man who was in my room?"

"Yeah, sure can. He was tall, quite slightly built with dark hair."

Carter nodded. The security man's description was undoubtedly accurate but a bit vague. Lots of people could fit the description he had given of the intruder.

The security man left the room, closing the door behind him. As soon as he had gone, Carter extracted his phone and called Detective Birch to tell him what had happened, that his room had been broken into, that the thief had been interrupted but had escaped, and that nothing was missing from the room.

Having brought Detective Birch up to date, Carter cleaned up the mess in his room, replacing the last of his clothes in the drawers and closing them. When he had finished, he looked around the room and fingered the memory stick in his pocket. As he did so, he mentally ran through the progress he had been able to make with the case so far. Was he any closer to finding out who had killed John? No, he wasn't. Was he any closer to finding out why John had been killed? Yes, he thought he probably was. When Lucy had told him about John's success with his work, that had pretty much settled the matter. John had been killed because of what he had achieved. He sat heavily on the end of his bed, deep in thought. John had achieved his objective; he had indeed created a reliable, cheap, portable synthetic diamond detector. As a result, there was no shortage of people who, if they knew about it, would want to stop it becoming known that such a thing existed and, more specifically, how it worked.

As long as it was accepted that there was no economical way for jewellers or members of the public to tell the difference between a synthetic diamond and a natural one, they could go on making a fortune out of the man made gems. But all that would change if John, or anyone else for that matter, solved the problem. And that would cost them billions.

If John had succeeded, then for those people, it was critical that all trace of his work be obliterated. John was dead, so he couldn't tell anyone about it, that was the first step accomplished. Now they just needed to track down, and eliminate, any traces of his research. But as far as Carter knew, no one, other than Lucy, was aware that John had achieved his objective. Was it possible that John had given her a backup of his work to look after?

Carter was still turning these thoughts over in his mind when his phone rang. He picked it up off the dresser and sat back down on the bed. It was Jacques.

"Jacques, hi," said Carter. "What's up?"

"I have made some enquiries today, about Pierre LeBlanc, as you asked," began Jacques. "To begin with, everyone I asked said that they didn't know anyone by that name. But then I saw Juliette in the Place. She used to work in the charter agency, you know, the one which Gilles Rénard ran for Phillipe."

"Yes, I remember,"

"Well, when I asked her, she said she was sure that she had taken calls for Gilles from someone of that name and that she thought he probably worked in Gilles' diamond cutting business, in Ste Maxime."

"I see."

"But she didn't know anything else about him or even if he still worked for Gilles."

"OK. Thanks, Jacques, that's very helpful. Let me know if you find out anything else."

Carter ended the call. It seemed that maybe his instinct had been right and that Pierre might not be an innocent bystander after all; not just a chance acquaintance of Lucy's. Maybe there was more to Pierre than met the eye. And, although it was a bit vague, he did fit the security man's description of the man found in his hotel room.

Chapter 11

After he had wandered the streets of Santa Monica for an hour, checking from time to time that he was not being followed, Pierre called in at a coffee shop on the 3rd Street Promenade and ordered a large cappuccino. As he sat and sipped his coffee, he looked out at the mass of shoppers walking up and down the broad promenade carrying bags containing their most recent purchases. He had been lucky to escape the clutches of the security man, he knew that. If he had been caught in the hotel, he would have had a lot of explaining to do and would have failed to avoid being locked up in a police cell.

When he had finished his coffee, Pierre made his way along the Promenade and turned right, heading away from Ocean Avenue towards the small hotel where he was staying. He thought it best not to hang around anywhere near Carter's hotel in case he was unlucky enough to run into the hotel security man again, or one of the maids who had reported him and who would probably recognise him.

Pierre entered his bedroom at the hotel and fell back onto the bed, flinging his arms wide as he did. After a few minutes relaxing in this position, he sat up and got off the bed. He walked to the window and looked out. His room was on the third floor and he had a reasonable view over Santa Monica looking west towards the coast. After a couple of minutes thought, he decided to make a call to Daniel Blundell. When Daniel answered, Pierre explained what had happened in Carter's hotel room.

"One of the maids must have realised it wasn't my room and reported it," he said. "And before I could search the room properly, there was a security man at the door. I forced my way past him and got away but I didn't find anything useful."

"So we still don't have a clue what Jefferson knows," said Daniel.

Pierre shook his head. "No, but I would be very surprised if Sprague did not make a secret back up copy of everything. And, if he did, it must be somewhere." He paused for a moment before continuing. "And I think Jefferson will most likely be of the same opinion and will be trying to find it as well."

"Do you think Sprague's girlfriend might know where this secret backup is?"

"She has never mentioned it to me, but then why would she?"

"Maybe we need to find out if she knows anything about it," said Daniel and Pierre understood immediately what he was suggesting. "Could be she does know where it is, and that she has already told Jefferson."

"Yeah, maybe," responded Pierre, considering the possibility for a moment before continuing. "I'll see what I can find out from her tonight."

"Good, that's great. And get back to me as soon as you can if you find out anything that might be useful, OK?"

"Of course." Pierre ended the call and continued to stare out of the window. After a few moments had passed, he sighed and tapped Lucy's number into his phone.

Later that day, Lucy was waiting outside the restaurant on 2nd Street, not far from her apartment block, when Pierre arrived. They embraced and kissed each other on the cheek before going in. Lucy had been surprised to hear from Pierre as she thought he had already returned to France but she was always ready for a nice dinner in a good restaurant.

Throughout the meal, Pierre was at his most charming, causing Lucy to recall the time they had spent together before she had met John. They had become quite close and she had reached the point where she looked forward to his visits and to spending time with him before he headed off to make another delivery somewhere else. They had also been physically intimate on more than one occasion. Lucy played back in her mind the first time that had happened. They had dined together, as they were doing that night, and had then gone back to her apartment. They had both had quite a lot to drink but that had not seemed to hamper Pierre's performance in bed. In fact he had taken her to some new places with his sexual preferences, places she had enjoyed visiting with him.

As the two of them downed the last drops of their coffee, Pierre called the waiter over. He settled the bill while Lucy paid a visit to the ladies' room. When she returned, they left the restaurant. As they came though the door onto the street, Pierre put his arm round Lucy's waist.

"Can I walk you home?" he asked as he withdrew his arm and turned towards her.

"Sure, I'd like that," responded Lucy. "You can't be too careful at night these days. Never know who you might meet." She smiled and they set off to walk the short distance to her apartment.

As they walked along the street towards California Avenue, Pierre took Lucy's hand in his and squeezed it.

Lucy wasn't sure how to react to Pierre's advance and didn't respond. When, after she had met John, she had avoided having Pierre back to her apartment at night, he had taken it well. In fact he had taken it better than she had expected and, as a result, she had concluded that, to him, their relationship had never been more than a transitory convenience, one in which he could indulge when he was in town.

After a few minutes walk, they reached Lucy's apartment building and stopped. As they turned to face each other, Pierre let go of Lucy's hand and put both of his hands on her waist.

"May I kiss you?" he asked.

Lucy didn't respond immediately. John had not been dead for long and she missed him. But the fact remained that he *was* dead and nothing that she did, or didn't do, would change that. And she had always found Pierre fun to be with. Maybe this was what she needed following the sadness of John's demise; maybe it would make her feel better.

Lucy decided to give it a try and nodded shyly before they kissed. It was a long, deep kiss and it stirred Lucy. When their lips parted, they were both clear about what was going to happen next but Lucy decided to formalise it anyway.

"Would you like to come in for … something?" she asked suggestively. Pierre nodded slowly as a smile crossed his face and they walked into the building arm in arm.

An hour later, following an exciting and enthralling reminder of what Pierre was capable of doing to her, Lucy lay back in her bed, exhausted. Pierre was also completely spent. As Lucy lay beside him, he leaned over her. He kissed each of her nipples and then her lips

135

before lying back, a satisfied smile on his face. Lucy wasn't so sure. Yes, she had enjoyed making love with Pierre, she had always enjoyed their sexual encounters, but she felt that she had betrayed John. He had been dead for less than two weeks and she hadn't hesitated to hop into bed with Pierre. Actually, she had hesitated, she reminded herself, but not for long. She looked at the gold locket John had given her, which was lying on the bedside table next to her. She had removed it from around her neck as soon as she and Pierre had entered the room.

"Coffee?" Asked Lucy as she dragged herself out of the bed and put on her dressing gown.

Pierre nodded and threw back the covers as he also got up. Not having a dressing gown available, he put on his shirt and boxer shorts before joining Lucy in the kitchen as she made the coffee.

"That was good," he said. "I have missed making love to you."

"Yeah, me too."

Lucy poured boiling water from the kettle into the cafetiere and carried the tray through to the living room where she put it on the coffee table before sitting down. Pierre followed her and sat in the chair opposite her.

"I'm sorry if it was too soon after … you know," said Pierre.

"It's OK. John was a man of the world. He would understand," said Lucy, hoping she was telling the truth; she wanted to believe that she was but in her heart of hearts she knew that she wasn't.

"Have the police made any progress with the case?" asked Pierre, remembering why he had arranged to meet Lucy that evening.

"Not that I know of," replied Lucy as she poured the coffee. "Carter Jefferson, you remember you met him here briefly last week, when you called to see me?

He says they think John's death had something to do with his work, but that's as far as they've got."

"He was developing a synthetic diamond detector, wasn't he? That was his work."

Lucy nodded. "Yes but he was very secretive about it. He didn't want anyone to know how it was progressing, not even me."

"So he never told you if he had succeeded?"

Lucy wondered if she should continue this conversation but, as John was now dead, she concluded that it didn't really matter any more who knew what.

"I dragged it out of him eventually," she said, "He told me that he was preparing a paper to present to the Royal Society in London. And he was pretty excited about it. I worked out that he had probably done what he had set out to do. So, I challenged him about it and he confirmed it. But everything was destroyed in the fire, so we will never know exactly how far he had got."

"Surely he made backups of his work, didn't he?"

"I don't know. If he did, he didn't tell me about it."

"If he did make a backup , he would probably have kept it somewhere safe, somewhere no one would think of looking."

"I guess," said Lucy, losing interest in the topic.

"He didn't give you anything to look after for him?" pursued Pierre.

Lucy looked at Pierre, a questioning look on her face. "Why are you so interested in John's work? And whether or not he made a backup? And where it is, if he did? Is there something you're not telling me?" Lucy was sitting up straight in her chair challenging Pierre. "Tell me you don't know more about this than you're telling me."

Pierre tried to defuse the situation and forced a smile onto his face before responding. "Of course not," he said. "I am just interested, that is all. Diamonds are my business, as you know."

Lucy's suspicions were now aroused and she wouldn't let it go. "I know you distribute synthetic diamonds, Pierre, but I've always understood you to be involved in the industrial side of the business, you know, the stuff we use for our micro processors." Lucy stared Pierre in the eyes, daring him to lie, as she continued. "Tell me you're not involved in gem quality synthetics, Pierre." She paused, waiting for him to respond. He didn't. "Tell me!" she shouted as she slammed her fist down onto her knee.

Pierre still did not speak. Instead he looked down at his hands for a few moments before getting up from his chair and going to the window. As he stared out of the window, Lucy rose from her chair and stood staring at him.

"You are, aren't you?" she said, as Pierre continued to stare out of the window. "You sell gem quality synthetics as well, don't you?"

Slowly, Pierre removed his hands from his pockets and turned to face her. "It is just a side line," he began, "Nothing important."

Lucy looked down and took a deep breath. She shook her head in disbelief, before looking up at Pierre, the anger in her eyes clear for him to see.

"And you never thought to tell me that."

"It just never came up when we were together," he responded as he walked slowly across the room, his hands palm upwards suggesting that he was innocent of any wrong-doing.

"And after John was killed?" Lucy paused for a moment, staring at Pierre, "You didn't think it was worth mentioning then?"

"I knew how upset you were."

"So tell me now. Why are you interested in John's work?"

Pierre moved around behind Lucy. He put his hands on her shoulders and began to massage them.

"You are much too stressed about this," he said in a gentle voice. "You need to relax and chill out."

Lucy stood still as Pierre continued to massage her shoulders. It was strangely relaxing, given the way their conversation was going, and when she spoke her voice was more relaxed.

"Tell me you didn't have anything to do with John's death?" she said quietly, without looking round at him. When he didn't reply, she drew her own conclusion from his silence. "You did, didn't you? And it was all because of what you found out from me, wasn't it?"

Still there was no response from Pierre so she turned her head to look at him. His eyes were glazed over and, for the first time, Lucy became afraid. He was looking straight through her, a fixed expression on his face.

"Haven't you got anything to say?" she asked, her voice now a bit shaky.

Pierre did not answer, his only response was to put his hands round Lucy's throat and to start to squeeze the life out of her. Realising what was happening, Lucy tried to break free, striking out at Pierre's arms, but his grip was solid. She coughed as Pierre's hands tightened round her throat and she struggled to breathe. She tried to look at him, a pleading look in her eyes, but he was standing behind her, his eyes fixed, staring ahead of him. She made one last effort to get free, twisting her head and neck in the hope that Pierre would lose his grip. But he didn't, and as her eyes closed, her last thought was of John and how she had let him down by trusting this man. As her body went limp, Pierre adjusted his grip. With one arm firmly across her chest, he wrapped his other arm around her head and wrenched it round. There was a loud crack as Lucy's neck broke and her body fell to the floor, beside the coffee table.

Chapter 12

After Carter and Conrad had failed to find the key-code to enable them to decrypt the data on John's memory chip, Carter had begun to think about what John would have done with the key-code. If he had gone to all the trouble of encrypting the data and copying it onto a memory stick, so that he would have a safe backup if he needed it, surely he would have made certain that he could get to the key-code. Otherwise the data would be useless.

As he pondered the matter, Carter tried to put himself in John's shoes. John had wanted a secure backup of his work, hidden somewhere safe, but why? He could simply back up the data on his laptop and keep it on there as well as on the desktop computer in his office. He could have done that and probably had. So why did he need this extra secret copy?

Of course, Carter knew the answer before he asked himself the question. It was a fairly obvious one. He was sure that John was aware, as Carter was, that there were certain people who, if they knew that his research had been successful, or even if they just suspected that it might be successful, would stop at nothing to bring it to an end, even if that meant killing him and destroying all evidence of his work. That must have been a scenario that haunted John and which would have caused him to want to ensure that, whatever happened, his research was safe and available for someone else to continue; that would explain why he had created a complex and tortuous chain to be followed to reach the secret backup of his work.

The fact that John had successfully completed his work would undoubtedly be a major financial threat to those who were making and selling synthetic gem quality diamonds. An easy to operate, affordable detection mechanism would hit the value of synthetic gem diamonds hard, very hard. But would they have gone as far as killing John and destroying all the evidence of his work to eliminate the threat? Yes, they would, he concluded. Carter finally, and reluctantly, accepted that it had to have been John's work which had led to his death. All the evidence pointed in that direction.

Carter's thoughts then turned to the connection between Pierre and Gilles. Although he knew that Gilles was only recently out of prison, Gilles had been involved with synthetic diamonds before, and he had not hesitated to sanction killing people when it was in his interests to do so. Carter felt he needed to know more about Pierre but there was probably little that Jacques could add to what he had already told Carter. Maybe Lucy could throw some light on things. She had been in love with John and she also knew Pierre. Was it all just a coincidence? Possibly. But possibly not. Had Lucy spoken to Pierre about John's work? She had spoken to Carter about it, but that had not been until after John had been killed. He decided that he needed to speak to Lucy again and find out what she had told Pierre.

Carter arrived at Lucy's apartment at 10:00am. He knocked on the door. There was no reply so he knocked again. Still nothing. He walked a little further along the balcony and tried to look through the living room window but the curtains were drawn and he couldn't see anything. He was surprised that the curtains were still drawn at that time of day but not particularly concerned. He decided to try calling her on her phone. As he waited for her to answer, he realised that he could hear her phone ringing inside the apartment. But she didn't answer. Instead the call went to her voice mail and Carter hung up. He had one final attempt to see if he could see anything though the door or the window and then left the apartment. When he reached the little office in the archway leading into the block, he tapped on the window and the attendant came over and leaned on the counter.

"Hi there," he said. "Can I help you?"

"Yeah, maybe," responded Carter. "I was supposed to have a meeting at eleven with Lucy in apartment 16 but there's no answer."

"Maybe she's out," suggested the attendant sarcastically.

"Could be," said Carter restraining himself from reacting. "Thing is, I just rang her mobile and I could hear it ringing in the apartment."

"Maybe she forgot it. That happens sometimes."

"Well, I think there may be more to it than that. Do you have a key for the apartment?"

"Yes, I do. But I have to have a good reason to go into someone's apartment without their permission."

"You do have a reason. She isn't there but her phone is," said Carter, his anger becoming apparent to the attendant. "And her curtains are still drawn."

The attendant stood up straight and smiled. "Well why didn't you say that before? Lucy never leaves her curtains drawn in the daytime." He turned his back to Carter and reached for the key to Lucy's flat. "Let's go, shall we?"

The two men walked quickly past the pool, up the steps and along the balcony until they reached Lucy's door. The attendant knocked on the door loudly and, when there was no response, he took the key, inserted it in the lock and opened the door. As the door opened both the attendant and Carter, who was looking over his shoulder, immediately saw Lucy lying on the floor beside the coffee table. Her dressing gown had loosened and fallen away leaving her naked body exposed. Both men gasped. Carter reacted the quicker of the two and went over to Lucy's body. He touched his fingers to her neck, feeling for a pulse. Nothing! Carter looked round at the attendant and shook his head.

"She's gone," he said and got to his feet. "Time to call 911."

After the attendant had called 911, Carter called Detective Birch to tell him what had happened. As Carter and the attendant waited outside Lucy's apartment for the police to arrive, the attendant looked at Carter, his concern showing on his face.

"This is awful," he said. "She was such a lovely woman. Who could possibly want to kill her?"

Carter wondered whether to respond and, in the end, decided he should say something.

"Yes, she was, wasn't she," he began. "Of course I hardly knew her, we only met for the first time a few days ago, but she seemed a really nice girl."

"Then why is she dead?"

"Impossible to say but clearly there was something in her life that wasn't quite right."

As Carter finished speaking, the attendant saw the police come through the archway into the courtyard and called to them from the balcony.

"Up here, officers," he said.

The police officers and forensic team made their way up the stairs, along the balcony and into the apartment. Shortly afterwards, Detective Birch arrived and he and Carter went into the apartment.

"Any idea what's happened here?" asked Birch.

"Not really. But Lucy was connected with my case and I'm not a great believer in coincidence. So my guess is that there is a connection."

"What kind of connection?"

"Maybe she knew something. Or maybe she had something the killer wanted."

"Such as?"

"Such as an encryption key-code." Carter looked at Birch and realised he was losing him. "The code that will let us decipher what's on the memory chip Mikey had." Birch nodded before Carter continued, "But I'm only guessing. I could be wrong. They didn't have the memory chip, so they wouldn't know that it needs a key-code; it could be something completely different."

Carter and Detective Birch watched as the forensic team examined Lucy's body and then waited patiently for some useful information to emerge. When it did, it surprised them. One of the forensic team came over to speak to them.

"There is clear evidence that the victim engaged in sexual activity shortly before her death. More than that, it looks like it was a bit outside the mainstream as she had bruising to her wrists, ankles and," he paused, "to her buttocks." He held up some pieces of twisted white rope. "We found these in the bedroom. Looks like she was into a bit of S&M. Not that rare these days, but a bit unusual."

"Could that be the cause of her death?" asked Birch.

"Not a chance. She was strangled and then her neck was broken. The killer wanted to be sure she was dead."

Carter sighed and left the apartment. Outside, he leaned on the balcony rail and took some deep breaths. The attendant came out and stood beside him.

"Did you see anyone go to her flat last night?" asked Carter.

"No. But we close the office at six in the evening so I wouldn't have done."

"And you don't have any CCTV coverage of the building?"

"No. You have to understand, our remit is not security. We're only here to manage the building. Sure, if someone's visiting and wants some information, we provide it, within bounds. But we're not responsible for monitoring who comes in or goes out."

Carter stood up and went back into the apartment where Birch was still standing watching proceedings.

"When your guys have done, would it be OK for me to give the apartment the once over? See if there's anything around that will help to get to the bottom of this?"

"Sure, no problem. It will remain a crime scene for a few days but I'll do that with you. That way no one can object."

"Thanks," said Carter. "I need a drink. Could you give me a call when we're clear to go through her stuff?"

Birch nodded and Carter left the apartment block and headed for the nearest bar.

Once settled inside the 'Traditional English' pub, which was nearby and which was promoting genuine British beer, Carter went to the bar to see what they had. After a quick scan he ordered a pint of Boddingtons which he took to a vacant table and sat down. He had noticed, as he carried the glass to the table, that the beer was ice cold. He knew that in England, beer had been traditionally served at room temperature and he had acquired quite a taste for it during his time as a student at Oxford University. So, before he took even a sip from the glass, he wrapped the palms of his hands round the glass in an attempt to warm the contents. As he waited, he wondered if he would find anything useful to his case in Lucy's apartment. It had seemed very bare during the brief time he had been inside but there was no knowing what he and Birch might find during their search.

Before long, Carter's thoughts turned to Nicole and he wondered how she was getting on, staying with Jacques and Eloise in Port Grimaud. He looked at his watch, it was 11.00am. He thought for a moment; 11.00am in Los Angeles meant it would be 8:00 in the evening in France. He took his phone out of his pocket, chose Nicole from his contact list and pressed the button to call her. When she answered, he smiled at the sound of her voice.

"Carter! How's it going? Are you OK?"

"Yeah, I'm good thanks. I was wondering how you guys are getting on?"

"Good. Yeah, good thanks. It's been nice to spend some time with Eloise and Jacques although they're out on a charter tonight and tomorrow."

"So what are you doing?"

Nicole smiled. "I'm in Munroe's." She knew Carter would smile at this; it was one of their favourite places in Port Grimaud, an Irish pub run by a Frenchman and largely populated by local customers who appreciated the pub atmosphere.

"Are you going to have an Asian Plate?" he asked and Nicole laughed.

"I thought about it but I've decided to go to La Table des Pecheurs for dinner."

147

"Without me!"

Carter and Nicole had had many meals at La Table; it was considered to be the best restaurant in Port Grimaud, located beside one of the canals, but he would not expect her to go there on her own.

"I will be able to concentrate on the food instead of having to make conversation," she said, the smile on her face broadening.

"Not if Monique sees you, you won't." Monique was the owner of the restaurant and she and Nicole had become good friends.

"Yeah well, we'll see." There was a pause for a few moments before Nicole decided to enquire about Carter's progress with the case.

"Are you getting anywhere with your enquiries?" she began, "Have you found out who killed John yet?".

"We're making some progress, but nothing is ever that simple. The case is getting more and more complicated as we dig into it."

"But you will find John's killer, won't you?"

"I hope so. For John's family's sake, as much as anything. Anyway, enjoy your meal. And say Hi to Monique from me."

Carter ended the call. He wrapped his hands round his glass again – it was warmer now so he took a long swig of the beer before putting it down and sighing.

An hour later, Carter and Detective Birch were wearing latex gloves and methodically going through all Lucy's things. They began in the living room where they found nothing other than the usual paraphernalia of day to day existence which would be found in any home. Apart from a framed photograph of John and Lucy, taken on the pier, the only other personal item in the room was a photograph of Pierre, which Lucy had put away in the drawer of the dresser. Carter looked at it briefly and then returned it to the drawer.

A quick run round the kitchen cupboards revealed even less of note and the two men moved on to the bedroom. Although the Santa Monica Police's crime scene people had examined it, the room was pretty much just as it was when Pierre and Lucy had left it to go to the living room. The duvet was scrunched up in the middle of the bed and it was obvious the bed had been used shortly before Lucy's death.

As Birch examined the contents of the chest of drawers, Carter looked inside the wardrobe. Finding nothing of interest there, his eyes wandered around the room. On the floor by the bed were some clothes. He assumed that these were what Lucy had been wearing before she had got into the bed. The clothes were scattered and looked as if they had just been dropped or carelessly thrown onto the floor. He picked up the blouse Lucy had been wearing and examined it briefly before letting it drop back onto the floor. Next, he picked up the rest of the clothes and it was then that he noticed the gold locket on the floor. He remembered John telling him that he had given Lucy a locket. He picked it up and opened it and sighed deeply when he saw the small photograph of John inside. Then, suddenly, a thought occurred to him. The locket had been a present from John. So, maybe John had hidden the key code inside it. It was a long shot but Carter was struggling to come up with ideas about where the key-code could be. He quickly fiddled with the photograph until it came out of the locket. Slowly he turned the picture over. He nodded to himself when he saw what was written on the reverse. It was a mixture of numbers and letters, letters from both the English and Greek alphabets: $X\sum 2\pi 8M\beta 9$. Carter was no expert on encryption but it certainly looked like an encryption code to him. He turned to Birch.

"I think we might have something here," he said.

Birch turned and looked at him. He saw Carter holding the locket, and the photograph he had removed from it.

"Let's see," he said and held out his hand. Birch looked at the locket and then at the photograph. "Do you know who this is?" he asked.

"It's John Sprague." The penny dropped and Birch nodded as Carter continued. "Turn it over."

Birch turned the photograph over and saw the characters written on the back. He looked up at Carter. "That mean something to you?"

"No," said Carter shaking his head. "But I think I know someone who might be able to make use of it."

Carter took the photograph back from Birch and then extracted a small pad and a ball-point pen from his inside jacket pocket. He carefully copied what was written on the back of the photograph before handing it back to Birch.

"Better take good care of that," he said meaningfully. "It could be very significant."

Dr Eloden, a pathologist employed by the Santa Monica Police Department was in the mortuary examining Lucy's body when Birch came into the large room where the post mortems on murder victims were carried out. Dr Eloden's assistant stood close by. She was a youngish dark-haired woman who, like the doctor, was dressed in white and wearing latex gloves. Dr Eloden spoke as he worked, his words being carried from the microphone hanging above the body to a recorder in the office at the back of the room.

"Clear evidence of sexual activity prior to death," he said. "Bruises to both wrists and ankles, consistent with having been tied with a rope." He looked up when he became aware of Birch's presence in the room and gave him a cursory nod, which Birch returned. Dr Eloden continued his examination as Birch looked on. Birch had attended many post mortems in his career as a police officer but he still found them upsetting, especially when, as in this case, the victim was an attractive young woman.

After a few minutes had passed, with the doctor continuing his examination, Doctor Eloden came over to Birch.

"There is also some bruising to the vagina," he said. "Whoever he was, he certainly wasn't a gentle lover,"

"Anything that's going to give us a lead on who he is?" asked Birch.

"Not yet. But there is some evidence of semen in the vagina so we should be able to provide you with a DNA profile of whoever had sex with her. Of course that doesn't mean it was him that killed her."

"Pretty likely though, wouldn't you say?"

"Yes. Unless there was more than one person involved."

Birch had had enough. He thanked the doctor and left the room as Dr Eloden returned to Lucy's body to finish his post mortem examination.

Outside the room, Birch approached Carter who had been waiting patiently. Although he had been able to look through the window and see what was going on, Carter had not been able to hear anything, so he was keen to know what had been found out during the autopsy. He looked at Birch expectantly.

"Pathologist says she had sex shortly before she was killed and that there is semen in her vagina. So even if the killer cleaned up after himself, we should be able to get a DNA profile from that. Not that it helps, unless his DNA is already in the database so that we can identify him."

Carter nodded and the two men left the building together. As they came out into the sunshine, Birch stopped and turned to Carter.

"Do you know who might have done this to her?" he asked.

"Not really. I've got an idea as to who it might be but no real evidence."

Birch lifted his head and looked Carter in the eye. "If you know something, you need to tell me," he said.

Conrad was waiting in the lobby of their hotel when Carter arrived, walking quickly along Ocean Avenue. Carter was clearly quite excited as he approached Conrad and he walked past him as he spoke.

"Let's go to my room," he said.

Conrad followed on behind him. "You got something?" he asked.

"Wait and see," responded Carter as he climbed the stairs two at a time.

"There is an elevator, you know!" called Conrad as he began to lag behind Carter.

"Too slow," came the response and Conrad knew, at that point, that Carter definitely had some new information on the case.

Once they were in Carter's room and the door had closed behind Conrad, Carter turned to look at him. Then he took his notebook from his jacket pocket and opened it to where he had transcribed the symbols which were on the back of the photograph of John in Lucy's locket. He folded the notebook and held it up in front of Conrad.

"Does that look like an encryption code to you?" he asked.

Conrad took the notebook and looked at the combination of letters, numbers and symbols. "Could be," he said noncommittally.

"Only one way to find out," said Carter as he snatched the notebook back from Conrad and went over to the wardrobe.

Carter removed his laptop from the wardrobe and put it on the round table by the window. He opened it and pressed the button to start it up. As the laptop went through its start up procedures, Carter reached for the memory stick, which now lived in the pocket of his trousers. He removed the cap and looked at Conrad.

"Over to you," he said handing it to Conrad.

Conrad took the memory stick and sat in front of the laptop. He plugged it into the USB socket and Carter watched as his fingers flew over the keyboard. Carter had a broad smile on his face. He could feel a breakthrough in the case was about to happen. As Conrad continued to work on the computer, typing something in and then waiting and then repeating the process, Carter began to get impatient.

"Well?" he said. "Is it working?"

Conrad smiled. "Sure is," he said as his fingers moved across the keyboard, tapping the keys.

"So what have we got?"

Conrad's smile faded. He leaned back in his chair and looked at Carter. "Not much," he said.

"Meaning?"

"It's a step but only a step. All there is on this memory stick is a short note which says that he has put a complete back up of all his work in a safety deposit box."

"Where? Where's the safety deposit box?" Carter was becoming impatient.

153

"The note says that it's in a vault in Oxford."

"What vault?"

"It doesn't say."

"Does it say anything else?"

Conrad nodded. "It says that the key to the puzzle is in the music."

"And that's it?" he asked. Conrad nodded. Carter was clearly upset. "I thought we'd cracked it when we found the key-code. That John hadn't died in vain. That we would soon have the answer to the threat facing the natural diamond industry worldwide."

"This will have some meaning," said Conrad as Carter's mood quietened a little. "This was intended to guide *him* to where the key is, or maybe someone close to him. It was never intended to help a thief to find out where it was. Or us, for that matter"

"So?" responded Carter, still quite upset.

"So we have to find a link between John and something musical."

"Like what?"

Conrad shrugged. "Don't know. But when we find it, hopefully we will know, hopefully we will make the connection." Conrad waited a few moments before continuing. "Want to go get a beer?" he asked.

There was a few moments pause before Carter turned to look at Conrad. A smile spread across his face. "Why not. You never know, we might get some inspiration from it," he said and the two men left the room, but not before Carter had retrieved the memory chip and put it back in his pocket.

Chapter 13

Based on what Carter had told him about briefly meeting Pierre on his first visit to see Lucy, and also on what Carter had told him that Jacques had been able to find out about the man, Detective Birch had issued an APB for Pierre LeBlanc. In the APB, Birch had advised that Pierre should be considered armed and dangerous and should be approached with caution. The photograph of Pierre had been retrieved from the drawer in Lucy's living room and circulated with the APB.

As a result, it was only matter of a few hours before Pierre was spotted at LAX airport and arrested. He was driven from the airport to the police headquarters in Santa Monica, where he soon found himself in an interview room with Detective Birch and two uniformed officers, one on each side of the room. As Birch interviewed Pierre, he seemed calm and unperturbed.

"Mr LeBlanc," said Birch, "Were you with Lucy Adams last night?"

Pierre paused before answering. "Yes, I was with her. We had dinner together."

"Where did you have dinner and at what time did you meet her?"

"We met at the Olive Tree Restaurant on 2nd Street. It was about 8:00pm."

"And what happened next?"

Pierre smiled. "We had dinner of course! What else do you do when you are in a restaurant?"

"Don't try to be clever, Mr LeBlanc," responded Birch. "You know what I mean. What did you do after dinner?"

"After dinner, we went to her apartment," Pierre smiled mischievously. "And we had sex." He leaned forward, smiling. "Very good sex. Do you want all the details?"

Birch sat back and played with the pen in his right hand as he stared at Pierre; the man was annoying him intensely but he didn't want to show it. "And after that? What then?"

"After that we had some coffee and then I left. I had to go back to the hotel to pack my things."

"And how was Ms Adams when you left?"

Another leering smile appeared on Pierre's face. "Very satisfied, I think. No! Better than that! I know. She had a very good orgasm."

"What time was that?"

"When she had the orgasm?" Pierre paused and touched his chin with his finger. "I'm not sure." The smile was back again. He was playing with Birch and he was enjoying it.

"What time was it when you left?" asked Birch doing his best to remain calm.

"About 11:00pm."

Pierre stared at Birch and Birch stared back before pressing the button to stop the recording.

"We will need to keep you here for now," said Birch as he got up from his seat. "While we make further enquiries."

As the uniformed officers went to escort Pierre to a cell, Birch left the interview room and made his way to the little room where Carter had been watching through a one-way window and listening to the interview.

"We haven't got any evidence that he killed the girl," said Birch. "If he sticks with that story, we'll have to release him.

"Surely there must be something," said Carter in frustration.

"Not so far. He's not denying being there. Nor that he had sex with her. But he says she was fine when he left. And there is a history of a relationship between them, as you know."

"I suppose it's conceivable that someone else killed her. But he looked far too sure of himself when he was answering your questions. As if he'd already thought his whole story through in detail."

"We could check with his hotel when he arrived back but the reality is it would only have taken a minute to kill Ms Adams before he left. So it wouldn't prove anything one way or the other."

"I guess it's down to motive then," said Carter. "We need to prove that he had a motive. He had the opportunity, and the means, so if we can prove motive, that might be enough to convince a jury."

"Yeah, maybe," replied Birch. "But if he gets himself a good lawyer, which I'm betting he will do, very soon, then what we've got is not going to be enough to hold him."

Carter looked at his watch as he left the police station. Even though he had no further news on Mikey, Alice had agreed to see him at 4:00pm, and it was nearly that time already. He drove the short distance to her house and parked outside.

Alice answered the door almost as soon as Carter had knocked on it; she had been waiting for him to arrive and, from the living room window, she had seen him approaching the door.

"Come in Mr Jefferson," she said and then closed the door before leading Carter through to the living room.

"Thank you for seeing me," said Carter as he and Alice sat in the armchairs. "I am so sorry that we still have no news about where Mikey is."

"I understand," said Alice, as she struggled to hold back her emotions.

"The police are doing everything that they can to find him," said Carter, trying to reassure her that Mikey would be found alive and well, but failing to do so.

There was a few moments of silence before Alice, remembering why Carter was there, continued the conversation.

"You said you needed to ask me something?" she said.

"Yes," responded Carter, finding it difficult to raise the matter he had gone to see Alice about. "It may sound a bit off the wall, but I was wondering… When John visited you the last time, when he gave Mikey the owl, did he also give you a key?"

Alice looked bewildered. "A key?"

"Yes, a small key?"

Alice shook her head. She had no idea what Carter was talking about. "No, not that I recall. He gave me a music box, but that's all."

Carter's ears pricked up! A music box. Maybe that was the connection, maybe that was where the key was hidden.

As Carter considered this possibility, Alice continued speaking. "He knew how much I liked music, especially Dvorak." She smiled slightly. "Would you like to hear it? It plays the Slavonic Dances."

"Yes, I would. That would be nice," enthused Carter, keen to follow this thread and see where it led.

Alice got to her feet and retrieved the music box from the cupboard in the dresser. She presented it to Carter proudly before returning to her seat.

"Just lift the lid and it will play," she said, the smile disappearing from her face as she remembered the reason for Carter's visit. Mikey was still missing and she felt a heavy weight of responsibility for that, even though there had been nothing that she could have done to prevent it. She began to fill up with tears as Carter opened the box.

The two of them listened as the music box played the first of the Slavonic Dances. Carter looked at Alice. He could see how upset she was and he wished he hadn't needed to bother her again. But he had needed to. If he was to find Mikey, and also find out why John had been killed, he had to follow every lead.

When the music had finished playing, Carter closed the lid. The clue on the computer chip had said 'the key to the puzzle is in the music' but nothing about what he had just listened to took him any further. Rather mindlessly, he turned the box over and saw where there was a removable cover. He assumed this was where the batteries were located.

"Do you mind if I open this," he asked and Alice shook her head.

Carter removed the battery cover and the two batteries. Underneath the batteries, a small key was sellotaped in the space. He removed it and held it up.

"What's that doing there?" asked Alice, a little shocked at the discovery.

"I think it might be what John was referring to when he said that the key to the puzzle was in the music."

"The key to the puzzle?" Alice was totally confused and Carter decided it was time he explained himself.

159

"Yes. John was working on something, something really important. And secret. He wanted to make sure that if anything happened to him, we would be able to find a copy of his work. It's like this, Alice, there are some people out there who didn't want John to succeed with his work. People to whom it was very important that he didn't succeed. People who, if he did succeed, would want to make sure no one ever found out about it."

"Are they the ones that killed him? And took Mikey?" she asked.

Carter nodded. "Almost certainly, yes."

"Are you going to catch them?"

"I hope so."

"Please make sure you do," said Alice pleadingly as she reached out and held Carter's hand. And if I can do anything to help, you just have to ask me."

"May I take this key?"

"Of course. I hope it helps." Alice nodded and Carter pocketed the key.

Having received a telephone call from Detective Birch as he was leaving Alice's house, informing him that Pierre was about to be released on condition that he did not leave the area, Carter contacted Conrad and told him to go to the police headquarters and keep watch. Carter then drove there himself and parked close to the entrance to the building. As Conrad waited for Pierre to be released, he stood in a doorway across the street from the entrance, hoping that Pierre would not see him. From there, he had seen Carter arrive and park a little way up the street. He had waved to him and Carter had waved back.

When Pierre came out of the police station, carrying his small suitcase and backpack, he looked at his watch.

Then he looked up and down the street and hailed a passing cab.

"To the pier," Conrad heard Pierre say as he got into the back seat of the cab and dragged his small suitcase in after him.

Conrad signalled to Carter to pick him up and when Carter pulled up next to him, Conrad got into the car.

"He's going to the pier," said Conrad before adding, "Maybe." He was well aware that the instruction to the cab driver to go to the pier might just have been for the benefit of anyone who happened to be listening.

The cab soon changed direction and began heading in the direction of the airport with Carter and Conrad following it at a discreet distance. As the cars approached the airport, the cab stopped at the drop off point at Terminal 2 and Pierre got out of the car with his baggage. Carter and Conrad watched from where they had stopped, about fifty yards behind the cab. Carter got out of the car and followed Pierre into the terminal building.

As Carter followed, trying to keep some travellers as a screen between himself and Pierre, he noticed that Pierre was not heading for the check-in desks. He knew that Detective Birch had told Pierre not to leave the Los Angeles area without checking with him first. He also knew that Birch would have made sure that any attempt to leave via LAX would be detected and stopped but he was at a loss as to why Pierre had come to the airport at all. Until he saw Pierre approach the car rental kiosk. With a hire car, Pierre could go where he liked, unnoticed, as long as it was within driving distance. But where did he want to go? And why go all the way to the airport to hire a car?

Carter knew from what Lucy had told him that Pierre supplied her company with industrial quality synthetic diamond wafers, one of the raw materials used in the latest micro processors the company was making, but there was nothing sinister in that, nothing that could possibly lead to Pierre wanting to kill her. But what if his connection with synthetic diamonds went wider than that? What if Pierre also dealt in gem quality synthetics? That would change things. That would mean that, because of her connection with John, she might have information that Pierre wanted. Information that he wanted enough to be willing to kill for it.

Carter decided that he would continue to follow Pierre and find out what he was up to, what he was involved in, other than the straightforward and perfectly legal delivery of synthetic diamond wafers. When he got back to the car, he told Conrad what his plan was and then they waited for Pierre to come out of the terminal.

———

Six hours later, when night had followed day and sunshine had been replaced with moonshine, Pierre was driving along the freeway in the hire car he had picked up at the airport. He was approaching the outskirts of San Francisco. Carter and Conrad were following a little way behind and saw the bright lights come into view as they reached the top of a hill and began the descent into the city.

A few miles further on, they turned off the freeway onto a smaller road leading into the city suburbs. Another couple of miles and Pierre pulled into the floodlit car park of a motel and stopped. Carter had stopped a little way up the road and he and Conrad watched as Pierre went into the motel. When they could no longer see him, Carter drove into the motel car park and parked the car in a position where they would have a good view of both the motel and Pierre's car. He turned the engine off and they sat and waited. Before long, Pierre emerged from the motel office and walked along the line of rooms until he reached his room. Carter and Conrad watched him go into the room and then Carter leaned back in his seat, relaxing, physically if not mentally, for the first time that day.

"You can take the first shift," he said as he closed his eyes. It was about 9:00pm.

The next thing Carter knew was Conrad punching his arm to wake him up. He opened his eyes and looked through the windscreen. He couldn't see anything that would justify Conrad waking him so he looked at Conrad inquiringly.

"He just got a visitor," said Conrad pointing in the direction of Pierre's motel room.

"Anyone we know?"

Conrad shook his head. "Nice car though," he said, as he pointed to a red Aston Martin V8 Vantage which was parked near Pierre's car.

Carter and Conrad watched the door to Pierre's room for nearly an hour during which, Conrad sneaked out of the car to make a note of the Aston Martin's licence plate. When Pierre's visitor finally left the room and walked towards his car, Carter sat up and stared at him. He reached inside his jacket pocket and removed the photograph of the man who had been driving the car into which Mikey had been dragged. He looked at the photograph and then at the man, who was closer now. He passed the photograph to Conrad.

"It's him," he whispered. "Take a look."

"It sure is. What now?"

"You wait here while I follow him," said Carter, almost pushing Conrad out of the car.

Carter started the car and followed the Aston Martin as it left the motel car park. Conrad, now stranded in the car park, all alone, wondered what to do. He couldn't just wait in the car park for Carter to get back. He could be gone for hours and Conrad would have been a bit conspicuous, no matter how hard he tried not to be. He decided to get a room at the motel and keep watch on Pierre's room as best he could from there.

A few minutes later, Conrad came out of the motel office with a key in his hand. His room was two rooms further along from Pierre's and once he was inside, he decided to call Detective Birch and ask him to put a trace on the licence plate number he had copied from the Aston Martin.

While Conrad was calling Birch, Carter followed the Aston Martin as it drove into San Francisco. When it reached the city centre, the car turned into a car park beside a tall office building. At the car park barrier, the driver punched in some numbers. When it rose, he drove into the car park and the barrier closed behind him. Carter drove past the barrier and pulled up at the side of the street. He knew he was parking illegally but it was late at night and he needed to find out who this man was, so he decided to take the risk.

Once the man had entered the building, Carter got out of his car and walked into the car park. He hadn't noticed on the way past, but there was a sign outside the car park saying that it was a private car park for the employees of a company called Shiny New Diamonds Inc. He nodded and smiled to himself. He had heard of Shiny New Diamonds Inc. They weren't one of the biggest makers of synthetic diamonds but they were the hungriest, never missing a chance to publicly run down the natural diamond business. The stream of articles they produced damning the natural diamond industry, or the 'Blood Diamond Industry' as they chose to call it, and blaming it for most of the human rights atrocities perpetrated in Africa, was never ending. And whilst Carter knew that some of the vitriol levelled at the diamond industry was justified, particularly in West

Africa, it was by no means as widespread as these stories suggested. If Pierre was supplying the company, not only with industrial diamonds, but also with gem quality diamonds, that could explain a lot.

Carter looked into the car park, and noticed that many of the parking bays had signs on them, indicating who could park there. Trying to look as nonchalant as he could he wandered over to where the Aston Martin was parked. The sign said: Daniel Blundell, CEO. Carter left the car park and got back into his car. He had found out what he wanted to know and now he needed to pass it on to Birch, but not before he had spoken to Conrad. He extracted his phone and tapped in Conrad's number.

"Conrad. Hi, it's Carter here. Is it all quiet on the western front?" Carter's voice was upbeat and Conrad noticed.

"Yeah, he's still in his room. I took a room too. For us. I thought I would look a bit dodgy just standing in the car park watching the motel. We're in room number 8 when you get here."

"OK, see you soon," said Carter. "I'll fill you in when I get back, OK."

Carter ended the call and started the car. He would be back at the motel within half an hour, he thought, and Conrad could wait that long to hear what he had found out about Pierre's visitor.

By the time Carter had returned to the motel, Conrad had heard back from Detective Birch regarding the owner of the Aston Martin and Carter felt somewhat deflated when he told Conrad his news only to be met with a smug "Yeah, I know" from Conrad.

Chapter 14

Just to be sure that Pierre didn't pull a fast one on them, Carter and Conrad took turns to sleep in the motel on the outskirts of San Francisco. At 7:00am, Conrad woke Carter. Not because anything was happening but because he thought it would be a good idea for the two of them to be ready if it did. Carter had slept in his clothes, although he had taken off his jacket and shoes before throwing himself onto the bed, exhausted, as Conrad took the first watch. He stirred as Conrad now shook his shoulder.

"What time is it," he asked, once he had remembered where he was, "Is it my turn again?"

"No, it's seven o'clock," responded Conrad, smiling. "Time to rise and shine and see what the day has in store for us."

Carter got off the bed, rubbed his eyes and went into the bathroom to splash some water on his face. He returned to the room looking remarkably awake and ready for action. Conrad was sitting at the window watching the space in front of the door to Pierre's room.

"Anything moving?" asked Carter.

"Yep. But nothing of interest to us. There's a coffee on the table for you."

Carter was just about to sit down and enjoy his first coffee of the day when Conrad suddenly stiffened.

"Strike that! I think he's on the move."

Carter walked over to the window and peered over Conrad's shoulder. Pierre was leaving his room. Carter and Conrad watched as he headed for the motel office to drop off his key.

"Time to go," said Carter as he picked up the car keys. "You go and drop off the room key, he doesn't know you. And I'll go and get the car started."

Carter and Conrad waited until Pierre had walked through the door to the office and then they bolted from their room. Conrad walked quickly towards the office. Not only did he need to drop off the room key, he also needed to delay Pierre long enough to allow Carter to get to the car unseen. As he entered the office, Pierre, dropped his key in the slot provided on the counter. As Pierre walked towards the door, Conrad blocked his way, as casually as he could.

"Excuse me," said Conrad, smiling at Pierre. "Do you know what I should do with this?" He held up his key.

"You have to put it in the hole on the counter. Over there," replied Pierre as he went to walk round Conrad.

"Oh, OK. Thanks," said Conrad, as he moved to block Pierre again. "Do I need to tell the man I've done that?"

Pierre sighed and shook his head. "No," he said as he put his hand on Conrad's arm and moved him to one side, out of his way. Conrad walked quickly to the counter and posted the key in the slot before following Pierre out of the office and making his way to the car park. Carter had already started the car and Conrad slid into the passenger seat. A few minutes later, they were following Pierre out of the car park on their way to the West Side Freeway.

While Carter and Conrad were taking the long drive back to Los Angeles from San Francisco, with Conrad having taken over the job of driving the car, Birch was doing some checking. After he had received Conrad's call the night before concerning Daniel Blundell's licence plate, and had called Conrad back to tell him the car was Blundell's, he had decided to call it a day and had gone home for some rest. When he had returned to the station that morning, around eleven o'clock, he had decided to call the department of motor vehicles to see if there was anything recorded against the car, any driving offences committed by its driver, anything which might help his murder enquiry. When the DMV finally called him back, they said that Blundell's Aston Martin had three driving offences recorded against it, one for illegal parking and two for speeding. One of the speeding offences was on Interstate 5, about ten miles north of Los Angeles, heading south. Birch's ears pricked up.

"Do you have a date and time for that one," he asked.

"Sure, let me just check," said the clerk and Birch waited as the clerk looked up the offence on his computer. "It was two days ago and the time was . . . 10:45pm."

Birch smiled. "Interesting," he said. "Thanks for your help. Can I get the record number for that one? So I can look it up on our records?"

The clerk gave Birch the number and Birch wrote it down on his pad before ending the call. He was about to look up the record of the speeding offence on the police computer when his phone rang.

"Detective Birch," he said.

"Hi Alex, it's Carter here. Me and Conrad, we're on Interstate 5. We're following LeBlanc."

"What's he doing on Interstate 5? He's not supposed to leave L.A."

"Yeah, I know. Last night he took himself off to San Francisco. We followed him."

"What was he doing in San Francisco?"

"He met up with the guy whose car Conrad asked you to check last night."

"Funny you should say that. I was going to ask you what your interest in that car was. It was stopped for speeding ten miles outside L.A. a couple of nights ago."

"Yeah well there's more to tell you about on that, but for now, it looks like LeBlanc is heading back to L.A. We'll stay on his tail and keep you informed, OK?"

"OK but I'd like a full update, as soon as you can."

"Sure. I'll call you." Carter ended the call. He looked at Conrad. "How much longer before we get to L.A.?"

"About another two hours, give or take," answered Conrad.

Carter leaned back and closed his eyes. "Wake me up when we're getting close," he said and Conrad smiled.

———————

As Carter and Conrad continued following Pierre, Detective Birch did some more checking into Daniel Blundell's background. The fact that he had met Pierre, a murder suspect, in what could only be described as a clandestine manner, suggested that there was something illegal going on. He wanted to know what it was. Carter, unable to sleep in the car, had called him again and told him about the factory building and that Blundell appeared to be the CEO of a company called Shiny New Diamonds Inc. but Birch wanted to know more about his past.

A little over two hours later, Birch's phone rang again. It was Carter. "We're on San Diego Freeway," he said. "Looks like he's heading for LAX where he hired the car yesterday. We're following him and it could be he's just going to return the car to the hire company but you might want to alert your people there, just in case."

"If it looks like he's going to skip the country, we'll pick him up," replied Birch. "We can hold him on the grounds that he left L.A., if nothing else. I'll inform the airport police and then get over to LAX myself. Keep me posted about where he's at and what he's doing, OK?"

Birch ended the call and got up from his desk. He almost ran out of the building and hailed a cab. He didn't want to be delayed by having to find somewhere to park at the airport. Ahead of him, Carter and Conrad turned off San Diego Freeway onto West Century Boulevard. There was no longer any doubt about where Pierre was headed.

When Pierre's car stopped outside Terminal 2, in the bay provided for returning hire cars, Conrad pulled over. "You'd better follow him," he said as Pierre got out of the car, taking his baggage with him,. "I'll go and park somewhere and then come and find you."

As Conrad drove off, Carter followed Pierre into the terminal. He made sure he kept a good distance behind him. He didn't want Pierre to see him and recognise him. Once inside the terminal building, Pierre went to the car rental desk and returned the key to his hire car. Next, he approached a KLM kiosk in the terminal and spoke to the clerk. As he did so, Carter called Birch again.

"Are you here yet?" he asked.

"Almost. Which terminal are you at?" responded Birch.

"Terminal two. He's at the KLM booth. Looks like he's buying a ticket."

"I'll be there in a few minutes. Don't lose him."

By he time Birch reached Carter, he had picked up two uniformed airport police officers. He strode up to Carter. "Where is he?"

Carter pointed to the KLM booth, where Pierre was finishing buying his ticket. Birch immediately set off towards the booth. The two officers followed on behind, their right hands resting on their handguns. They were ready for action.

Pierre turned away from the booth. As he did so, he was met by Birch and the two airport police officers. He looked shocked and, after a couple of seconds, he realised what was happening. He raised his arms, as if to surrender, and then pushed Birch away with both hands. Birch fell backwards, into the two officers behind him and Pierre saw his opportunity. He started to run, as fast as he could, towards the exit.

One of the uniformed officers side-stepped Birch and drew his pistol from its holster. He aimed it at Pierre. "Police, stop!" he shouted.

Pierre didn't even look round. He just kept on running as fast as he could and was soon in the crowd of people milling around in the terminal. The officer lowered his gun.

"Too risky, Sir," he said to Birch.

Birch nodded and then smiled at what he saw as Pierre continued to run. "He ain't going nowhere," he said, just as Conrad launched himself at Pierre, knocking him to the floor and falling on top of him. Pierre turned his head to look at Conrad and Conrad took the opportunity to punch him hard in the face. Pierre grunted and went limp as Birch, Carter and the two officers arrived on the scene.

"Nice one, Conrad," said Carter as he offered Conrad his hand.

Conrad took the hand and pulled himself to his feet. The two uniformed officers lifted Pierre from the floor and handcuffed him.

"Take him to the station and book him for murder," said Birch to the officers who were holding Pierre. Each of them held one of Pierre's arms in a firm grip.

"You have nothing on me," spat Pierre.

"We'll see about that," retorted Birch before indicating with a nod to the officers that they should leave. When they had gone he turned to Carter.

"Time we had a conference, I think."

Carter nodded and he, Conrad and Birch left the terminal building.

Back at the Santa Monica Police Department, Carter and Conrad settled into two chairs in the meeting room as Detective Birch closed the door. Birch smiled as he also sat down.

"He had a false passport on him," said Birch. "An American one! Which probably explains what he was doing in San Francisco."

"Not that anyone would be suspicious of someone with a French accent having a U.S. passport," joked Carter.

"Whoa! Just a minute, my fine friend! In the USA we welcome people from all cultures."

"Sure. Course you do. Hell, I'm a prime example."

Birch looked shocked. "You have US citizenship?"

Carter laughed and shook his head. "Just kidding. I have Belizean and British nationalities but not American."

"Thank goodness for that! I was getting worried about our immigration policies."

They all laughed. As their laughter subsided, they became serious. Carter was the first to speak.

"Well, I guess I'd better fill you in on what we've found out in the last twenty-four hours, yeah?"

"You bet."

"You already know a lot of it, so I'll restrict myself to the stuff you don't know. And the main thing is that it's all beginning to make some sense now. The killing in Oxford. The burning of the lab. And even what's been happening here."

Carter went on to tell Birch about Shiny New Diamonds Inc in San Francisco. He explained what a threat to the company's business it would be if synthetic and natural diamonds could be distinguished easily and cheaply. He reminded Birch of the huge sums of money involved.

"Do you have any idea what the value of a one carat natural diamond is?" asked Carter. Birch shook his head. "Well," continued Carter, "It varies depending on quality. But the average retail value is around ten thousand bucks."

"And the synthetic equivalent?"

"Currently, at wholesale prices, about forty percent of natural. But if there was a portable, cheap, reliable detector, that would drop sharply. Probably to below ten percent."

"That's a big difference," observed Birch.

Carter nodded. "Especially if you're selling … let's see … say around ten thousand of them a year."

"Ten thousand times … ," Birch looked at the ceiling as he did the math. "Thirty million bucks less!"

Carter nodded. "At retail prices, yes. And serious producers are making a lot more of them than that."

"OK, so that gives us a powerful motive for them wanting to stop your friend Sprague," said Birch. "But what about Lucy? Why kill her?"

"Maybe she knew something," suggested Carter. "Or just got caught up in the middle of it. By accident. Same with Mikey's kidnapping."

Birch brought his hand down on the table with a loud bang. "OK! It's time we nailed the rest of these mother-fuckers!" he said.

"You betcha!" responded Conrad as Carter looked at Birch. He had not seen the man so worked up before. "Where would you like to start?" he asked.

Birch smiled. "I had my guys do a bit of digging," he said. "While you were relaxing in San Francisco."

"They come up with anything?"

"Blundell's company has another property in L.A. Assuming he's as wrapped up in this whole business as you seem to think he is, maybe that's where Mikey is."

Carter got to his feet. "Well let's get over there. See what we can find."

"I'll get us some backup first," said Birch as he and Conrad also got to their feet. "Wait for me here."

Chapter 15

After three days of sitting alone in the corner of the basement room which was the furthest from the door, Mikey was tired, hungry and scared, very scared. He had been interrogated twice and the silent man, the one who had stood at the door during his questioning, had come in a couple of times each day and dumped some sandwiches and a plastic bottle of water on the table. Apart from that, he had been left on his own. He had come to the conclusion that he was never going to get out of that dark, miserable place. He wondered what his father had done to result in his son being dragged into a car and locked in what was effectively a prison. He guessed it must be something important but he had no idea what it was. When they were together, his father had always wanted Mikey to have a good time and Mikey always did. But he had seen his father infrequently and he knew little about his life and work.

The sound of the key in the basement door roused Mikey and his head jerked upwards as his two kidnappers came in. The one who always asked the questions looked at him.

"Get up!" he snapped at Mikey.

Mikey did as he was told.

"Come over here and sit there," continued the man, pointing at the chair by the table.

Mikey obeyed and walked towards the table hesitantly. He sat down and stared at the man. It was a cold stare, no emotion. The man sat down opposite him.

"The last time your Dad visited you, the time he gave you the owl with the memory stick inside it, what else did he give you?" asked the man.

"Nothing," replied Mikey.

"Nothing?" repeated the man and Mikey nodded. "You sure about that? No other presents?" Mikey shook his head.

"What about your Grandma? Did he give her a present?" Mikey didn't answer so the man continued. "What was it?"

"What was what?"

"What was the present your Dad gave your Grandma?"

"He didn't give her anything."

The man sighed and then he reached out and slapped Mikey hard across the face. Mikey winced but did not cry out.

"There's no point in me keeping you alive if you're not going to tell me the truth," said the man as he stood up and leaned towards Mikey. "Last chance," he said but Mikey did not respond and the man stood up straight and stared at him.

Mikey watched as the man who had been interrogating him went over to the man by the door and whispered in his ear before leaving the room. The other man, the nasty looking one, looked at Mikey and shook his head. He sighed and left the room, locking the door behind him.

Carter sat beside Detective Birch as Birch drove into Los Angeles heading for the building owned by Blundell. Conrad was in the back seat along with

176

another detective from the SMPD. Behind their car, two police cars, one marked and one unmarked, followed. The marked police car had not turned on its flashing lights and siren as Birch had decided on a silent approach. Having decided to search the building to see if Mikey was being held there, he wanted the element of surprise on his side. In the unmarked police car were two more detectives from the SMPD homicide department and in the other one were four fully armed, uniformed LAPD officers wearing bullet proof vests. Birch didn't know what to expect when they got to the building and he wasn't taking any chances.

As the three vehicles approached the two storey building on East 3rd Street, they pulled up about a hundred yards away and everyone got out.   Birch positioned two of the armed officers at points along the street in front of the building, covering the entrance, and two in the street behind the building. Carter, Conrad and the three detectives followed Birch into the building.

Birch walked briskly up to the reception desk and held up his hand in which he was holding his police ID card. The young female receptionist did not know how to respond to this and simply stared at him, dumbfounded.

"We're here to search this building," he said.

The receptionist did not speak. She just picked up the telephone receiver on her desk, punched in a couple of numbers and waited for her call to be answered. Birch turned to the detectives. He pointed at two of them in turn and said, "You two take the top floor." Then he pointed at the third. "You and Conrad take this floor. And we'll take the basement."

The first two detectives immediately headed for the stairs to the top floor. Conrad and the third detective headed for the door leading into the large open plan office on the ground floor. Birch turned back to the receptionist just as she started to speak on the phone.

"Mr Johnson, there's some police officers here. They want to search the building." She paused before continuing. "OK, I'll tell them." She looked at Birch. "Mr Johnson is on his way down."

As the two detectives who had been allocated the top floor started climbing the steps, a man appeared at the top of the stairs. He saw them and tried to block their way.

"You can't go up there," he said, an air of desperation in his tone. "You're not signed in."

"Sure we can," replied one of the detectives as they both pushed past him. "We have a search warrant."

Johnson descended the stairs and approached Birch and Carter.

"What's going on?" he asked.

Birch held up a piece of paper. "We have a warrant to search this building," he said.

"What for? What are you looking for?"

"That's our business, Sir. Now, please, just get out of the way and let us do our job."

Birch and Carter headed for the stairs leading down to the basement of the building as Johnson looked at the receptionist and then followed them down the stairs. At the bottom of the stairs was a large, solid door. Birch tried the handle. The door was locked. He turned to Johnson.

"Open this door, please," he said.

"You can't go in there, it's a secure area. And there's nothing there but a load of files anyway."

"Just open it."

"I don't have the key."

"Then get it! Carter, can you wait here while we get the key, please."

Carter nodded and, after a few moments' thought, Johnson turned and headed back up the stairs, closely followed by Birch. When they reached the reception area, Conrad and the three detectives were gathered together. As Birch approached them, one of the detectives who had been allocated the top floor spoke.

"There's nothing up there," he said.

"Nothing on this floor either," added Conrad.

"Which just leaves the basement," said Birch, whereupon Johnson decided to make his escape. He ran towards the entrance door and out through it onto the street with Birch and Conrad in hot pursuit.

Once in the street he looked up and down, trying to decide which way to go. As he did, a voice rang out.

"Stay where you are!" It was one of the armed officers who had been watching the entrance. "And put your hands on your head."

Johnson had no choice but to comply and as he stood there, Birch came out onto the street behind him with Conrad and one of the other detectives. The detective went up to Johnson and carried out a quick search, during which he removed an automatic pistol from the shoulder holster under Johnson's suit jacket and handed it to Birch.

"OK, cuff him, and have him taken in for questioning," said Birch to the uniformed officer who had crossed the road and was standing in front of Johnson with the muzzle of his gun a few inches from his chest.

As the uniformed officer spoke into his radio arranging for Johnson to be picked up and taken to the police station, Birch, Conrad and the detective went back into the building. By this time, Carter had returned to the reception desk and he watched as they came back in.

"I think we need to take a look in that basement," said Birch as they walked towards the receptionist. She was in shock and just stood motionless as they approached her. "Do you have a key for the basement?" he asked.

The receptionist just nodded and opened the drawer beside her. She reached into the drawer and extracted a large key which she handed to Birch.

"You stay right where you are, lady, OK?" instructed Birch. She nodded, still unable to speak.

Carter, Birch and Conrad descended the steps to the basement door and Birch inserted the key. He looked at Carter as he opened the door and then went into the room. It was pitch black, the only light being that coming through the open door. Carter looked for a light switch and found it on the wall beside the door. He flicked it and the fluorescent strip lights came on, illuminating several rows of filing cabinets in the main body of the room and bookcases along two of the walls. A quick inspection told them that no one was being kept prisoner in the basement.

"There's no one in here," said Carter, turning to leave.

"Maybe not," responded Conrad quickly, "but we should check it out anyway."

Carter turned back and nodded. "You're right. Never know what we might find."

The three men split up and went down three different alleyways of filing cabinets, pulling one open from time to time and looking inside it.

As they were about to give up and leave the basement, Conrad, who by this time was at the far end of the basement, called out.

"Got something here," he shouted, indicating with his hand for Birch and Carter to join him.

When Carter and Birch reached Conrad, they saw what had attracted his attention. While Mikey wasn't there, nor any human remains, there was a crumpled blanket on the floor with a half full bottle of water next to it. Clearly someone had been there, even if only for a short time.

Birch sighed. "Looks like we're a bit late. Unless someone just used the place as a hotel after a late night's work."

Carter nodded. "If they're still holding Mikey, it isn't here!"

Birch extracted an evidence bag from his pocket and reached down to pick up the bottle, using the bag to prevent any contamination from his hand. He also picked up the blanket.

"Better take these with us, see if they give us any clues."

Carter nodded and Birch then led the way out of the basement, switching off the lights as they left the room.

When they reached the reception desk, the receptionist was sitting in her chair, pretending to do some work. Birch approached her and she looked up.

"Find anything?" she asked.

Birch looked away, towards the main entrance before speaking. "Not for sure," replied Birch before holding up the evidence bag and blanket, "But we'll be taking these with us for forensic examination."

"Why?" asked the receptionist, a surprised expression on her face.

"It looks like someone has been sleeping there."

"I don't know anything about that," said the receptionist. "The building is locked from 6:00 at night until 8:30 in the morning.

"I'd like to speak to Mr Blundell. Is he here?" asked Birch

"No, he only comes in for a few days each month," responded the receptionist coldly, looking up from her desk.

"Any idea where we can find him?" asked Carter. It was a throwaway comment but it produced a response.

"Sure. He'll most likely be sunning himself on the deck of his beach house," said the receptionist with an air of superiority.

"His beach house?" queried Birch.

"Yeah, if he's not here or at the factory in San Francisco, that's where he usually is."

Birch raised himself to his full height. "So, where is this beach house?" he asked.

"Don't know if I should tell you that." The receptionist was now in command and she knew it.

"Trust me. You should tell me. It's not like I can't find out if I want to," said Birch dismissively. The receptionist looked at him, her sense of supremacy fading.

"I think you should tell him," said Carter with a gentle voice and a smile.

The receptionist gave in. "OK, it's along the coast a bit, on Pacific Coast Highway, about ten miles north of Malibu."

"Address," demanded Birch and the receptionist looked through her address book until she found the address.

"I'll write it down for you," she said, her attitude now much more compliant as she scribbled the address in her notebook before tearing out the sheet and giving it to Birch.

Birch looked at the detectives who had been standing a few yards away watching the process.

"You stay here," he said to one of them. "I don't want her making any phone calls, OK? Not to anyone."

The detectives nodded and one of them walked round behind the reception counter so that he could see everything the receptionist did.

"And no one leaves here until I say. OK?" continued Birch before looking at the remaining detectives. "The rest of you? Looks like we're going up the coast a ways."

When the man guarding Mikey returned to the basement of the house, he locked the door behind him and put the key in his pocket. Mikey was back in the corner of the room again with his knees pulled up to his chin. He hadn't been expecting the man to be back so soon. Mikey looked at him as he came in. He was carrying some thin rope, a sack and a large piece of rock. The rock was smooth, like a pebble only much bigger. It was the size of a small child's toy football, about six inches across. As the man put the rope, the sack and the rock on the table, Mikey plucked up the courage to ask the question which was burning a hole in his mind.

"What's all that stuff for?" he asked.

The man looked at Mikey. "None of your business," he said, as he patted his pockets, clearly looking for something and not finding it. He reached his hands into his trouser pockets and then withdrew them, empty. "Where the fuck ..." he whispered to himself before a thought occurred to him just as Mikey spoke.

"Are you going to tie me up?" Mikey's voice was a little shaky now.

"Maybe," came the reply as the man looked at the sack, the rope and the rock on the table.

"Why?"

The man spun round. He took a few steps towards Mikey, who was still sitting in the corner, and then bent forward to speak to him.

"Because we're finished with you."

"So... are you going to kill me?" There was clear apprehension in Mikey's voice as the reality of what was happening dawned on him.

The man stood up straight and looked Mikey in the eye. "We're just going for a boat ride, that's all," he said, pausing for a moment, before turning away and heading for the door.

Mikey smiled a weak smile. He didn't know what to believe but, if they were going for a boat ride, he was sure it was going to end badly for him. The man unlocked the door and turned back to Mikey.

"Don't you go anywhere now," he said, a false smile on his face. "Or you'll miss all the fun."

The man went out and locked the door again as Mikey looked around the room, wondering what the man had been looking for. He couldn't escape the thought that something bad was about to happen and, for the first time, he thought there might be something he could do about it.

Mikey got to his feet and went over to the table. He picked up the smooth rock, it was heavy. He put it down again and looked towards the door. Then he picked up one of the chairs and moved it next to the door, on the side where it would be hidden when the door opened. Back at the table, he picked up the rock again before returning to the chair and, with some difficulty, climbing up onto it. He stood there with the rock in his hands and waited.

When, a few minutes later, Mikey heard the key in the lock, he took a big breath and lifted the rock above his head. The door opened and the man came in. He turned towards where Mikey had been sitting and his eyes narrowed when he saw that Mikey wasn't where he had left him. He looked quickly round the room and when he failed to see Mikey he realised where he must be. He slowly pulled the door towards him and peered round it. As he did, Mikey, with all the strength that he could muster, brought the rock down onto the man's head. The man let out a grunt as the rock hit him with a cracking sound before he fell to his knees. He looked at Mikey for a few moments, as he tried to get up, but then his eyes closed and he crumpled onto the floor.

Mikey was almost crying with fright as he got down from the chair and walked slowly and tentatively round the motionless body of the man. When he got to the open doorway, he took one last look at the man before quickly turning back and running up the stairs. As he approached the ground floor, he suddenly realised that the man might not have been alone. His pace slowed and quietened. The top of the stairs led into the kitchen. Mikey could now see that he had been held in the basement of a house. Across the kitchen, through the open door, he could see the living room of the house. Through the large picture window at the far side of the room, he could see the sea glinting in the sunlight. He moved slowly and silently round the edge of the kitchen towards the door to the living room. Along the way, he picked up a large kitchen knife which was on the work surface. He wondered if the man now lying in the basement had planned to use it on him. He peeped through the doorway and looked round the living room. There was no one there. He breathed a sigh of relief and went into the room. He walked towards the glass door next to the picture window and looked out at the sea, wondering what to do next. Suddenly the phone rang. He froze. It rang several times and then stopped. Then he heard the sound of the man's mobile phone ringing in the basement. He panicked and dropped the knife. He looked around the room and spotted a small ornamental Buddha. He picked it up and threw it at the glass door. The glass shattered. Quickly, Mikey used his foot to clear a space large enough for him to get through. Before he left the house, he turned and looked back through the kitchen to see if the man was coming after him. There was no one there.

Outside the house, standing on the decking which faced the sea, Mikey looked around. At one side of the decking a wooden pathway led to a pier where a small power boat was moored. There was also a way round the side of the house but he didn't know what he would find there. So he decided to see if he could get away from the house using the boat.

After another quick look round, Mikey ran along the wooden path to the pier and jumped into the boat. He found the starter button and pressed it. Nothing happened! He pressed it again, several times. Still nothing. Although Mikey had never driven a speedboat himself, since moving to Santa Monica with his grandmother, he had seen lots of people get into their boats and start them up and he couldn't understand why the boat would not start. Then he saw the keyhole next to the starter button. He sighed as he realised that he needed a key to turn on the engine's ignition.

By now, the stress of what was happening had left Mikey short of breath. He wondered what to do. He was panting, taking quick deep breaths and looking around, as if suddenly out of nowhere a solution would emerge. Then he remembered what the man had said. He had told Mikey that they were going for a boat ride. If they were going for a boat ride, then he must have had the key to the boat. It was the only boat in sight. His brow furrowed as he realised what he had to do.

Slowly, Mikey made his way back to the house and through the broken glass door. Once inside the house he looked round the living room and kitchen for anything that might be the key for the boat. There was nothing. Then it occurred to him. Maybe his kidnapper had the key in his pocket. He went to the top of the steps leading down to the basement and listened. He couldn't hear anything. Slowly, he started walking down the steps, one at a time but pulled up sharply as the man's mobile phone rang again. Mikey thought his heart would leap out of his chest if it beat any harder or faster. Then the phone stopped ringing. Mikey listened. He was ready to run for his life if he heard any movement coming from the basement. But it was silent. Slowly, one step at a time, and always ready to turn and run back up the stairs at a moment's notice, he descended to the basement door. The man was still sprawled on the floor where Mikey had left him. Mikey went and kneeled down beside him. He waited a few moments and then, plucking up his courage, he took a deep breath and started to go through the man's pockets. He didn't have to search for long. In the second pocket he reached into, one of the pockets in the man's leather jacket, he found what he thought must be the boat's key. He sighed with relief. As Mikey put the key into his own pocket, he heard a grunt. He froze, for the second time that day. His eyes moved to look at the man's face. There was a slight movement and another grunt. So the man wasn't dead. Mikey had mixed feelings about that. He was glad he hadn't killed the man but he was terrified that he might get caught. He got to his feet and ran up the steps into the kitchen.

In the space of a less than a minute, Mikey had negotiated the broken glass door and was back in the boat. He tried the key in the lock. It fitted! He couldn't stop himself from smiling as he turned the key and pressed the starter button. The boat's engine burst into life and the boat began to pull against its mooring ropes as the engine ticked over. Mikey untied the ropes and returned to stand in front of the steering wheel. He reached out with his right hand and thrust the throttle lever forward. As the boat began to pick up speed and head out to sea, he looked back at the house. He saw the man appear at the broken glass door. He looked back at the sea, and smiled. For the first time since he had been dragged into that car, he was free.

"I'm freeeeeee!" he screamed above the noise of the boat's engine and began to laugh unrestrainedly, the euphoria taking him over completely.

Chapter 16

Having left Malibu a few miles behind them, Birch, Carter and Conrad approached Blundell's beach house. They were closely followed by the car containing the two detectives and two uniformed police officers.

When they reached the turn off from the highway, Birch turned down a small unmade road and they weaved their way down towards the sea and the rocky outcrops which littered the beach. There was only one house at the end of the road, a bungalow with white painted walls and a red tiled roof. When they reached it, Birch parked the car.

"We don't know what to expect here," he said to Carter who was sitting beside him. "You and Conrad wait here while we check it out."

Carter nodded and Birch got out of the car. He was quickly joined by the other police officers. They approached the door of the house.

Birch looked at the uniformed officers. They were holding their automatics, they were ready for action.

"You two stay here and cover the back," he said. They nodded as Birch and the two detectives drew their hand guns in readiness for whatever might be behind the door.

"OK. Let's do it," said Birch

One of the detectives raised his leg. He kicked the door with the sole of his shoe. It didn't open. He changed tack, took a few steps back, and ran at the door, hitting it with his shoulder. It still didn't open. Birch looked at him. He reached out and turned the handle of the door; it opened. They all smiled for a moment at the comedy of the situation as, back in the car, Carter and Conrad were creasing themselves.

Once inside, the detectives quickly established that there was no one in the house. As they searched the house for any evidence, they discovered the basement at the bottom of the stairs leading down from the kitchen. The presence of the ropes, the sack and the rock in the basement, not to mention the shattered glass door in the living room, convinced them they were in the right place. As they gathered in the living room, Birch looked out of the picture window and saw a man running, rather unsteadily, along the beach. He quickly turned to his colleagues, pointing at the man as he spoke.

"Get after him!" he instructed them. "I'll call it in."

The two detectives made their way gingerly but as quickly as they could through the broken glass of the door before jumping over the rail at the front of the decking and making their way across the rocks to the beach. They ran as fast as they could after the man, shouting: "Stop! Police!" as they did. Not far behind them, one of the uniformed officers was also giving chase. The man was still more than a hundred yards ahead of them and he was still running as fast as he could but they were running faster. The uniformed officer stopped. He dropped onto one knee and raised his automatic rifle. He aimed it at the man and fired three shots in quick succession. The man faltered and reached down to his leg. One of the bullets had penetrated his thigh. He stopped running. Slowly, he fell to his knees and lifted his hands above his head.

When Carter and Conrad had seen the uniformed officer run down the side of the house, they had got out of the car and gone into the house. They found Birch in the living room and he turned to them as they came in.

"Got him!" he said and the satisfaction he felt was obvious from his broad smile. "Now maybe we can find out who's behind all of this."

"Any sign of Mikey?" queried Carter and the smile quickly left Birch's face.

"Well," he began, "he's not here, that's for sure. But there's stuff in the basement that suggests ..."

"We need to find him," interrupted Carter. "They must have moved him to another location."

"Unless he managed to escape." Suggested Birch.

"Yeah, sure," responded Carter, "Why didn't I think of that?"

"I grant you that it seems unlikely, but you never know. And it might explain the smashed door."

Carter and Birch stopped talking as they watched the policemen dragging the injured man towards the house. They could see that he was in no state to be questioned and they knew that they would have to wait until he had been medically examined but Carter couldn't resist asking one question.

"You got a name?"

The man looked at him and then at Birch before answering.

"Ben Blake," he said as the two policemen led him past Carter.

When Carter and Conrad had been dropped off at their hotel by Birch, with a promise to keep them informed about the man they had caught and about Mikey's whereabouts, they decided they needed a break and quickly changed into more casual clothes. Carter put on blue jeans and his fawn lightweight jacket over a dark blue shirt. Conrad wrestled his legs into a pair of tight tan trousers, topped off with a white shirt, no jacket.

Ten minutes later they were sitting in the café at the end of the Santa Monica pier, looking out to sea and enjoying a beer. Inevitably, the break was short lived. Before long they were discussing the case and what to do next.

"One of us should get back to Oxford and check out the safety deposit box," said Carter. "Could be there's a few answers in there."

"Want me to go?" offered Conrad

Carter looked at him and thought for a few moments. "Yeah, why not? If you're OK with that," he said.

"Sure, no problem. I'll book a seat on the next flight to London." Conrad got up to leave.

"Finish your coffee first!" said Carter, putting out his hand and touching Conrad's arm.

Conrad sat down again and they both laughed. It had been a manic ten days for the pair since they had met up in Oxford and they were both tired and in need of some relaxation. But it couldn't last. Carter's phone rang.

"Hi there. What's new?" said Carter and mouthed 'Detective Birch' to Conrad. "Interview finished already?"

"Yeah," responded Birch. "We didn't get much out of him. He's just low level muscle."

"What's his connection with Blundell?"

"He's employed by Blundell's Shiny New Diamonds company. Said he was responsible for security at the company's offices in L.A."

"So why was he at the house? How did he explain that?"

"He said he was doing the boss a favour."

"By kidnapping a kid?"

"He said he didn't know anything about any kidnapping. Or about any kid."

"So, if Mikey was there, and it looks like he was, where is he now?"

"Don't know. But maybe he did escape."

"So, what happens next?"

"We'll charge him with kidnapping. We have enough for that. And we've already started a search of the area to see if we can find Mikey."

"And Blundell?"

"We'll pick him up too. We've got more on him. The kid's photo for a start. And his connection with LeBlanc."

"Is there anything I can do to help?" asked Carter as the conversation drew to a close.

"Just make sure you're here for the trial," responded Birch. "If I need anything else, I'll let you know."

Carter ended the call. He looked at Conrad. "Looks like we've done all we can here," he said, " And, much as I would like to wait until Mikey has been found, I think I might as well go back to Oxford with you. But not until we've finished our coffee." He raised his cup and they both smiled.

Having gone in a variety of directions, not sure of which he should choose, Mikey continued to drive the speedboat across the sea. He was now heading south from where he had been held captive in the basement of Blundell's beach house and, as he did, he kept looking behind him to see if he was being followed. Each time, when he saw there was no one behind him, he smiled and punched the air again. He was driving the boat more slowly now but, before long, he had rounded the cape at Point Dume and was heading east towards Santa Monica, keeping fairly close to the coast.

A couple of hours after he had started the boat and made his escape, Mikey saw Santa Monica beach ahead of him. His heart started beating at a more normal pace as he realised that he would soon be back on dry land and on his way to his grandmother's house. In his excitement, Mikey pushed the throttle forward and ran the boat at full speed onto the beach before turning the engine off. A few people enjoying the sunshine watched him, a bit shocked by the way he had beached the boat and then just left it. He totally ignored them and walked quickly up the beach towards Pacific Coast Highway.

When he reached the highway, he crossed the small area of grass and trees to get to Ocean Avenue. Once there, he relaxed and took a few deep breaths before starting to walk along the sidewalk towards his home.

As Mikey reached Ocean Avenue, Carter and Conrad, on their way back from the pier, were walking along the road towards their hotel and they saw him. Carter recognised him at once and became excited.

"Mikey!" he shouted as loudly as he could. But Mikey, who was about twenty yards in front of them, simply took fright and began to run, too terrified to even look to see who was calling his name.

"Mikey! It's me, Carter!" shouted Carter as he and Conrad began to run after Mikey.

When Mikey realised that it was Carter who had shouted his name, he looked round. But he was still running as fast as he could and, as he did, he caught one of his feet behind the other and fell heavily onto the sidewalk. As he tried to get to his feet, Carter reached him and helped him up.

"I'm sorry, Mikey," he said as he pulled him to his feet, "I didn't mean to scare you. Are you alright?"

Mikey got to his feet and dusted himself down before speaking. "Yeah, I'm good." He looked at Carter and Conrad before continuing. "But I need to get home and see my Gran, tell her I'm OK."

Of course you do," responded Carter. "We'll take you there."

Conrad began trying to hail a cab as Carter checked that Mikey was not physically damaged as a result of his fall.

"They had me in this basement and they were going to kill me!" said Mikey, tears in his eyes as he looked at Carter.

"Yeah, we know. We found the place where they held you." Carter smiled. "I'm just so glad that you're safe."

A cab pulled up in response to Conrad's incessant waving and shouting and the three of them got in before Carter gave the driver Mikey's grandmother's address. As they drove to Alice's house, Mikey told Carter and Conrad what had happened at the beach house and how he had managed to escape.

Alice happened to be in the hallway as the cab carrying Carter, Conrad and Mikey pulled up outside her house. When she saw Mikey get out of the cab, she opened the front door and Mikey ran up to her before wrapping his arms round her waist. Alice burst into tears, so relieved to see him alive and well. She put her hands round his head and pulled him towards her, tears streaming down her cheeks as she looked up at Carter and Conrad. They were both smiling as they walked along the path to the front door. Alice looked up at them and mouthed 'Thank you' before separating herself from Mikey and inviting them into the house.

When they were all sitting comfortably in the lounge, Alice asked the inevitable question. "What happened?"

Carter sat back in his chair and took a deep breath before replying. "Well," he said, "they took Mikey because they believed that he had something they wanted They didn't know what it was but they suspected that John had given Mikey something which would ensure that his work was safe. And they were right. it was the memory stick that he found inside the owl John had given him." Alice shook her head in disbelief as Carter continued. "They kept him in the basement of a beach house while they tried to get what they could out of him. But they under-estimated him." Carter gave Mikey a look and Mikey smiled. "It's hard to believe this, but Mikey managed to escape! Using all the resourcefulness he could muster, he knocked the man who was guarding him unconscious before jumping into an outboard powered little boat and heading out to sea."

Alice looked at Mikey. She shook her head in disbelief and smiled at him before reaching out and pulling him over to hug him. "You are one clever boy, Mikey!" She kissed him. "And I am so happy to have you home again." She looked at Carter as she cuddled Mikey. "Thank you!"

Carter smiled back before he spoke. "Well, I think we should leave you to enjoy some alone time with Mikey but if you need any more information, please call me. We'll see ourselves out."

As Carter and Conrad rose, Mikey turned to look at them and offered a high five and they both patted hands with him before leaving him, still cuddled up to his grandma.

Daniel Blundell's Aston Martin raced along Route 101, away from San Francisco, heading south by the coast road towards Los Angeles. Inside, Blundell checked his mobile phone. No messages. He threw the phone onto the passenger seat and stared ahead. Ben Blake should have phoned him by now. His instructions were to check in every two hours to confirm that all was as it should be. Blake had now missed two calls. Blundell checked his watch. It would be another two hours before he reached the beach house, assuming he didn't get a speeding ticket before then. As he drove through Santa Maria, he decided to stop for something to eat. He also wanted to call Pierre, who he hadn't heard from for twenty-four hours. In fact, what seemed to be a conspiracy of silence was beginning to get to him. He pulled off the highway into the car park of a burger bar. Before he went into the building, he tried Pierre's phone again. It was still going straight to voicemail.

Birch was in his office when Eddie Tronda, a uniformed officer, knocked and opened the door. Birch looked up and waited for him to speak.

"Sorry to disturb you Detective but I thought you would want to know," said the officer.

"Want to know what?" queried Birch.

"Daniel Blundell just left Santa Maria. The cell phone trace shows that he stopped there, at the In-N-Out Burger about twenty minutes ago."

"Looks like he's still heading for the beach house then."

"Yeah, it looks that way."

Birch rose from his seat. "Then I guess we'd better get out there so we can give him a warm welcome," he said and the officer smiled.

"Me and Officer Crane are ready when you are."

An hour later, Birch, Tronda and Crane were driving along Highway 101 towards the beach house, with Malibu behind them. When they reached the house, Birch asked Tronda to open the garage door. He wanted their car out of sight when Blundell drove up to the house. When the car was safely stowed in the garage, Birch looked around, checking that there was nothing to indicate that anything had happened at the house. He turned to Officer Crane.

"You wait out here," he said. "But make sure you're out of sight when he gets here. Once he's inside the house, move round to cover any escape attempt. OK?"

Crane nodded. "Gotcha," he said as he surveyed the area around the house looking for a good hiding place. There was a hedge running along the left side of the road which led to the house. It ended as it reached the garage. Crane forced his way through between the hedge and the garage wall and took up position behind the hedge.

Inside the house, Birch and Tronda stood in the hallway. To the right was the kitchen, with the steps leading down to the basement, and to the left were the bathroom and bedrooms. Straight ahead, a short corridor led into to the living room which ran the whole width of the house and looked out over the sea. Birch decided that they should wait in the kitchen. From there they would be able to see anyone approaching the house from the highway. He and Tronda sat at the breakfast counter and waited. Birch looked at his watch.

"Could be another hour yet," he said. "Let's make some coffee."

Outside, Crane sat on the ground facing the sea. He knew he would be able to hear if a car drove along the road to the house.

198

In the end, they didn't have to wait long. Blundell was a fast driver. He had a long list of speeding tickets to his name and he wasn't about to change his ways. He still hadn't heard from his man, Blake, and he was in a hurry to find out why.

Officer Crane lifted his head as he heard the deep throated sound of the Aston Martin approaching the house. He stood up and turned round, remembering to crouch so that he couldn't be seen from the road. Inside the house, Birch put down his coffee cup as he saw the car approaching. He tapped Tronda on the arm and indicated for them to go into the hallway. There, he pointed to the bedroom door. Tronda opened it and stood in the doorway, out of sight from the front door of the house. Birch backed into the kitchen slightly. He peeped round the door jamb so that he could see the front door.

The Aston Martin slowed and pulled up in front of the house. Blundell got out of the car and walked towards the house. He had a bunch of keys in his left hand and in his right hand was a Smith & Wesson Magnum revolver. He was prepared for anything, or so he thought. He inserted one of the keys into the lock and turned it only to find that the door wasn't locked. Then he put the keys into his trouser pocket and paused. He put his hand on the door handle and took a deep breath. A moment later, he turned the handle and threw the door open. As he did so, he held his gun out in front of him, using both hands. He was ready to confront whoever was in the house. He stepped into the hallway. Nothing happened. He lowered his gun and breathed out. He began to relax and, just as he did, Birch stepped out of the kitchen into the hallway. He stood with his legs apart, his gun raised and pointing at Blundell.

"Drop the gun," said Birch, quietly but firmly, as Tronda appeared from the bedroom, his gun also at the ready. "Do it now," advised Birch.

Blundell looked at Birch and then at Tronda. He nodded and made as if to drop his gun on the floor. Birch took a couple of steps forward, anticipating the gun falling to the floor but, as he did, Blundell lurched round and ran out of the house. Before Birch or Tronda could react, Blundell came running out of the front door, heading for his car. Crane watched from behind the hedge. A shot rang out as Tronda let off a round in the direction of Blundell. It missed its mark. Crane lifted his gun and reached out over the hedge, pointing it at Blundell.

"Stop! Police!" he shouted.

Blundell looked over at Crane. Without hesitation, he raised his gun, pointed it at the officer, and fired. Crane felt the shot hit his bullet proof vest. He narrowed his eyes and pulled the trigger of his own gun. Birch and Tronda came out of the house just as Blundell collapsed in a heap beside the open door of his car. All three officers gathered around Blundell and looked down at him. He looked up at them pleadingly as he drew his last few breaths.

"Shouldn't have done that," said Crane. "You tried to kill me, you little shit."

Blundell's eyes closed and he stopped breathing.

Chapter 17

Inside the Tom Bradley international terminal at LAX airport, Carter and Conrad queued to check in for their British Airways flight to London. Neither of them was looking forward to the ten hour flight, especially as they were due to arrive in London at 7:30am the following morning. That meant that whatever sleep they wanted before travelling to Oxford would have to be taken on the journey and neither of them was small enough to make sleeping on an aeroplane easy.

After they had checked in, they made their way to the departure lounge and eventually to their departure gate where they found two comfortable soft black seats which were not already taken. They dropped into the seats and waited for the flight to be called. As they sat, mindlessly watching the people come and go, Carter's phone rang.

"Carter Jefferson," he said, wondering who was calling him.

"Carter, it's Detective Birch here."

"Oh! Hi. What can I do for you?"

"No, nothing. I just wanted to update you. Blundell's dead. He came to the beach house, as we thought he would, but he decided to try and make a run for it. He took a shot at one of my officers who, thankfully, was wearing protection. The officer fired back and wounded Blundell. Fatally."

"We're not going to get any information from him then," said Carter, his tone indicating his disappointment.

"No. But it was him who took the first shot. The officer had no choice," replied Birch, a touch annoyed by Carter's tone. "Anyway, have a good flight. And let me know what you find in the safety deposit box."

"Will do," said Carter as he ended the call. He looked at Conrad. "Blundell's dead," he said.

"Yeah, I figured." Conrad looked away, his eyes following an attractive girl as she strutted across the lounge in high heels and a short skirt.

The following morning, at half past eight, after the long flight from LAX to Heathrow, Carter walked up to one of the car hire kiosks at London Heathrow airport. He signed the form to hire a car and returned it to the desk clerk with a smile. Then, he and Conrad left the building to await the arrival of the car outside. When it pulled up in front of them, Carter gave the driver his ticket and got into the driver's seat. He was tired, but so was Conrad, and they had agreed that Carter would take the first shift at the wheel.

Two hours later, having enjoyed a hearty breakfast of fried eggs, sausage and bacon at a motorway service centre, Carter drove into Oxford. Conrad had fallen asleep again after the meal. Carter smiled as he glanced at him before parking the car on Woodstock Road as usual. After he had turned off the ignition, he put his hand on Conrad's shoulder and shook him.

"What? What?" said Conrad as his eyes opened. He looked around and saw that they were parked. "Are we there already?"

Carter nodded. "Yup. And you didn't drive a single mile!"

"Sorry," apologised Conrad. "You should have woken me."

"I just did! Come on lets go find a policeman."

They walked down Woodstock Road towards the Thames Valley Police station in Oxford. It was on St Aldates, opposite the Oxford Combined Court Centre where many of its inhabitants spend a lot of their time. Continuing along St Giles and Cornmarket Street, they came to the junction with High Street and crossed over into St Aldates.

Carter looked around as they walked. Oxford was a city he enjoyed visiting. Since he had first arrived there as a Masters student, nearly thirty years earlier, he had loved the place. The old buildings were not just old buildings, they were infused with a mass of history. You could spend your whole life here, he thought, and never learn all there was to know about the city's history. They walked past the impressive entrance to Christ Church College and Carter couldn't help smiling as he looked up at the ornate entrance, Tom Tower, which had been designed by Christopher Wren.

Before long, they were standing outside the main Thames Valley Police station in Oxford. Carter checked his watch and led Conrad into the relatively modern-looking stone built three storey building. After they had signed in at reception, they were led by a uniformed policewoman to the stairs.

On the second floor of the building, Detective Chief Inspector Murray sat at a table in one of the many small meeting rooms which lined the corridor. Before leaving, the policewoman opened the door for Carter and Conrad to enter the room. They were greeted by DCI Murray and sat opposite him, across a wooden table. The table was bare apart from a tray bearing three cups of coffee.

When Murray had passed the coffee cups round, he sat back in his chair and looked at Carter. "So, how was Santa Monica?" he asked. "Hot and sunny, I expect."

"Of course," answered Carter. "Not that we had much time to enjoy the delights of the Californian coast."

Carter proceeded to fill Murray in on all that had happened on the far side of the United States of America, concluding with Mikey's safe return home to his grandmother and the discovery of the safety deposit box key.

"So that's why we're back here in Oxford again," said Carter. "We need to take a look inside that box and see what's there. It will almost certainly also have a bearing on the case of John Sprague's murder." Carter looked Murray in the eye. "Have you been able to make any progress with that?"

"Not much," admitted Murray. "But we did manage to lift some finger prints from the keypad by the door to the building. The killer would have had to use that to contact Sprague and get him to open the door."

"Any match yet?"

Murray shook his head. "No. If it's someone in this country, he hasn't crossed our path before."

"What about Interpol?"

"They're checking. But nothing yet. And it's quite possible that the prints have nothing to do with Sprague's killer anyway. Someone else could have left them."

"Then I guess the next step is to take a look inside the safety deposit box," suggested Carter.

Murray nodded and got to his feet. "Well, let's get on with it, then, shall we? We've checked out probable locations and we think the box is probably in the vault of the bank that Mr Sprague used."

The three men walked the short distance from the police station to where the bank branch which had been used by John was located. It was at the crossroads between St Aldate's and the High Street. When they got there, they went into the building and asked to see the manager. He took them down to the basement where the safe was located and to the desk where the clerk responsible for the safe was sitting.

"These people are from the police," he said to the clerk. "They have a key to a safety deposit box which they think is one of ours."

"May I see the key?" asked the clerk.

Murray nodded and looked at Carter who took the key out of his jacket pocket and handed it to the clerk.

"Yes, it's one of ours," confirmed the clerk.

" That's great," said the manager. "In which case, they would like to look inside the box."

"Do they have a warrant?" asked the clerk.

"No, but it's a murder enquiry. The box is in the name of the murder victim, John Sprague. And they do have the key."

"OK, but nothing can be removed from the box without a warrant."

"It's in hand," lied Murray as he, Carter and Conrad started to lose patience. "If we need to take anything, we'll come back with the warrant. For now we just need to take a look inside and see what's there."

The manager nodded to the clerk, who got up from his desk and went to the steel grill which kept the contents of the safe secure once the main safe door was opened each morning. Noisily, he unlocked the grill and led the party along a corridor and then into a room at the end of the corridor. The room was lined from floor to ceiling with a grid of grey metal flaps, each one about nine inches square. In the centre of the room was a small table surrounded by four very functional looking chairs.

"Number one, four, seven," said the clerk as he examined the key closely. He looked up and ran his eyes along the wall of boxes.

When he found the correct number, the clerk inserted his master key into one of the keyholes and the key Carter had given him into the other keyhole. He turned both keys and opened the flap before removing the box inside. The box was about eighteen inches long and fitted neatly behind the flap. It had a handle at each end, one of which the clerk used to pull the box out before placing it on the table. He removed the keys from the flap and gave the one that Carter had given him to Murray. Then he stepped back.

"Do you want me to stay, or leave you to it?" he asked.

"You can go," said the manager, "thanks for your help."

The clerk left the room to return to his post at the desk outside the grill.

"You too, if you don't mind," said Murray to the manager.

"I'm sorry but I have to stay."

Murray looked at the manager. He hesitated and looked at Carter. Carter shrugged.

"OK. Let's get on with it," said Murray as he handed the key back to Carter. Not only did the key open the flap, it also opened the box itself. The four men sat round the table, Conrad opposite Carter, and Murray opposite the bank manager. Carter looked at each of them in turn. Then he directed his attention to the box. He inserted the key into the lock and turned it.

Carter lifted the lid of the safety deposit box. He sighed deeply when he saw what was inside. Slowly and carefully, he removed the black metal box that had made him react in that way. Underneath the black box was a binder containing a large sheaf of papers. He removed that too, and placed it on the table next to the black box. Lastly, he reached into the bottom of the safety deposit box and took out a bound document. He surveyed the items now laid out on the table in front of him and looked at Conrad. He pushed the black box across the table towards him.

"See what you can make of that," he said.

Conrad smiled as he reached out and drew the box towards him. As he lifted the box and turned it in his hands, Carter began to leaf through the papers in the binder. The papers were in sections and were clearly marked with tabs. Next, he had a quick glance at the bound document. Across the top of the light green front cover, there were some words written in bold black letters: 'Presentation to the Royal Society'. Underneath that, were some more words, also written in bold black letters: 'Diamonds – Natural or Man-Made. What's the Difference'.

Carter leafed through the document. He closed it and exhaled deeply before speaking. "Wow!" he said. "Looks like he really had cracked it."

Conrad looked up from the black box which he had been examining. "Sure does," he responded. "And I reckon this is his prototype synthetic diamond detector."

"You sure about that?" asked Carter.

"I'll need to test it. But, yeah, I think so." Conrad tilted the box so that Carter could see the top clearly. Then he lifted the lid of the box to reveal a dial. "See here," he said, "There's a little dial with a needle. The needle can only give one of two results. Natural or Man-Made. No in-between reading. So no room for doubt."

"How does it work?"

"Not sure yet," said Conrad as he pulled the box back towards him. "I need to get inside to have a look at the mechanisms he's used."

Carter pushed the sheaf of papers across to Conrad. "You'll probably find everything you need in there. By the look of it, it's pretty comprehensive." Then Carter picked up the bound presentation document again and opened it at the first page. He smiled. "And you're gonna love the name he gave it."

Conrad looked at Carter for a few moments, waiting for him to continue, until he could wait no longer. "Go on then, spill the beans," he said, holding out his hands in front of him.

"Guess," taunted Carter and both DCI Murray and the manager smiled.

"Come on, Carter! Just tell me, OK?"

Carter smiled and put the opened document down in front of Conrad so that he could see for himself. "DiamondProof," he said. "Don't you just love it?"

Conrad smiled back. He picked up the little black box and held it up. "Does what it says on the tin."

All four men laughed. When they had regained their composure, Carter turned to Murray. "Can you make the arrangements for us to take all this stuff? We need to go through it all in detail."

"Give me a couple of hours," said Murray as he got to his feet.

"We'll put everything back in the box for now," said Carter to the bank manager, as he picked up the presentation document and binder. "And then come back for it once the paperwork is all in place."

Carter opened the lid of the safety deposit box so that he could replace the papers and the black box which was DiamondProof. As he did so, he noticed a black memory stick, similar to the one Mikey had found in the owl. He held it up in his hand as he spoke.

"And there's probably a lot more on this," he said before returning it to the empty safety deposit box, along with everything else. Then he closed the box and locked it.

Back in Santa Monica, Detective Birch was concluding his interview with Pierre. "Why would Mr Blundell have killed her?" he asked, not at all convinced by Pierre's repeated assertion that Blundell was responsible for Lucy's murder.

"Simple," responded Pierre, "he knew what Sprague was working on and that he was likely to do what he was trying to do. And that would mean the end of his synthetic diamond business, at least the part of it that was making him a rich man."

"And he knew all this because you told him?"

"There's no law against that, I think."

"But you knew that he would want John Sprague dead, didn't you?"

"I thought we were talking about Lucy Adams." Pierre smiled. He knew Birch could not prove he had killed Lucy and he was quite enjoying the way the interview was going.

Birch slammed his hand on the table and gave Pierre an angry stare before speaking again. "Interview terminated," he said as he pressed the button to stop the recorder, got up from the table and left the room, leaving the uniformed policeman who had been in the room during the interview to take Pierre back to his cell.

Eventually, after a few hours had passed, Birch had to accept that he had no choice but to release Pierre. He was very reluctant to do so as he was convinced that Pierre had killed Lucy but he had no proof. Pierre had freely admitted to being with Lucy that night and to having sex with her, quite violent sex, but he continued to claim that she had been fit and well when he had left her apartment. Birch couldn't prove otherwise. With Blundell dead, he had lost the only possible route to a conviction. If Blundell had not been killed at the beach house, he could have denied Pierre's claim that Blundell must have killed Lucy while trying to get information out of her about John's work. Both Pierre and Blundell had a motive, so it could have been either of them. Or both of them. Or someone employed by them.

Pierre smiled as he left the police station in Santa Monica and hailed a cab to take him to the airport. He was a free man, free to leave the USA and travel home to the south of France. It had been a messy business but it was over.

Carter and Conrad went to the pub across the road from the bank to wait for DI Murray to get the paperwork sorted out so that they could take the contents of the safety deposit box out of the bank. They both felt they needed to celebrate the success of John's work. If he truly had developed a reliable, easily portable system, then he had not died in vain and the natural diamond industry would owe him a huge debt of gratitude.

The barman was a little surprised to be faced with two men asking for a bottle of champagne and two glasses. After all, it was mid afternoon and no degree results were expected to have been announced yet. Not that these two looked anything like your typical Oxford University students. It would be different once the results came out, of course. Then the bar staff would be pouring champagne like it was going out of fashion. He put the champagne and the two flutes on the bar and watched as Carter and Conrad wandered away to find a seat.

When they had settled into a bench seat under one of the bay windows and Carter had filled the two glasses with the champagne, they both lifted their glasses and clinked them together.

"To John," said Carter. "A man we can both be proud to have known."

"To John," echoed Conrad.

Carter was still taking his first sip when his phone rang. He put his glass down on the table and pulled the phone from his pocket. He looked at the display and then at his watch.

"It's Birch," said Carter as Conrad looked at him enquiringly. "He's up early." He pressed the receive call button and put the phone to his ear. "Detective Birch! What can I do for you?"

"I thought you would want to know that we had to let LeBlanc go."

"Seriously?" Carter was shocked.

"Yeah. We had nothing we could prove. Especially after Blundell's death."

Carter nodded. "I guess."

"He claimed Blundell was responsible for the girl's murder."

"Do you know where he's headed?"

"Yes. We've had eyes on him since he left the station and we know that he has booked a KLM flight to Amsterdam Schipol, leaving later today. But he's booked through to Nice. Should get there tomorrow morning, my time. That would be afternoon, your time, I guess."

"OK. Thanks for letting me know," said Carter as he ended the call. He looked at Conrad. "They've released LeBlanc. No evidence. He's on his way home."

Carter pondered the news from Birch as he sipped some more champagne. It tasted strangely bitter now and he put his glass down.

"I think I should head out over there, see what I can find out about him," said Carter. "We may not be able to get him for Lucy's murder but the police here are still looking for whoever killed John. And it all started here in Oxford, remember." Carter paused for a moment, deep in thought, before continuing, "Or did it?"

"If you want, I could stay here and help Murray do some digging into John's work and contacts?" suggested Conrad. "And I could check out DiamondProof as well. See if it's everything it seems to be."

Carter looked at Conrad. "Good idea. Let's go with that plan. You stay here and I'll see what I can dig up in the south of France."

"Guess who got the short straw!" said Conrad. They both laughed and sipped some more champagne.

Chapter 18

The next day, Carter smiled as he sat in his seat on the Air France flight from London Heathrow to Nice. He was looking forward to seeing Nicole, after ten days apart from her. But he was still sad about what had happened to John. His colleague and friend had done the natural diamond industry a huge favour, one that would ensure its long term survival, and he had been killed for it. But at least his work had survived him. Those who had conspired to stop him had failed. His son, Mikey, had also survived, despite his kidnapping and probable death if he hadn't taken matters into his own hands. Carter wished that he could do something for Mikey. He was a good boy and clearly had inherited his father's fighting spirit. It had crossed Carter's mind that he and Nicole might adopt him but that wouldn't have been fair on his grandmother, even if she had thought it was a good idea. And a life on Ambergris Caye, whilst it might be an idyllic existence for some, including Carter, would offer little to a growing boy; one who would soon turn into a man with aspirations and ambitions. Carter wondered what else he could do for Mikey, what contribution he could make to Mikey's life, in honour of his father.

The plane crossed the French coast and headed out over the Mediterranean sea before making a left turn to point in the direction of Nice. Carter had telephoned

Nicole to say he was on his way and she had promised to meet him at the airport.

When Carter came through the final barrier into the concourse at Nice Airport, he saw Nicole smiling at him. Beside her were Jacques and Eloise. He gave Nicole a big hug and a kiss before they made their way to the car park and began the drive to Port Grimaud. Jacques had driven Nicole to the airport in his blue Peugeot 508. He had upgraded to a more expensive car when he had been in a position to do so, after Philippe's death. As Carter squeezed his large frame into the back seat next to Nicole, he was glad that he had.

"It's good to be back," said Carter as he looked out of the window. "Can we take the coast road?"

"Of course!" responded Jacques with a quick glance at Eloise beside him. "It's the only way I would go."

Carter smiled as Jacques turned off La Provençale, the main autoroute from Nice to Marseilles, onto the Route Nationale, from which they would be able to join the Route du Bord de Mer.

They drove past the marina in Nice in which dozens of boats were moored, including large yachts moored at the Quai des Grandes Yachts. When they reached the coast, Jacques slowed down to allow Carter to make the most of the drive, with only the beach now separating the road from the sea. Carter took a deep breath through the open window. He looked at Nicole, a smile lighting up his face. She smiled back and put her hand on his.

"I wish I didn't still have to work on this case," said Carter, becoming more wistful. "I want to spend some time with you guys, here in Port Grimaud." He squeezed Nicole's hand as her smile faded, her expression now tinged with a little sadness.

"Then why don't you do that?" she asked.

"You know I can't."

"I know you, that's for sure. And I know you can't leave a job unfinished."

Carter nodded. "Yeah. A real pain, isn't it?"

"You said it!" Nicole smiled and paused before continuing. "Is there anything more you can usefully do, anyway?"

"I don't know. But we still don't know who killed John. And until we do, I can't stop. I have to find out who was responsible for killing one of the nicest men I have ever met."

"Yeah, I know," said Nicole, lifting Carter's hand to her mouth and kissing it. "That's what makes you the man that you are. And I love you for it."

Eloise looked round at Carter and Nicole. "Will you two please give it a rest! There are other people in this car you know!"

They all burst out laughing and Carter's gaze returned to the sea as they approached Antibes, with Le Fort Carré high on the hill ahead of them.

By the time Jacques' car and its occupants were approaching Ste Maxime, the mood had become more sombre with little being said. Carter's mind was working on what his next steps would be. Detective Birch had given him Pierre's flight number and time of arrival in Nice and he knew he still had a few hours before Pierre would be back in France. He assumed that Pierre would have left his car at Nice airport before his flight to America and that from the airport he would drive to Ste Maxime, where he lived. But Carter wanted to know every move that he made, from the moment he arrived in Nice. He checked his watch and decided that he had just about enough time to enjoy lunch with Nicole in Port Grimaud but, before that, he needed to pick up a hire car which he could use to return to the airport and await Pierre's arrival.

Conrad sat at a table in one of the meeting rooms at the police station in Oxford. In front of him were the contents of the safety deposit box. Although he was alone in the room, his examination of the black box, the documents and the memory stick was subject to the supervision of the Thames Valley police. As a consequence, every now and then, DI Murray or one of his colleagues would pop in to see how he was getting on.

So far that morning, he had spent three hours going through the documents in the binder and examining the contents of the memory stick which, thankfully, were not encrypted. There was a lot in the documents, ranging from single pages, containing handwritten notes made during experiments, to a long and detailed account of how the black box, DiamondProof, worked. And there was even more on the memory stick which contained all the detailed results of John's experiments.

As he closed the binder and removed the memory stick from his lap-top, he was keen to have a detailed look at the black box. He knew from what he had read how it was supposed to work, the theory, but now he wanted to see it in action. He wanted to understand in practice, as well as in theory, exactly how the prototype of the instrument which was so vital to the survival of the natural diamond industry, worked. If John really had created what he appeared to have created, it would sound the death knell of the potential to make huge fortunes from gem quality synthetic diamonds.

Conrad smiled as he stroked the black box. He lifted the lid and ran his fingers over the indicator dial with its needle, a needle which could confirm, unequivocally, whether or not the item being tested included synthetic diamonds. According to what he had read, the system could analyse any piece of jewellery placed into it and, if any part of the item, brooch, ring, whatever, was a synthetic diamond, the needle would immediately swing to the red area at the left hand side of the dial. If the dial swung to the green area on the right, then the item contained no synthetic diamonds.

In the middle of the box, spanning the dial, was a small handle. Conrad took the handle between his thumb and forefinger and pulled it upwards. A circular section, including the indicator dial, came up with it and, suspended from four tiny supports attached to it, was a round glass-like plate, shaped like a shallow bowl. This was the place where the item to be tested had to be placed. Conrad connected the power cord and plugged it into the socket on the wall of the room before reaching into his pocket and removing two small cloth pouches, one blue and one black, which Isaac at the FIDT had arranged to be delivered to him. He opened the blue one and removed one of the diamonds it contained, which he then put on the plate. Slowly he lowered the plate back into the box and pushed the handle back so that he could see the indicator dial. Then, he took a deep breath and flicked the switch next to the dial, to turn the box on, before pressing the button next to the switch to start the assessment. There was a whirring sound as the semi-circular 180 degree laser gun rotated slowly round the item being examined. This was followed by a pause. Conrad waited expectantly for what he was hoping would be a correct assessment of the diamond. The needle swung to the left, into the red area.

Conrad smiled. "So far so good," he said to himself.

Slowly and carefully, he removed the diamond from the box and replaced it with another one, this time taken from the black cloth pouch. He lowered the plate, pressed the button again, and waited. As before, there was a few moments of whirring but this time, when it stopped, the needle swung into the green area of the indicator.

"Two out of two," said Conrad to the box. "Very good. I'm convinced."

Conrad removed the diamond from the box and put it back in the pouch. As he returned both pouches to his pocket, Murray came into the room.

"Are you going to be much longer," he asked.

"No, I'm done," answered Conrad. "But I would like a copy of all these documents, if that's possible, and everything on the memory stick as well.

Murray picked up the DiamondProof box, the folder, the bound presentation document and the memory stick. "I'll get that organised," he said. "Could take a bit of time though. Come with me, if you like, and while you're waiting, I'll update you on the investigation into the fire at the lab. We've got some new information from the crime scene."

———————————

Having asked Jacques to drop him off in Sainte Maxime, on their way to Port Grimaud, so that he could hire a car, Carter parked the hire car in the car park outside Port Grimaud before going through the archway into the town to join Nicole. A few minutes later, Carter was sitting opposite Nicole at the restaurant which overlooked the canal between the Place du Marche and the Place des Artisans. They had decided to sit outside on the canal side, where they could watch the boats passing by.

Carter looked at Nicole and smiled as he finished the last morsel of his crêpe.

"Just as good as ever," he said.

"Glad you enjoyed it," responded Nicole, smiling back at him as he checked his watch. "When do you need to leave?" she asked.

"Not yet. Let's get some coffee."

While they were enjoying their coffees, an americano for Carter and a cappuccino for Nicole, they watched the boats going to and fro along the canal.

"Maybe we can have a few days here after you've wrapped your case, before we go home?" suggested Nicole.

"Yeah, that would be nice. Do you think Jacques and Eloise would be OK with that?"

"Absolutely. They'd love us to stay on for a bit."

Carter's phone rang and he reached into his pocket as he spoke. "That's settled then." He saw that the call was from Murray in Oxford and mouthed 'excuse me' to Nicole. "Hi there Inspector. What's new?"

"As it happens, there is some new information," replied Murray. "I've got Conrad here with me and he suggested I call you."

"Tell me more."

"I don't know why I wasn't informed about this earlier, it got missed, but it seems that during the post mortem on Mr Sprague, a foreign object was found in his throat."

"A foreign object?"

"Yes. He must have swallowed it just before he died."

"What was it, this foreign object?"

"You're not going to believe this but ... it was a plastic locket. The kind you might give to your girlfriend, except that it was made of plastic, not gold."

"How would that have got into his throat?" asked Carter. This new information was interesting but he wasn't sure that it led anywhere.

"Well that's the thing. It seems the only rational explanation is that he deliberately swallowed it just before he died."

"Which means ... ?"

"Difficult to say," said Murray, "But the most likely explanation that we can come up with is that he swallowed it to leave a clue as to who his attacker was."

"So how does this help us?" Carter could not see how finding the locket was going to help.

"Well, there was a picture of a girl inside the locket."

"Have you identified the girl?"

"No not yet."

"So we need to identify her, and then what? Are you thinking that she might be the killer?"

"It's a possibility. That might have been the clue. But if all we had to go on was her picture in the locket it would prove very little, and we wouldn't have much to shout about. But it isn't"

"Go on," pressed Carter, wondering what more there could be.

"There was some residual DNA on the picture inside the locket which was not attributable to the victim or to the girl."

"So that could be the DNA of the killer?"

"That seems possible, likely even. We've run a check through our database and nothing has come up. But if we can get DNA samples from any of the suspects, we can check them and if one matches, then we've probably got our killer. We've checked with Detective Birch in Santa Monica to see if they took a DNA sample from LeBlanc but he said that, currently, they are not allowed to do that at such an early stage of an investigation."

"What about testing the semen found in Lucy's vagina?"

"Yeah, I thought of that and Conrad has just spoken to Detective Birch in Santa Monica. Birch said that he would look into it and get back to us."

"Would it help if I could find a way to get a sample from LeBlanc when he gets back here later today?"

"It would certainly give us a back up in case Birch doesn't come through. And it might speed things up a bit."

"OK, I'll see what I can do and, if I can do that, what do you want me to do with the sample? Send it to you or get the police here to profile it?"

"Call me when you've got something and I'll let you know. I need to check here what would be the preferred way to get the profile."

Carter ended the call and looked at Nicole. She looked back at him, a quizzical expression on her face.

"Did you get the substance of that?"

"If I understood your end of the conversation correctly, you need to get a DNA sample from someone called LeBlanc." Carter nodded. "Is that the same as the Pierre LeBlanc you asked Jacques to look into? The one you're going back to the airport to follow when he gets back here?" Carter nodded again and Nicole's expression became stern. "Just make sure Jacques and Eloise don't get dragged into this, Carter, OK?"

Carter nodded for a third time. "I think I'd better go. I've got a potentially concrete reason now for following that piece of shit around so I'd better get on with it."

Carter rose from the table, kissed Nicole on the cheek and left the restaurant. Nicole sighed. She picked up the bill and watched, as Carter disappeared through the door, before reaching for her handbag.

Murray was sitting at his desk with Conrad opposite him. He replaced the telephone receiver and leant back in his chair. "He's going to try and get us a sample," he said.

"Good," responded Conrad. "I'll give Detective Birch another call to see if they can also provide us with DNA profiles for Blundell, Blake and Johnson."

"OK, thanks," said Murray. "I suppose those are the only other people we know of who are involved in this case."

"And Blundell is dead anyway," observed Conrad. "If we're done, I'll get going. I have a meeting in London this afternoon."

Conrad reached for his bag and got to his feet. He shook hands with Murray and left the office. As he walked to the train station, he checked his phone. No messages.

As the train made it's way to Marylebone station in London, Conrad read through his copy of the bound presentation document John had left in the safety deposit box. It was a comprehensive analysis of what sort of instrument was needed to enable the average jeweller to detect synthetic diamonds economically. But it went further. It went on to describe in detail how the little black box, which he had named DiamondProof, did this. Inside the box, a hemi-spherical collection of ninety-six tiny laser guns each fired a beam of light aimed at the specimen sitting on the plate. The specimen could be a single diamond or a piece of jewellery containing diamonds. After the lasers had fired their beams at the specimen for a few seconds, the hemisphere would rotate around one hundred and eighty degrees so that the laser guns were replaced by a hemisphere of light sensors, tuned to different light wavelengths. The data from the light sensors was fed into a tiny computer processor, made from synthetic diamond wafers so that it was not affected by the heat generated by the lasers. Here the data was analysed to determine if the specimen included any synthetic diamonds. The result was then shown by the indicator on the top of the box, with green indicating no synthetic diamonds and red indicting that a synthetic diamond had been detected in the sample.

As he turned the last page, Conrad shook his head in wonder at the technical detail and comprehensiveness of the presentation John had been going to make to the Royal Society. Suddenly his eyes widened and he moved his head forward to take a closer look at the last page. Not only had John written this detailed description of the problem, and the solution, but he had actually reached the point where he could apply for a patent for DiamondProof! The last page of the presentation was a copy of the patent application! He leant back in his seat as his hands, which were holding the document, fell into his lap. He couldn't stop himself from letting out a yelp followed by an unrestrained laugh. Not only had John solved the problem, and built a prototype, but he had laid the foundations for a hugely profitable business making the machines! And nobody had known about it! How on earth had he stopped himself from shouting it from the rooftops? Actually, thinking about it, maybe that was exactly what the presentation to the Royal Society was about.

An hour later, Conrad emerged from the taxi which had taken him from Marylebone station to the home of the Royal Society on Carlton House Terrace, a few hundred yards from Buckingham Palace. He clutched his bag close to his chest as he approached the door.

Inside, he was led to a luxurious office on the top floor of the very impressive looking four-storey building, where he was introduced to the society's Events Secretary, Sir Stephen Balding, a man in his sixties who himself had been a scientist of some note, specialising in palliative medicine. Sir Stephen led Conrad to a leather armchair by the window, which overlooked The Mall, before sitting in a similar chair opposite.

"Thank you so much for coming to see me," said Sir Stephen.

"Hey, it's my pleasure," responded Conrad. "I can't believe I'm actually sitting inside the Royal Society!"

"Well, you are most welcome." Sir Stephen smiled and then he became more serious. "It was awful news about John. I knew a little bit about his work of course but I had no idea it was laced with so much danger."

"Thankfully, John was very well aware that there were people who would prefer him to fail. And who would go to considerable lengths to make sure he did. But he was ahead of them all the way. He made sure that whatever happened, his work was safe."

"It's such a shame that he won't have the opportunity to present the results of his work to the world. I was looking forward to having the presentation here. We often have scientific presentations, that's part of what the society is all about, but presentations on subjects which are, at one and the same time, ground-breaking in their use of cutting-edge technology and very, very sexy, are rare," Sir Stephen smiled, "If you know what I mean."

Conrad nodded. "I do. I've worked in this area for most of my life and I still find it ... sexy, as you put it!" They both smiled before Sir Stephen continued.

"Nearly a hundred people booked to attend the presentation," he said, "But we will have to cancel it now."

Conrad held up his hand at this. "Well, I've been thinking about that and I would like you to go ahead with the presentation." Sir Stephen's face conveyed the doubtfulness he was feeling at Conrad's suggestion but Conrad continued anyway, "I'm sure John would have wanted it. And I would be happy to do the presentation on his behalf. I understand the subject matter and John was a personal friend. I would like to do it for him. As a sort of memorial." Conrad paused, trying to gauge Sir Stephen's reaction to his proposal before concluding with "What do you think?"

Sir Stephen thought for a few moments, looking out through the window as he did. Then he turned to face Conrad. "I think that is a splendid idea and I think that I speak on behalf of everyone at the Royal Society in thanking you for being willing to do that. Splendid!"

Conrad smiled a broad smile, he was pleased with the outcome of his meeting. "That's great! Thank you Sir Stephen. Thank you the Royal Society." Conrad's smile left his face as he continued. "Would it be OK for John's mother-in-law and son to attend the presentation? Mikey's only twelve years old but his grandma would take care of him."

"Of course. We would be pleased to welcome them both."

"Well, I think I have taken up enough of your time," said Conrad as he got up from his chair, "And I now have some homework to do before Friday."

Sir Stephen smiled as he shook hands with Conrad. "I look forward to your presentation."

Chapter 19

Carter was standing inside Terminal 1 at Nice airport as Pierre LeBlanc came out of the baggage collection area pulling his small suitcase behind him. Carter had made sure that he was inconspicuously positioned, something that was not easy given his height and build but he had found a good position behind the information kiosk. From this vantage point, he had spotted Gilles Rénard who, he assumed, was also waiting for Pierre to arrive.

Carter watched as Pierre came into the arrivals area. He was greeted by Gilles and the two men set off towards the exit doors. They were not expecting to have to evade anyone tailing them and Carter was able to follow them unnoticed at a discreet distance. Gilles led Pierre across the road to the short stay car park and Carter was thankful that he had parked his hire car in the same car park. It would make it easier to follow them.

An hour later, Pierre and Gilles entered Sainte Maxime. They turned into a car park off the Avenue Charles de Gaulle, closely followed by Carter who reversed his car into a space that would allow him to see where they went without getting out of the car. He wasn't sure whether Gilles would recognise him after more than two years but, given a good look, Pierre almost certainly would. He watched as they got out of the car, crossed the road and sat at a table outside a roadside café.

A few moments after they had taken their seats, Gilles and Pierre were approached by a waiter.

"Un verre de Merlot, s'il vous plait," ordered Gilles before looking at Pierre to see what he wanted to drink.

"Et un Cabernet Sauvignon pour moi," requested Pierre

"Quelque chose pour manger?" asked the waiter.

"Non, merci."

The waiter disappeared inside the café as Gilles and Pierre talked animatedly to each other. When the waiter returned, he put the two glasses of red wine on the table along with the bill. As Carter watched from his car, his view was obscured by the waiter but when the waiter left, he saw Pierre pick up one of the glasses, take a sip and nod to Gilles.

Pierre then took an envelope out of his jacket pocket and handed it to his boss. Gilles opened the envelope. He looked at the cheque inside and smiled.

"A worthwhile trip, I would say," said Gilles. "Regardless of the problems."

Pierre nodded. "Let us hope that all that is done with now."

Carter watched as Gilles and Pierre sat and talked to each other. About ten minutes later, when they had finished their wine, Gilles put some money on the table and they left, walking round the corner past the café towards the town centre. Carter saw his opportunity and leapt out of his car. Not bothering to lock the car, he strode across the road, heading for the café and the table where Gilles and Pierre had been sitting. As he approached the café, his pace slowed and when he got to the table, he stopped and pretended to look inside, as if he was wondering whether to go in for a drink. As surreptitiously as he could, he put his hand on the glass from which Pierre had been drinking, gripping the rim between his thumb and forefinger. Slowly he drew the glass towards him and turned towards the road before walking away from the café, holding the glass in front of him so that it could not be seen from the café. Once back in his car, he placed the glass into an evidence bag and smiled to himself as he put the bag into his black holdall on the passenger seat.

"Gotcha!" he said out loud as he started the car, ready to drive to the police station in Sainte Maxime. He hadn't seen Inspecteur LeGrande, the local chief of police, for a while but they had parted on good terms and he was sure he could count on him to cooperate.

When Carter reached the police station at Sainte Maxime, he parked the car in the small space outside before walking into the building. A few moments later he was seated opposite LeGrande. The wine glass, still in the evidence bag, was inside his holdall. LeGrande looked at Carter inquisitively.

"It has been some time since we last spoke, Monsieur Jefferson. What can I do for you this time?" he asked, a smile on his face. "Something to do with diamonds, I am guessing."

Carter smiled back and waited a few seconds while LeGrande's interest grew to the point where he needed to adjust his position in his chair. This prompted Carter to speak.

"My friend, and colleague in the diamond business, John Sprague, is dead," began Carter. That was enough to pique LeGrande's interest.

"And what does that have to do with me?" he asked.

"Well," replied Carter, "He was murdered. In Oxford. And we think he was killed because of the work he was doing."

"What work was he doing?"

"He was developing a cheap synthetic diamond detector."

"I was right then. It is to do with diamonds."

"Yes. And we think someone from the south of France is involved in his death."

"Gilles Rénard?" queried LeGrande.

"No, not him. But the person who we think may be involved in John's death is connected to him. We believe he works for Rénard."

"So what can I do to help?"

"Well, it seems we now have some DNA evidence relating to John's murder. The police in England found a small locket in his throat and it had some DNA inside it which wasn't John's." Carter paused as LeGrande sat up straight in his chair and leaned towards him, expectantly, waiting for him to continue. "They think it is probably the DNA of the killer," said Carter.

LeGrande leaned back in his chair and touched the tips of his fingers together, thoughtfully. He waited for Carter to continue but when he did not, LeGrande spread out his arms, questioningly, as he spoke.

"So, who is the murderer? Who killed your friend?"

"Ah, well, so far we have not been able to establish that," answered Carter. "The DNA that was found inside the locket does not match anything on the UK police records.

"Then you are no further forward," responded LeGrande, relaxing back into his chair.

"Maybe not," responded Carter. A smile crossed his face as he opened his holdall and pulled the evidence bag out of it. "Unless we can check the DNA on this glass. Can you arrange that for me?"

LeGrande took the bag from Carter and smiled back. "I am sure that even here in France, we have the technology for that."

"If you can send the results to Inspector Murray in Oxford, he will be able to check them against the DNA from the locket. And that could be enough to identify John's killer. Is it OK for you to do that? I can give you Inspector Murray's contact details."

"Yes, of course. It will be as you ask," said LeGrande as Carter reached into the inside pocket of his jacket and extracted a piece of paper on which were written the contact details for the Oxford police. He offered the piece of paper to LeGrande who took it and nodded. There was a short pause before LeGrande looked into Carter's eyes. He had a question to ask, one that Carter had been waiting for him to ask.

"So whose DNA is on the glass?" he queried.

"Pierre LeBlanc," answered Carter, "Our main suspect."

"Ah yes, he is known to us," said LeGrande, "Is there anything else I can do for you at this time?"

"No, that's it for now," replied Carter as he got to his feet, "Thank you for your help with this, Inspecteur, it is very much appreciated."

"No problem," responded LeGrande as he rose from his chair and shook hands with Carter before Carter left the office and returned to his car.

There was a big smile on Carter's face as he got into the car. Not only was there now a strong possibility of identifying John's killer but he would soon be back with Nicole, in Port Grimaud, as well.

Half an hour later, Carter was sitting with Nicole on the patio outside Jacques and Eloise's house, looking across Le Lac Interieur towards the harbour in Port Grimaud and enjoying a glass of Sancerre. Nicole could not help but notice that Carter was more jovial than usual. Everything he had said since arriving at the house had been positive.

"So," she said, "I assume you achieved your objective?" Carter nodded.

"I certainly did," he said, "A wine glass from a café in Sainte Maxime. So, it could be that we will soon be able to identify John's killer! Assuming it is Pierre LeBlanc, of course."

"That would be good," Nicole responded. Carter nodded as he took a sip from his wine glass before she continued. "And if that proves to be the case, then maybe I'll have you all to myself for a bit, yes?"

"Hopefully. But, even if we can prove that Pierre LeBlanc killed John, we still have nothing on Gilles, his boss. And that's a guy who should not be roaming around, free as a bird. I feel sure that he has a connection with this case and I'd like to prove it, but I'm not sure that I can."

Nicole leaned back in her chair and looked out across the harbour before she spoke. "OK, so I probably shouldn't book our tickets back to Belize just yet then, eh?"

"Maybe just wait a few days. But it won't be long, I promise."

Nicole looked at Carter, her face clearly showing how unconvinced she was, before they both started laughing loudly. Jacques and Eloise were out on a charter in Jacques' yacht so they had the house to themselves and, much as they missed having Jacques and Eloise with them, they were enjoying each other's company.

Then, just as a small inflatable boat passed in front of the house, breaking the quietness for a few moments with it's noisy engine, Carter's phone began to ring. Nicole's gaze moved quickly from the little boat to

Carter, as he reached into his pocket and answered the call.

"Carter Jefferson," he said.

"Hi Carter, it's Conrad here. How's it going? Are you enjoying the French Riviera?"

"Yeah, it's great, thanks. But I don't think you're calling me to ask about the weather, are you?"

Conrad smiled to himself before responding. "What do you mean?"

Carter sighed, "Just get on with it will you. Nicole and I are enjoying a nice bit of peace and quiet here, with a lovely glass of wine of course."

"Yeah, sorry man. It's just that I've got some news for you," said Conrad, "Do you recall that John was going to do a presentation to the Royal Society in London next week? If you remember, we found the presentation document in the safety deposit box."

"Oh, yeah, of course," replied Carter, "I guess they'll have to fill that slot with something else now."

"Well …. maybe not," hinted Conrad, keeping Carter waiting and trying to build some suspense for his announcement. "The thing is, I've offered to do the presentation myself," he continued, "And they've agreed! So, John's work will be properly appreciated, after all!" Conrad was smiling as he spoke, he could imagine the look of surprise on Carter's face.

"You sure you're up for that?" asked Carter, aware that Conrad would have a lot of work to do to prepare for the presentation.

"You bet! There's no way, I'm not doing it."

"Well, good for you, Conrad. John would have appreciated that."

"And that's not all," continued Conrad, "They've also agreed that it's OK for Mikey to be there. And Mikey's grandma, of course. And the Society will be happy to pay their expenses."

Carter smiled a broad smile. "Brilliant!" he said. "And I'll be there too. I wouldn't miss it for the world."

There was a slight pause before Conrad spoke again. "There's one more thing."

"What else can there be?" queried Carter, feeling that he had heard all the news there could possibly be about John's work.

"John had applied for a patent for DiamondProof. The last page of the presentation document we found, was a copy of the application form."

"Yeah, and…?"

"Sir Stephen at the Royal Society has checked with the UK Intellectual Property Office and the patent was approved yesterday. We should have the certificate confirming it by the time I do the presentation."

"What are the implications of that?"

"Well," said Conrad, "It means that John left Mikey a bit of a legacy. If Mikey wants to, he can sell the patent for a big chunk of money, or he could invest in a business which would make the DiamondProof boxes. Either way, he's not going to need to worry too much about money."

"Well, I guess that's good news then," responded Carter, hesitating slightly before continuing, as a thought crossed his mind, "But how's he gonna feel about making money out of something that ended up killing his Dad?"

"I can see where you're coming from, Carter, but Mikey should be mega-proud of what his Dad achieved. And we need to make sure he realises that. It might have cost his Dad his life, but he did something that no one else has been able to do."

"Yeah, I guess you're right. We need to emphasise the achievement, not the tragedy. But it doesn't make it any less tragic."

There was a pause as they both thought about this, not knowing what to say, before Conrad broke the silence.

"So, I'll see you in London on Friday, yeah?" he asked, bringing their conversation to an end."

"I'll probably arrange for us to arrive on Thursday, so we can make sure Mikey and his grandma are looked after properly. And I'll give Alice a call and arrange everything with her," said Carter before ending the call and looking at Nicole. "Did you get most of that?" he asked.

Nicole nodded. "Yup. You'd better get on with getting our travel arrangements sorted, hadn't you?"

"Yeah, I guess. I'm sorry to be leaving Jacques and Eloise so soon but they'll be back tomorrow, so at least we will have a last day with them."

Nicole smiled. "Yes. And we'll be able to say goodbye to them properly for once." They both laughed.

The next day, when Jacques' yacht approached the harbour in Port Grimaud, the sun was shining, as it usually did in the Bay of St. Tropez. Carter and Nicole were waiting at the berth opposite the fuelling station, which had been allocated to the boat. They were talking to Bernice, the lady who ran the Capitainerie. It was her job to oversee all the arrivals and departures from the small harbour, which could accommodate about fifteen yachts of around twenty to thirty metres in length.

"Here they are now," said Bernice, as she spotted the Esprit turning into the harbour.

"Only half an hour late!" responded Nicole, "Not bad that, for Jacques."

"You cannot be that precise when you are at sea." Said Bernice, a smile on her face. "We always allow a few hours each side of the time booked."

The Esprit approached the quay before turning back to face the harbour entrance and then slowly reversing into the space reserved for it. Once the boat was safely docked, Jacques and Eloise disembarked. Carter spoke to them as they approached the group.

"What, no guests?"

Jacques smiled as he replied. "We dropped them off in Cannes," he said, "They are staying there for a couple of days before we pick them up again and take them back to Monte Carlo."

Nicole already had her arm around Eloise's shoulders as Jacques approached her and kissed her on the cheek.

"It's good to have you here again," he said.

"It's good to be back," she replied before removing her arm from Eloise's shoulders.

Jacques looked at Bernice. "Everything OK?" he asked.

"Sure, I just need to know when you are planning to leave."

"Of course. It will be at 9:30am on Friday, OK?"

Bernice nodded and said her goodbyes to Carter and Nicole before returning to the Capitainerie office behind her. Jacques watched her go for a few seconds before turning to speak to Carter and Nicole.

"So, what do you want to do today?" he asked.

"Oh, nothing in particular. We just want to spend some time with you guys," answered Nicole, before Carter chipped in.

"Actually, I'd quite like a little trip on the Esprit. Maybe this afternoon? How about a little cruise along the coast to Cavallaire, that would be nice."

Jacques gave Carter a quick look before turning and running after Bernice. Carter looked at Eloise questioningly.

"Did I say the wrong thing?" he asked.

"No," answered Eloise, smiling, "But, if we're going to do that, he needs to tell Bernice, that's all."

"Ah, yes! Of course. Silly me!"

Two hours later, Carter, Nicole, Jacques and Eloise were enjoying an early lunch at La Table des Pecheurs, their favourite restaurant in Port Grimaud, near the entrance to the town. As Carter was digging in to his meal, Eloise decided to enquire about his investigation into John's death.

"How's it going?" she asked, "Have you been able to make any further progress?"

Carter finished his mouthful before replying. "Yes, as a matter of fact, I think we have. And that's part of the reason for my return to the south of France."

"Really!" responded Eloise, a bit surprised at the news, "So, did Gilles Rénard have something to do with it then?"

Nicole chipped in quickly before Carter could reply. "Darling, this is a murder investigation. I'm not sure that Carter can share information about it with you."

Carter raised his hand as he spoke. "It's OK, I know the boundaries but I can fill you in a little bit." Carter took a drink from the glass of white wine he had ordered to go with his fish dish. "I'm here to see if I can find out a bit more about this Pierre LeBlanc guy, see if there's anything to link him to what happened to John. We know that he's involved to some extent but we're not too sure just how deep it goes. The fact that he has worked with Gilles Rénard for some years, helping to run his diamond cutting business, means that he could be involved. It just depends on what's been happening with that business while Gilles has been in prison. Our understanding is that it now only deals with synthetic diamonds, in which case LeBlanc might well have had a motive for killing John. But that assumes that he knew about John and what he was working on, and that we can't prove at the moment."

"Well I hope you catch whoever it was that killed your friend," said Eloise. "When I think about that poor little kid, already without a mother and now without a father, it makes me so mad!"

"Don't worry," responded Carter a slight smile on his face, "We'll get whoever did it. And, in the meantime, little Mikey will get to celebrate his Dad's achievements on Friday. At the Royal Society in London."

"What do you mean?" queried Eloise, "What's happening at the Royal Society?"

"Conrad is presenting the results of John's research there?"

"Are you sure Mikey will be OK with that?" queried Eloise

Carter nodded. "Yes. He will understand what a brilliant man his father was. Not many people get to present a paper at the Royal Society. It's probably one of the most prestigious scientific institutions in the world, so I think he will be really proud of his Dad."

A few hours later, Carter, Nicole and Eloise were sitting on the bridge of the Esprit, as it cruised west along the French coast toward Cavallaire, with Jacques at the helm in front of them. Although the original plan had been to dock at Cavallaire, and perhaps get something to eat there before returning home, Carter had asked Jacques to take them to La Plage de Bon Porteau, a beach he particularly liked and, as a result, Eloise had prepared a picnic for them to have on the beach instead.

As luck would have it, however, after they had passed Cavallaire and were heading towards La Plage, Carter's phone rang. He looked at Nicole and mouthed 'sorry' before taking the phone out of his pocket and going down the steps to the rear deck to answer the call.

"DCI Murray. I wasn't expecting to hear from you today. What's up?"

"Well, you know that wine glass you gave to the French police for DNA analysis?"

"Yes."

"We've just received the profiles from them."

"Wow! That was quick. What did it show?"

"When they analysed the various traces on the glass, excluding what they assumed to be your DNA, on the edge of the rim, they came up with three sets of DNA, so, apart from you, three people had contact with the glass."

"Three sets!" Carter thought for a moment. "For sure, there would be the waiter's DNA there, and LeBlanc's, they both touched the glass. But a third set! I guess someone else must have touched the glass too, maybe the barman."

"Well, the good news is that one of the three sets of DNA was a match to the DNA we found inside the locket in Sprague's throat."

Carter's spirits rose. "That's great!" he said, his excitement noticeable, "So one of those three people was John's murderer?"

"Well, not for certain, but most likely, yes." Murray paused as Carter listened, waiting for him to continue. When he did his voice was a bit lower key. "The bad news is that, as you might guess, we don't know who the matching DNA belongs to."

"Well surely it must belong to LeBlanc, mustn't it."

"In all likelihood, yes. But we need to know for sure whose it is before we move."

"It will be LeBlanc's, I'm sure of it," said Carter. "We need to get the French police to bring him in and question him and then it will all come out."

"OK, maybe you're right," replied Murray. "I'll contact LeGrande and fill him in but I think it would be good if you were in on the interrogation as well. You will have a better idea of what questions to ask him."

"Yeah, of course. I'll get over to LeGrande as soon as I can and then we can work on this together. When you speak to him, let him know that I'm on my way."

After he had ended the call, Carter walked slowly up the steps to the flybridge. He knew that he was going to be in trouble with Nicole. She looked round as he approached her and saw the guilty look on his face.

"Everything OK?" she asked.

"Yeah, all good," he replied, "But …."

"So why the long face?" Nicole turned in her seat and stared at him.

"I'm really sorry. But we have to go back to Port Grimaud." Carter paused before continuing. "Now."

"You're kidding me!" exclaimed Nicole, "We haven't even had our picnic yet."

"Maybe we can eat it on the way back." responded Carter as he sat beside her.

By now, Eloise had turned to look at Carter and even Jacques was becoming aware of something going on.

"But what's happened?" challenged Nicole.

"The DNA on the glass matches that of John's killer," said Carter, as he looked Nicole in the eye, "I have to go back and help with the interrogation of Pierre LeBlanc."

Nicole sighed deeply and nodded, accepting the logic behind the decision. She looked at Eloise who got up and went to speak to Jacques.

Carter telephoned Inspecteur LeGrande from the boat on the way back to Port Grimaud and, by the time he arrived at the police station in Sainte Maxime, Pierre LeBlanc had already been picked up and brought in for questioning.

Carter and LeGrande sat at one side of the table in the interview room while LeBlanc sat at the other and a uniformed policeman stood at the door. On the table was a recording device which LeGrande set recording. He stated the date and time before he began the interview.

"Monsieur LeBlanc, as you can see, this interview is being recorded. Please ensure that you tell us the truth in all that you say." LeBlanc did not respond to this and LeGrande continued, "Where were you on Thursday 12th June?"

LeBlanc thought for a few moments before removing his diary from his pocket and opening it. He leafed through a few pages before finding the 12th June. Carter and LeGrande looked at each other, a little surprised.

"I was at a conference in San Francisco," he said, "It is an annual conference. I attend every year. This year it was about the use of synthetic diamonds in the manufacture of computer chips."

"Then you will be able to give us the names of some people who saw you there," responded LeGrande.

"Of course. I was speaking on that day so there would be about one hundred and fifty people who saw me."

LeGrande looked at Carter, his shocked expression demanding an explanation. Carter was only aware of one conference in San Francisco which might include the topic of synthetic diamonds in its programme. He looked at Pierre as he spoke.

"If you are talking about the CompTech Science Fair, that took place three months earlier. In fact, I was there."

"I was not at CompTech this year. The conference where I spoke was after that. It is much smaller and always happens about three months after CompTech. It is a follow up conference where computer scientists can learn more about the scientific background of what they might have seen at the science fair. This year, they concentrated on the use of synthetic diamond materials."

Carter was struck dumb by this revelation so Legrande stepped in.

"We will need the names and contact details for the people who run the conference," he said.

LeBlanc removed an address book from his pocket and opened it. He found the page he was looking for and, as he stared at Carter, he passed the address book to LeGrande.

"Can I keep this?" asked LeGrande.

"No. I will need it. But you can make a copy of this page."

LeGrande nodded and looked at the policeman at the door. The policeman came over to him and took the address book from him before leaving the room.

With the interview concluded, and after LeBlanc had left the police station a free man, LeGrande looked at Carter waiting for him to say something. Carter threw his hands up in the air.

"I don't understand," he said in desperation, "His DNA was inside the locket!"

"Well it is not possible that he was there," responded LeGrande, "He was in California at the time that your friend was killed."

241

"Unless … ," Carter's face lit up a little as a thought occurred to him, "Unless, the DNA in the locket belonged to Gilles Rénard."

"How could that be?"

"It's possible that Gilles touched the glass that we got the DNA from, the DNA which matches that in the locket. There were three sets of DNA on it, remember. I assumed the third set of DNA belonged to the person who poured the wine into the glass, the barman. But I couldn't see inside the café so maybe that was the waiter. And I couldn't see clearly when the waiter was at their table, so maybe Gilles also touched the glass. I remember seeing Pierre nod to Gilles when he drank from the glass so maybe the glasses were mixed up and they both touched them. Maybe Gilles was given the wrong glass and he passed it to Pierre. That could explain why there were three sets of DNA on the glass."

LeGrande nodded. "Yes, that is possible."

"We need to check Gilles' DNA to see if it matches. You will have that on record from before, won't you?" LeGrande nodded before Carter continued. "And then we will need to bring him in for questioning."

"I agree. I will let you know when it has been done."

"Gilles must have killed John. It must have been him. It's the only possible explanation now."

LeGrande smiled. "Unless the waiter was wearing gloves. Then it could have been someone else, someone you did not see."

"The waiter was not wearing gloves! This I know for sure."

"Then Gilles must be the one."

Carter nodded and got up to leave. "Thank you Inspecteur, it has been good working with you. And I'm sorry for the confusion over the DNA."

"No problem," responded LeGrande as the two men stood up and shook hands before Carter left the room.

When Carter got back to Port Grimaud, Nicole was sitting on the patio with Jacques and Eloise. They each had a glass of wine and there was a bottle of wine and a fourth, empty, glass on the table. Carter poured some wine into the empty glass and sat down. He took a sip of the wine and looked out across Le Lac. Nicole looked at him expectantly and when he didn't speak, she did.

"Well?"

"Well what?"

"Aren't you going to tell us what happened? We had to give up our picnic so that you could go to the police station, remember."

Carter smiled. "Sorry about that. Shall we have it now?"

"What! The picnic? We've already had it."

"Oh, OK, Shall I just eat my share then?" Nicole gave Carter an 'I don't believe you' look before Carter continued. "Where is it?"

"There's none left, we ate it all. We assumed you would get something at the police station." Nicole sat back in her chair angrily and stared at Carter, waiting for a response.

"It wasn't him," said Carter, shaking his head, "It wasn't Pierre LeBlanc."

"What do you mean it wasn't him? You had certain proof! You had his DNA on the glass. And it matched the DNA in the locket in John's throat, for goodness sake."

There was a pause as they all looked at Carter. "He has a cast iron alibi," he said, "He was speaking at a conference in California at the time John was killed."

"Then whose was the DNA in the locket?" queried Nicole.

"The only other possibility is that it was Gilles Rénard's. They're checking it now, as we speak."

Nicole sat up straight in her chair, a shocked expression on her face. "Gilles Rénard!" she said, "The shit who was responsible for my father's death? And who they let out of prison way too soon a month ago?" Carter nodded as Nicole continued. "So what's going to happen now?"

"If Gilles' DNA matches the DNA in the locket, LeGrande will arrange for him to be picked up." Before he could say any more, Carter's phone rang and he answered it. "Inspecteur, what's up?"

"We have checked Gilles Renard's DNA with the DNA from the locket. And they are the same. I have sent a car to arrest him."

"Wow, that was quick. Thanks for letting me know."

As Carter ended the call, Nicole could not wait for him to speak. "What's happened?" she asked, looking at him expectantly.

"The DNA matches. LeGrande has arranged for Gilles to be arrested."

Nicole jumped up from her seat and headed for the front door of the house. As she did, she spoke very emotionally to Carter.

"That I want to see!"

"Nicole! Where are you going?"

"To his house! This I want to see for myself."

Carter followed Nicole out of the door as Jacques and Eloise watched, struck dumb by what was going on.

Within a few minutes, Nicole, almost running, had reached the Place des Artisans where Gilles Rénard lived. Carter followed close behind her and, as they entered the Place, they saw a police car outside Gilles' house. They walked, more slowly, towards the police car and, almost immediately, two police officers came out of the building, each of them holding one of Gilles' arms. As they marched him towards the car, Nicole could not restrain herself. She pushed past Carter and ran towards the policemen who stopped walking when they saw her approaching. When Nicole reached them, she stood in front of Gilles and stared at him, her eyes only inches away from his. Then, without any warning, she threw her arm back and swung it round, slapping Gilles in the face with a loud clap. She continued to stare at him as she spoke.

"There! Take that, you bastard! You killed my father and my son. You might have got away with that but this time they are going to lock you up for ever! You will never get out!"

Gilles' face was expressionless and when Nicole had finished her tirade, she turned away from him and walked back to Carter. The two police officers resumed taking Gilles to the police car. A third police officer opened the rear door of the car and they pushed Gilles into the back seat.

Carter and Nicole looked at each other as the police car left the Place and went through the arch leading out of Port Grimaud. Nicole turned to look at Carter, a huge smile on her face.

"YES!" she exclaimed loudly, clearly happy to see Gilles back in police custody. Carter put his arm round her shoulders and pulled her towards him before giving her a kiss on the forehead.

Chapter 20

Keen to be there when Conrad delivered John's presentation at the Royal Society in London, Carter and Nicole arrived at London Heathrow airport in the early afternoon of the day following Gilles' arrest. It was the day before the presentation was to take place, so they checked into a hotel within walking distance of the Royal Society's premises on Carlton House Terrace.

Soon after they had checked into the hotel, they set off to meet Conrad at the Royal Society. He had promised to give them a tour and to show them the Kohn Centre where the presentation would be held. He had told them that nearly two hundred people had booked to attend the presentation so the room would be almost full.

The Kohn Centre was the Royal Society's most prestigious room and was, to say the least, very spectacular. There were wood panelled marquetry walls with a range of old paintings of past presidents of the Royal Society in carved wooden frames between the windows. These windows overlooked St James's Park.

After Conrad and a representative of the Royal Society had given Carter and Nicole a tour of the Kohn Centre and also the Marble Hall, where a reception would be held with snacks and drinks after the presentation, Conrad took Carter to Sir Stephen's office and knocked on the door.

Once inside Sir Stephen's luxurious office, Carter and Conrad sat down facing him across his antique wooden desk.

"I'm pleased to say that the event is now fully booked," said Sir Stephen, "So you can expect a full house for your presentation."

"Excellent," said Carter, "But there will still be room for John's mother-in-law and son as well, won't there?"

"Yes, of course. Will they be saying anything?"

"No, but I would like Conrad to present Mikey with the patent certificate for DiamondProof. Would that be acceptable?"

"Absolutely."

"Thank you. We are so grateful to you for being willing to continue with the event, given what has happened," said Carter, "It will be something that both Mikey and his grandmother will remember for the rest of their lives."

"And they will be justifiably proud of their father and son-in-law, respectively," added Conrad. "John's discovery is going to protect the natural diamond industry from being undermined by cheap, synthetic, gem quality diamonds. Once again, a diamond will be forever!"

"Not that we're against synthetic diamonds," continued Carter, "Far from it. They have their place, especially for making such things as computer processors. And as long as gem quality synthetics are labelled as such, so that the buyers know what they are getting, we have no objection to that either. It's the practice of selling synthetic diamonds as natural diamonds that is the problem. And it's a problem for every owner of an item made using natural diamonds."

Sir Stephen stood and held out his hand to Carter. "It's been good to meet you both and I hope you have a really special day tomorrow."

"Thank you, we owe you, and the Royal Society, big time!" said Carter as he shook Sir Stephen's hand before he and Conrad left the office.

As Carter and Nicole sat in the hotel bar, enjoying a relaxing glass of wine, Carter's phone rang. He sighed before reaching into his pocket and extracting it. He looked at the caller ID before pressing the button to answer the call.

"Inspecteur LeGrande, bonjour," he said

"Bonjour, Carter, I just wanted to tell you that we have been checking Gilles Rénard's movements at the time of John Sprague's murder," said LeGrande.

"And what have you found?" queried Carter, hoping for some positive news.

"He was in the UK on the day that Sprague was murdered, we have proof of that,"

Carter smiled. "Excellent!" he said. "Thanks for letting me know."

"We will arrange for him to be transferred to the Oxford police as soon as possible."

"Thank you Inspecteur, I am most grateful to you. And John's family will be pleased to hear that we now have his killer in custody."

Carter brought the call to an end and looked at Nicole, whose smile could not have been broader.

"Hopefully he will get life this time," she said.

"If I have anything to do with it, he will," responded Carter. "But there will be some more work for me to do to make sure everyone else involved in John's murder, and Lucy's, gets what they deserve. So I may be spending some more time away from home until that's all sorted."

Nicole took Carter's hand in hers and kissed it. "That's OK. I'll cope."

The next day, the sun was shining brightly as Carter and Nicole, accompanied by Conrad, walked from their hotel to the Royal Society. They were looking forward to a day when all John's hard work would be revealed. Of course, they were sad that he wouldn't be there to enjoy it with them but he had left something behind that would never be forgotten, by his son, by his mother-in-law, by his friends and by his work colleagues, not to mention by everyone involved in the diamond business. And in leaving a worldwide patent of his invention to his son, he was ensuring that Mikey would never need to worry about money.

The three of them walked into the reception hall, got their name cards and then went to have a look inside both the Kohn Centre and the Marble Hall, where everyone attending would be able to enjoy some snacks and drinks after the presentation. When they had seen all they wanted to see, they went back to the Kohn Centre and sat down to await the arrival of the people who had booked to attend the presentation.

After a few minutes, people began arriving and twenty minutes later, at 2:00pm, the room was full. In fact the organisers had to bring in some extra chairs to accommodate all the people who had turned up. When they were all sitting down and Sir Stephen had entered and taken his seat at the table on the platform at the front of the room, it was time for the presentation to begin. Sir Stephen rose to his feet.

"Good afternoon, everyone," he began and then paused briefly before continuing, "I would normally say that it gives me great pleasure to welcome you to this presentation, and in a sense it does. But it is also with great sadness."

The audience moved and looked at each other, wondering what was coming next. Sir Stephen continued.

"Today, we were hoping that John Sprague would be delivering this presentation. It is, after all, based upon his work and the presentation itself was written by him. But the fact of the matter is that John Sprague is no longer with us. Only a few weeks ago, he was murdered, while working in his lab in Oxford. Not only that, it now appears that the reason he was killed was to try and prevent his work from being used to protect the natural diamond market from being significantly undermined by synthetic diamonds."

A hubbub of sound ran round the room as the audience whispered to each other. Sir Stephen paused until it died down and then continued his address.

"Nevertheless, it is with a feeling of honour that I now invite Conrad Saunders, John Sprague's close work colleague and friend for many years, to make the presentation that John would have made if he had not been so tragically taken from us."

Sir Stephen looked across the room to where Conrad was seated at the back and stretched out his hand.

"Ladies and gentlemen, please welcome Conrad Saunders."

Sir Stephen sat down and the audience clapped as Conrad made his way to the platform. Dressed in a dark suit and tie, he walked down the side of the room past the audience. He was carrying the presentation with him. Before long, he was at the microphone ready to begin.

During his presentation, or more accurately, the presentation prepared by John, Conrad stressed the size of the mountain that John had climbed in coming up with a small, reliable and relatively inexpensive synthetic diamond detector. Many had tried before him, and failed, and his achievement would be crucial in ending what was, effectively, a war which was taking place within the diamond industry. Whilst nobody in the industry had any problem with synthetic diamonds being produced and sold, not even gem quality synthetic diamonds, as long as the people buying them were aware that they were synthetic, it was the growing practice of using synthetic diamonds in jewellery which purported to have been made from natural stones that was the issue. Until the arrival of John's DiamondProof synthetic diamond detector, the expense of determining whether a diamond was natural or synthetic had not been cost effective for the average jeweller and had required the diamond in question to be submitted for testing in a lab full of very expensive scientific equipment.

When Conrad got to the end of the presentation, he concluded it by holding up the little black box which was DiamondProof and, at that point, the entire audience rose to their feet and applauded loudly. When the noise had died down, Conrad spoke again.

"I have one final thing to do before we conclude this meeting."

There was a hush as the audience sat down again and listened, wondering what else there could be.

"Before John died, he submitted his invention to the UK Intellectual Property Office who have now granted a UK patent for DiamondProof, which will, in the course of the next year, result in patents being granted worldwide."

Conrad paused for a few moments to allow what he had said to sink in. When it had, he picked up the patent certificate and held it in front of him with both hands.

"This is the patent, which we received from the UK Intellectual Property Office yesterday and which now belongs to a young man sitting here with us today."

The audience began to look around the room and Conrad waited a few seconds before continuing, raising his voice so that it could be heard above the hubbub.

"His name is Michael Sprague, John Sprague's son!" there was a hushed pause before Conrad continued. "Mikey, please come up here."

Mikey looked at his grandmother, wondering what he should do. She gave him a slight push as she spoke, "Go on. Go and get it. It's what your Dad would have wanted."

Mikey rose to his feet and walked down beside the audience until he reached the platform. Conrad was smiling as he handed the patent certificate to Mikey.

"There you go, Mikey. A present from your Dad."

Mikey turned and looked at the audience, wondering whether or not he should say anything. In the end he decided he would.

"My Dad was a great Dad," he said, tears in his eyes.

Conrad leaned across the table and patted Mikey on the shoulder to get his attention before handing him a microphone. As Mikey looked at him, he nodded, indicating that Mikey should use it.

"Like I said," repeated Mikey into the microphone. "My Dad was a great Dad. But not only that, he was a great scientist!" The audience rose to their feet, as one, and applauded before Mikey spoke again, "And I am one lucky kid to have had a Dad like him. I am so proud to be his son." Another pause as the audience sat down again. "And I will make sure that I make good use of this so that everyone who buys a diamond ring for their sweetheart, to show them that their love is forever, will know that the diamond in the ring was made in the ground, millions of years ago, and not in a factory last week."

The audience rose to its feet again, applauding and cheering loudly as Conrad took the microphone back from Mikey. And when Mikey's grandmother, with tears flowing down her cheeks, came running down the room and took him in her arms, there were even louder cheers.

An hour later, after everyone attending the presentation had enjoyed their food and drinks in the marble hall and left, only Mikey, his grandmother, Carter, Nicole and Conrad remained. Mikey and his grandmother said their goodbyes and left, promising to contact Conrad the following week concerning what they should do with DiamondProof. Then Conrad said goodbye to Carter and Nicole, leaving them alone in the room with one of the attendants. Carter looked at Nicole.

"Well, I think that went as well as it could have done," he said.

"It was wonderful!" responded Nicole, as she gave Carter a big hug. "So I guess its time for us to go home now."

"Yup, back to Ambergris Caye."

"Unless anything else comes up in the meantime," poked Nicole.

Carter looked at her, a hurt look on his face. "How was I to know that our visit to see Jacques and Eloise was going to be interrupted like that?"

"Because nothing we plan ever actually goes according to plan!" interjected Nicole, "But I guess that's what makes you such an interesting guy."

"Did you find me that interesting when we met at university in Oxford all those years ago?"

They both laughed as they collected their coats from the coat rack and left the room, leaving behind them the sad story of John Sprague, a dedicated and incredibly talented scientist.

THE END

23758390R00150

Printed in Great Britain
by Amazon